Frank Mysteries

Russell Fine

Other Novels By Russell Fine

Science Fiction Series
Future World History I
Future World History II
Future World History III.
Janus

Frank Carver Series
Frank Carver Mysteries II
The China Strategy
The Eternity Gene
Dreamscape
McBain's Redemption
New Terra

Political Fiction
The California Experiment
Quest For Power

Copyright © 2017 By Russell Fine
All rights reserved. This book, or parts thereof, may not be reproduced in any form without permission.

Dedication

This book is dedicated to all those people who assisted me in making this book possible.

First, to my wife Sherry, who is my primary editor. She read every word countless times to correct my frequent errors and provided a sounding board for my story lines.

My son, Randy, edited every story and not only corrected mistakes but also made helpful suggestions to make the stories better.

Suzanne Horsfall and John Binseel provided additional editing and error correction.

And B. J. Gillum, a friend and fellow author, who provided the final proofreading and editing.

Please accept my gratitude for the assistance each of you provided.

Russell Fine

Table of Contents

Backfire 1

The Antique Car Caper 37

The Armchair Prophesy 73

The Halloween Incident 111

The Fireman 145

The Disappearing Man 181

Backfire
A Frank Carver Mystery

My name is Frank Carver. I've lived in Norfolk County my whole life, except for the four years I spent in the Army. I was always athletic. In high school I played football and baseball, but off the athletic field I was shy and introverted. That was probably the result of being an only child, which made it difficult to even ask a girl for a date. So, aside from my athletic endeavors, my high school years were spent immersed in schoolwork. I graduated second in my class. I could have gone to almost any college, but since my parents didn't have a lot of money, I decided to go to the local university where I earned a BS degree in Electrical Engineering. After graduation, I joined the Army. Before starting basic training, they gave me a series of tests and told me I would be perfect for a position in Army Intelligence.

After basic they sent me to another school where I was trained as a spy. During that training, they realized I had a knack for languages, so they sent me to a school to learn Arabic. When they thought I was sufficiently proficient, I was sent to a base in Kuwait. As it turned out, I never had the chance to work on any secret missions. My job was to evaluate information supplied by the field agents.

As the end of my enlistment approached, I decided I wanted a change. The Army offered to pay for graduate school if I joined the reserve, so I agreed. After I was discharged, I went back home. My parents gave me a big "welcome home" party.

The day after the party, I went to the university to register for graduate school. It was April and classes wouldn't start until September, so I had some time on my hands. My parents had been planning to take a vacation for some time, but didn't want to board Chester, their collie. Since I was home, I would be able to take care of him while they were gone.

They were going to drive to Maine and spend a few days at Acadia National Park. Then, they were going to drive into Canada and spend some time in Quebec before coming home. They never made it to Canada. On Interstate 95, just south of Houlton, Maine, a truck driver on the south bound side fell asleep. His truck crossed the median and hit my parent's car head on. They were killed instantly.

I suddenly found myself on my own. I had very little money and my parents had no life insurance. I consulted a lawyer in anticipation of suing the trucking company, or the driver, but the driver was an illegal alien from somewhere in Central America and didn't even have a driver's license. The company that owned the truck carried minimal insurance. The small settlement from the insurance company paid the lawyer, and there was just enough left over to give my parents a decent burial. I made a small profit when I sold their house, but I knew I was going to have to go to work instead of school.

The Norfolk County police department was looking for people, and they preferred to hire veterans. I was hired immediately as a patrolman. I worked in that position for two years and became eligible to take the examination to become a sergeant. I passed the exam, and when a sergeant's position became available six months later, I was promoted. That was four years ago.

It was my first day as a homicide detective. After receiving my promotion two weeks earlier, I decided to use up some of my unused vacation time and go on a fishing trip that I been thinking about for a long time. I had been on the job only two hours when the call came in. A male victim was found in a motel room. I got into my unmarked car and made the short drive to the Goodnight Motel. When I arrived in the room, I saw Mike Stevens, the local beat cop, standing next to the bed. On it was a naked man, his buttocks exposed for all the world to see.

Backfire

It was hard to tell the victim's age without looking at his face, but I guessed he was in his mid-forties. There were no apparent signs of violence, so I was confused about why I had been called to the scene. Before I could ask, Mike said, "Hi Frank, if you're wondering why you're here, it's because this is victim number three. Since you were on vacation for a couple of weeks, I wasn't sure you knew there were two other bodies found in the past ten days under identical circumstances."

"You're right, I don't know anything about it."

"The other two victims were found in the Stardust Motel. They were both found naked on a bed in the same pose as our current victim. In all three cases, the rooms weren't rented for the night, there was no clothing or other personal items found in the rooms, and the desk clerk had never seen the victims."

I was thinking about the case and was about to ask Mike a question, but at that moment Jill Tanner, the smart shapely county medical examiner, walked in with her assistant. She looked at me, smiled, and said, "Hi Frank, I hope you had a good vacation, because I suspect this case is going to ruin the next several weeks for you."

"Hi Jill," I responded. "I was about to ask Mike about the cause of death in the other two cases, but since you're here, please tell me what you know about our victims."

"Obviously, I haven't checked out our most current one, but both of the others were middle aged males. We haven't been able to identify either of them. We tried both finger prints and facial recognition, but there were no hits. The autopsies revealed both men died because some of their internal organs disappeared."

"Please define 'disappeared'. I don't understand how somebody's organs can disappear. Were they surgically removed?"

"No, the organs weren't surgically removed. There was no indication on either victim they were cut open. In the first victim, his liver, left kidney, and right lung were gone.

Our second victim was missing his heart and a substantial portion of his brain. I have no idea how the organs were removed, so I thought the word disappeared would be appropriate."

"Okay, this is really creepy. Who has been investigating this so far?"

"The chief has been working on this himself, and he got the state police involved too. But there hasn't been much progress made as far as I know. I'm sure the chief will dump this case on you now that you're back from vacation."

"I haven't seen him since I returned, but I'll discuss the case with him when I'm at the station. Please let me know what you find out about victim number three as soon as possible," I said as I walked out of the room.

I had no idea where to even start. None of the victims had been identified. Their naked bodies were somehow placed into locked rooms, and they died as a result of having some of their organs removed. I suddenly remembered I hadn't asked Mike who found the body, so I turned around and started to go back to the room.

Before I got there, Mike walked out and I asked him my question.

"In all three cases, a call was received by the front desk to report a problem with the room. When somebody went to check out the problem, they found the body."

"Can I assume the calls were placed from the rooms?"

"Yeah, but the rooms were all thoroughly checked for fingerprints and we were able to match all the prints we found to people who worked at the motel in either maintenance or housekeeping. There were no other fingerprints, so the rooms must have been meticulously cleaned since the last guest had stayed there. Also, all the people from the motel staff who were in the room have been employed by the motel for several years. The forensics people will be here shortly. As soon as Jill is done, they'll get started."

"Thanks Mike. You know, the more I learn about this case the more confusing it gets."

I went back to my desk at the station and sat there thinking about the case. My mind was wandering. While I was sitting there I felt a tap on my shoulder. Chief Mitchell, a large heavy-set man with red hair, bushy mustache, and a loud gruff voice, asked, "Did I wake you up?"

"No chief, I was thinking about this case. Jill told me you were doing the investigation yourself. Can you tell me what you found so far?"

"So far we haven't found much. We questioned the employees at both motels, but none of them could provide any additional information. The night clerk at the Goodnight Motel said that a few hours before the body was discovered, a woman called the motel and asked to be connected with the room where the victim was found. The clerk told her the room was empty and the woman hung up."

"So, you think the woman called to find out if the room was occupied? I guess that makes sense, but how did she get into the room?"

"Frank, this is your investigation now. I put you into this position in homicide because I think you're probably the most intelligent and logical person in the department. I have confidence in you and I'm sure you will figure this out." The chief smiled and walked toward his office.

I found myself deep in thought again when the phone rang. It was Jill. She said, "I think you should know our latest victim wasn't from around here. During a quick examination I found evidence of recent dental work, and the materials used haven't been utilized in the United States for twenty years. I think the only place they're still used is in Eastern Europe and Russia."

"Maybe the Russian embassy can help us identify the guy. Please send some pictures of our victim along with his fingerprints to the Russian embassy in Washington."

"I'll do that in the next fifteen minutes. As soon as I'm done with the autopsy, I'll call you."

I suddenly realized I was hungry, so I went to a nearby a restaurant to get something to eat. I always think more clearly when I'm not hungry. I had the unhappy feeling that when we finally discover the identity of our victims, it wasn't going to help solve our mystery. Aside from the obvious questions, I was wondering why all of our victims were middle aged males.

When I returned to my desk, there was a message to call Jill, so I called her immediately.

"Hi Jill, it's Frank."

"Our latest victim had his larynx and pancreas removed. You don't need a larynx and you can live, at least for a while, without a pancreas, so I have to try and figure out what actually killed him. I think perhaps all of the victims were killed before their organs were removed."

"Do you still have the other bodies?"

"Yes, I plan on checking the first two victims shortly. I'll keep you informed."

"Thanks Jill," I said and hung up the phone.

I stuck around the office for another hour before I decided to go home. On the way home, my cellphone rang. It was Jill again.

"I found out what killed our victims. There was an almost microscopic incision made on the back of the necks of all the victims. All of them had their spinal cords severed at the base of the brain by something that was substantially thinner and sharper than a scalpel. In fact, I needed a microscope to find the injury. I've never seen anything like this before. I'm not aware of any medical instrument that could make a cut that small and precise. This makes a laser cut look like it was made with a chainsaw."

"The unknown seems to be par for the course with this case. Did you hear anything from the Russian embassy?"

"Not yet. You'll know as soon as I hear anything."

I know the chief wanted to keep the details quiet, but I decided I was going to send out a notification to all the police departments in the country. I should be able to determine if similar incidents occurred at any other place.

I had trouble sleeping that night. At 4:00 I gave up, showered, dressed, and was at my desk by 5:30. I sent a message to the chief asking him if he had any objections to sending out a request to other police departments asking for information. I was going to do it without his permission, but I thought that was probably not a good idea since I had only been on this job for one day.

At 7:15 my cellphone rang. I looked at the screen on my phone and saw it was Jill.

"Good morning Jill. I hope you slept better than I did last night."

"I probably didn't. I was up most of the night researching surgical devices that could have made the incision and sever the spinal cord in a way that matched our victims, but there's nothing I found that could do it. But the reason for my call is that I received a response from the Russians. They said the finger prints and the picture match a prisoner who is awaiting execution for murder in a prison near Moscow. His name is Stefan Petrowsky, and they indicated he was still there."

"So, does Stefan have a twin brother?"

"I doubt it. Anyway, I'm going to send them pictures and fingerprints from the first two victims this morning. Perhaps they were all from Russia and that's the connection between them."

"That sounds like a good idea. But, if they are all from Russia, how did they end up here?"

Jill laughed and said, "You're the detective, so detect. I only supply information."

"Okay, I promise I'll spend the morning detecting. Anyway, please let me know what you find out about our first two victims."

"I'll do that. Bye."

"Bye Jill."

It was as I suspected, knowing who the victims were wasn't very helpful. If all the victims were from Russia, it would explain why they aren't in any of our databases. Even if all the men were from a Russian prison, there's no explanation as to how they got here or into a locked motel room. I have no idea what weapon was used to kill them, or why they were killed.

A few minutes later the chief walked by. He looked at me and asked, "Have you found our killer yet?"

"All I have so far are more questions, and other than the cause of death, absolutely no answers."

"I thought the deaths were caused by organs being removed. Is that wrong?"

"Yes, Jill examined all three bodies and discovered they were killed by having their spinal cords severed at the base of the brain by some unknown device."

"What makes Jill think the murder weapon is an unknown device?"

"She said the cuts were made with a device much sharper and more precise than a surgical scalpel. She spent the night doing research and couldn't find anything capable of making those cuts."

The chief just shook his head and walked away. I decided to go to the Stardust Motel and examine the other two crime scenes.

I walked into the lobby of the motel and up to the front desk. A young woman looked up from the magazine she was reading and said cheerfully, "Good morning, sir. How can I help you?"

"Good morning." I showed her my badge and said, "I'm Lieutenant Carver. I would like to look at the rooms where the bodies were found."

"Sure, we've been waiting for you guys to tell us when it's okay to rent those rooms again, so they are still empty. The room numbers are 120 and 121. You can use my passkey," she said and handed me her card key.

I looked at the card key for a moment and then asked, "Will this open any room?"

"Yeah, actually it will open any room in any motel that uses the same key system, which is probably half the motels in the city."

Now I was fairly sure I knew how the bodies got into a locked room. I asked, "Are these rooms near another entrance?"

"Yes, there's an entrance at the end of each hallway and these rooms are located at the end of the hallway next to the outside door."

"Thank you, you've been very helpful."

I walked over to the rooms. There was nothing special about them except for the location. I went back to the front desk, returned the card key, and asked, "How hard is it to get one of these passkeys?"

"If you have an account with the company that makes the locks, you can buy them for $3.00."

"Thanks. We're done with the rooms, so you can rent them again."

I went back to my desk and found a message from the chief telling me it was okay to send out the request for information to other police departments. It took about fifteen minutes to complete the paperwork. I scanned it and sent it to the state police who would forward the request. By tomorrow morning it would be distributed all across the country.

Jill called me that afternoon to tell me she heard from the Russians again. The first two victims were also residents of the same prison as our last victim. There was obviously a pattern.

That evening I was home watching some lousy TV show when my phone rang. It was the dispatcher. She said, "There was another body found in the Goodnight Motel."

"Perfect," I responded with more than a little sarcasm. "That's just what I wanted to hear. I'm on my way."

When I got to the scene Mike was already there. He just waved when he saw me.

There was another naked man on the bed in the same pose as the other victims. He looked older, probably in his sixties. I couldn't tell if any of his internal organs were missing, but most of his left leg was gone. It appeared to be severed at mid-thigh. The wound on his thigh looked fresh, but there was no sign of blood. The wound appeared to have been cauterized.

Jill and her crew arrived a few minutes later. She said, "Hi Frank, I assume this is our fourth victim?"

"Yes, but look at the wound on his left leg."

Jill examined the wound for a minute and then looked at the back of his neck.

"The wound on his leg looks identical to the internal wounds we found on our other victims where their organs had disappeared. There is a small mark on his neck that's identical to our other victims as well. I'll bet you he has been a recent resident of a prison near Moscow."

"I won't take that bet. I'm sure you're right." Turning towards Mike I said, "I assume the forensics guys will be here soon. Ask them to send me a report as soon as possible."

"Okay."

Just like the other rooms where victims had been found, this room was next to an outside door. I was sure I knew how they got in, but there were still a lot of unanswered questions.

When I arrived at the station the following morning, there was a man sitting on the chair next to my desk. He was wearing a dark blue suit and appeared to be about thirty-five, black hair, tall, and very muscular. He looked like a cop. I walked up to him and said, "I'm Lieutenant Carver. Can I help you?"

"Yes, is there someplace we can talk privately?"

"Sure, follow me."

We went over to the interview room. He walked in and sat down. I followed him into the room and closed the door.

As soon as I sat down he showed me his identification. His name was Marvin Gerber and he was with the CIA. I asked, "What brings you here this morning, Mr. Gerber?"

"Your request for information regarding the bodies that have been found. I think I may have some information for you. However, some of what I'm about to tell you is classified and must not leave this room. I checked your record and found you worked in Army Intelligence for a few years, and you still have security clearance. So, I'm sure I can trust you with this information."

"Okay, I won't discuss what you tell me with anyone, but if the information leads to an arrest, it may become public knowledge."

"I understand, but that's a risk we have to take. Four years ago we learned Russia was developing a device that could transport objects electronically. I'm sure you have seen the transporters on Star Trek. It was something like that. The early tests with inanimate objects were reasonably successful. Things like wood blocks and metal tools worked perfectly. More complex objects were destroyed by the process. They continued to refine the technology, and about a year ago, they were able to transport everything except living things."

I didn't believe a word he said, but I thought I knew where his line of thought was leading.

"They began testing with things like apples and other fruit. The tests all failed initially. But as they continued to improve the device, these tests became successful. We knew they were going to begin testing on animals, but our contact, who was part of the development team, was killed in an auto accident. I think we have to assume they have now advanced to the point where they are experimenting with human subjects."

He paused for a moment to let the information he just gave me sink in. It was all beginning to make sense. "Why send the subjects here? Why not someplace inside Russia?"

"I suspect there are two reasons. They wanted to know if the device would work over a longer distance and the KGB has a known agent here. Her name is Samantha Clarke, or at least that's the name she is currently using. We've known about her for several years and have been watching her from a distance. We don't want her to know we're aware of her."

"I think we're going to have to keep a close watch on her now."

"I agree, but our ultimate goal is to destroy or steal the transporter device, and I think this may be an opportunity to do that."

"It obviously doesn't work with human subjects. Every one they transported lost body parts. The body we found yesterday was missing most of his left leg. Why would we want that technology?"

"Even if they are never able to send a human successfully, they may be able to transport a nuclear weapon here. We need the same technology to prevent that from happening. I'm sure you remember the idea behind 'mutual assured destruction'."

"Yeah, I do. But I don't understand how catching our spy gets us any closer to the device."

"I'm hoping our spy will be able to tell us where the device is, or perhaps, since we know they can transport non-living material, we can get them to transport a bomb back to their location."

"I'm guessing you have an address for Ms. Clarke?"

"Yes, I do. It's 1231 Avenue C. We have to find some ruse to get into her house. Then we can plant some devices that will let us keep track of her movements. I think she's too well trained for us to follow her. I'm going to assign two of my best guys to this case. I'll probably need your help too, but for now, just keep me informed regarding anything new in the case."

I handed him my business card and said, "This is my card. It has my cellphone number on it. Can you give me something with a number where I can contact you?"

He took a card out of his shirt pocket and handed it to me. Then he asked, "You never met me before, so why did you believe I worked for the CIA?"

"I wasn't sure until you mentioned I worked for Army Intelligence. That information isn't in my service record. It could only be obtained through classified channels."

"Good, I'm glad you were skeptical. Thanks for agreeing to help. I'll keep in touch."

"You're welcome."

We both got up and left the interview room. Marvin walked out of the station and I went back to my desk. I found a report from forensics on last night's murder. Like before, there were no unknown fingerprints found.

Nothing happened for two days. Then Jill called to tell me our latest victim was from the same Russian prison as the others. At the end of the day, Marvin called and asked me to meet him at a restaurant a few miles away. I told him I would be there in a half hour.

I arrived right on schedule. When I walked in I saw Marvin sitting in a booth at the back of the restaurant. The hostess began to ask me something, but I told her I was meeting a friend, and I walked past her to Marvin's booth.

I sat down and Marvin said, "Dinner is on me. We were able to install a few devices in Samantha's house. She just uses a cellphone, so we'll only be able to hear half the conversations, but we also placed a few video cameras in her house."

"I won't ask you how you did that, because if you told me, I'd probably have to arrest you. Anyway, what do we do now? Sit and wait for something to happen?"

"Pretty much, it looks like they test a prisoner every five or six days, so I don't think we'll have to wait very long. I'll bet you're getting pressure from your chief to resolve these murders."

"That would be a safe bet. I've told him we have names for all our victims, but they were all on death row in a Russian prison. He thinks space aliens are involved, so I told him so far that's the best explanation we have."

We stayed at the restaurant for more than two hours talking about a lot of different things, but neither of us mentioned the case again.

The following day there was a gang shooting that resulted in two deaths. By the end of the day I figured out that the two idiots shot each other over some deal involving a used car.

It was now a week since the last body was found and I was getting concerned that Marvin's assumptions about the case were wrong. I was driving home from the station when my cellphone rang. It was Marvin.

"I think our girl is going to make a pickup tonight. We're going to try and follow her. Do you want to tag along?"

"Yes, of course I do."

"Meet me in the 1000 block of C Street. I'm driving a black Hyundai Sonata sedan."

"I'll be there in fifteen minutes."

It only took eight minutes to get there. I parked behind Marvin's car and walked over to the front passenger door. I looked inside and Marvin waved at me. I got in.

After I sat down, Marvin said, "She received a phone call about two hours ago. She's going to the regular pickup spot to meet somebody at 8:00. I have no idea where the regular pick up spot is, so we have to follow her."

"Okay."

We had been waiting for about an hour when we received a call from one of Marvin's men. He said she left her house, walked to her car, and was driving in our direction. Marvin started the car, and after she passed us, he pulled out and began following her.

She drove a few blocks and pulled into a 7-11. We passed her and parked about two hundred feet farther down. I still had a view of the 7-11. I watched as she went into the store and came back out a few minutes later carrying a brown paper bag, got back into her car, and left. She turned in our direction again. After she passed us Marvin waited for fifteen seconds before he pulled out. Marvin's assistant, who had been reporting her movements, was a block behind us.

Either she wasn't as well trained as Marvin thought, or had become complacent. In any case, she led us right to an old warehouse. We drove past the warehouse and parked our car off the main road on a side street. Marvin's assistant parked there as well.

We got out of our cars and began to walk back to the warehouse. There was no way to approach it without being seen. It was almost nightfall, but as the day transitioned into night, lights around the warehouse lit the area surrounding it. While we were softly discussing the situation, two people walked out. They were carrying something that could have been a body, but we were too far away to be sure. They put whatever they were carrying into the back seat of Samantha's car, got into the car, and drove away.

I said, "If that was another body, they are going to either the Stardust or the Goodnight."

Marvin looked at his man and said, "We'll go to the Stardust. You go to the Goodnight."

We hurried back to our cars and headed to our destinations. When we got to the Stardust we found her car parked near a side entrance. We parked next to her and I ran over to the front of the motel. I walked up to the desk and was surprised to see the same girl there. She looked at me and asked, "Is something wrong?"

"Yeah, I think somebody is about to dump another body in one of your rooms. Are either 120 or 121 empty?"

"They both are."

"Give me your passkey."

She handed me the key and I ran back to Marvin's car. We walked together to the side door which I opened. We listened at the doors of both rooms and we could hear someone talking in room 120. We both took out our guns. I inserted the passkey and the door made a loud click. Marvin kicked in the door and entered the room, gun first.

Marvin yelled, "Get down on the floor and sit on your hands." Samantha began to comply, but the man with her reached into his coat pocket. Marvin shot him without saying another word.

I took out my cellphone and called for backup and an ambulance.

Marvin calmly said, "Ms. Clarke, this can go down two ways. You can agree to cooperate with us and we'll pin the blame on your friend here, or you can spend the rest of your life in a small, uncomfortable, prison cell. The choice is yours."

Samantha looked down at her dead companion and said, "I guess I'll cooperate, but I really don't know much about what's going on. He was just paying me to help him."

Marvin said, "Stand up, clasp your hands behind your back, and turn around."

Samantha complied and Marvin put handcuffs on her. He led her outside to his car. I waited inside with the body.

When Marvin walked back into the room he said, "I just drugged our lady spy so she'll be asleep for the next twelve hours or so. Toby, the guy I sent to the Goodnight, will be here shortly and he'll take charge of the prisoner."

I could hear sirens close by. I said to Marvin, "You have to stay here since you shot him. I'm sure you know there'll be an inquiry."

"Yeah, I'm not going anywhere."

Neither of us touched the body. Two minutes later two other detectives and two guys with a stretcher walked into the room. One of the guys with the stretcher checked the body and confirmed he was dead. They turned him over and found a 45 automatic clutched in his right hand. One of the other detectives took an evidence bag out of his pocket and carefully placed the gun inside. He looked at me and asked, "Hey Frank, who's the stiff on the bed?"

"You probably won't believe this, but he's a Russian who, until recently, was on death row in a prison near Moscow."

"Okay, if you don't want to tell me, that's fine. Who shot the suspect?"

Marvin said, "I did. I'm working with Frank on this case. My name is Marvin Gerber. I work for the CIA. Frank was telling you the truth about the guy on the bed." Marvin showed him his ID and put his gun into an evidence bag the detective was holding."

The detective said, "After we run a ballistics check, you can have your gun back. It's obvious this guy was reaching for his gun when you shot him, but I still have to follow procedures."

"It's okay, we have the same procedures. Just let Frank know when you're finished with the gun."

Marvin and Frank left the motel room and walked back to Marvin's car. After they were inside, Marvin said, "I'm going to interview our spy tomorrow. Do you want to be there?"

"Sure, as long as there are no other murders before then."

"How often do they occur here?"

"We average about twenty-five per year. Our population is about 75,000, so the murder rate is really low. More than half are drug related and the rest are usually domestic disputes. I'm the only homicide detective in the department."

"Well, if you want to be there, call me in the morning."

"Okay."

He dropped me off at my car and once I was inside I called the chief and filled him in. He listened but made no comment until I was finished, then he said, "I told you that you would figure this out. I didn't know it would involve the CIA, but that really doesn't matter. You did a good job Frank. I'll see you in the morning."

"Yes sir."

I didn't mention Samantha Clarke in my conversation with the chief and I was uncomfortable not telling him the whole story, but I couldn't tell him about her without also telling him about the Russian transporter, and that was a secret.

The next morning, I went to the station and spent an hour completing the paperwork required to report the incident. The chief wasn't in yet, so I left it on his desk. I told the dispatcher I would be out for a while and left the station. Once I was in my car, I called Marvin. He gave me an address and told me to be there at 11:00. I told him I would be there.

Something was nagging at me concerning the events of the previous evening. Why would a guy reach for his gun when there was a cop who already had a gun pointed at him? He had to know he was going to get shot. The other thing was, why did Marvin kill him? I was sure he was an excellent marksman; it was part of the CIA training. He could have shot him in the arm or shoulder which would have incapacitated him. That's what I would've done.

There was something else too. Why did Samantha give up so easily? Marvin never told me how he got the bugs into her house. When we followed her she made no effort to determine if anyone was following. When I was in Army intelligence, one of the rules stated that if you are working undercover, never go directly to a meeting. Make some unusual turns and check the cars behind you so you can be sure you aren't being followed.

It was all too easy. Something was going on, and if I wasn't careful I was going to be caught up in the middle of it. I decided to verify that Marvin worked for the CIA. I called one of my friends who still worked in Army Intelligence and asked him to check out Marvin Gerber. Then I called Marvin and told him I wouldn't be able to meet him to witness Samantha's interrogation because something came up at work.

I didn't want to go back to the station or go home, so I just drove around for a while. An hour later, my friend from Army intelligence called back. He said there was an agent named Marvin Gerber who worked at the office in New York. He was sixty-six years old and retired last year. Now I knew I'd been duped. I had to find out who Marvin Gerber really was.

I immediately called Jim Doyle who was in charge of forensics. When he answered I said, "Hi Jim. It's Frank. I need your help with something, and for the time being it's a secret, until after I talk to the chief."

"Okay, I can keep a secret. What do you need?"

"The gun that was used in the shooting last night is in the lab for the standard ballistics tests. I need you to check it for fingerprints. It would appear the CIA agent who shot the suspect last night is a fake. I have to find out who he is."

"I'll check the gun for prints myself. To your knowledge did anyone besides our phony CIA agent touch the gun?"

"No, Marvin just dropped it into an open evidence bag."

"We haven't done the ballistics yet, so I'll check it for prints first and then do the ballistics testing. I'll call you as soon as I get the results."

"Thanks. I'll be waiting for your call."

I thought that was the best chance we had to find out Marvin's real identity, but he also handed me his business card and that may have prints on it as well. I also remembered when we went to dinner he used a credit card. I would have to check on that too. I was beginning to think we would soon know who Marvin really is, so I decided it was time to face the chief and let him know how badly I screwed up.

I went back to the station and walked to the chief's office, half hoping he wouldn't be there. He was there talking on the phone. He looked up, saw me, smiled, and motioned for me to come in. I walked in and sat down across from him. A few seconds later he hung up the phone and asked, "Did you want to talk to me about something?"

I hesitated for a moment and said softly, "Yes, but I really don't want to."

"What's wrong?" he asked with a note of concern in his voice.

"I really screwed up. If you want me to resign or bust me down to patrolman, I'll understand."

Now he was a little annoyed and said, "Just tell me what you did."

"I'm sure you're aware of the CIA agent who shot our suspect yesterday. He's a fake."

The chief didn't say anything for a few seconds and then he said, more calmly than I expected, "Please continue."

"When he introduced himself he showed me his ID. I've seen CIA credentials before, and it looked perfect. And he knew something about me even you aren't aware of; I spent several years working in Army Intelligence. That information isn't on my service record; it's classified. Since he knew I assumed he was genuine."

The chief just stared at me so I spent a few minutes telling him the rest of the story.

"You were really snookered son."

"Yeah, I know. But there is more, and this part I believe is true. He told me the Russians developed a device like the transporters they used on Star Trek. It took years to develop to the point where they could transport complex inanimate objects. Then they tried to send living things, but they all died in the process. Apparently, at some point they were able to send animals successfully, so they decided to try humans. They took men from a prison just outside of

Moscow who were scheduled to be executed anyway and sent them through the device. However, in the process, every person who was transported lost part of their bodies. For reasons which are still not clear, they decided to send them here. Marvin said something about the Russians having an agent here named Samantha Clarke and she was involved somehow."

I stopped talking and the chief just looked at me for several seconds before he said, "This story sounds like a load of bullshit. Do you have any proof? Do we know anything about Samantha Clarke?"

"We have identified the victims and all of them were residents of the Russian prison until they were found here. I know how it sounds, but I have no other explanation. Marvin and I followed Samantha Clarke to the motel where the shooting occurred. Marvin took her to his car before our guys got there because he wanted to interrogate her."

"You do realize the more you talk the worse this gets. Can I assume that you are making an effort to find out who our fake CIA agent really is?"

"Yes sir. We have the gun he used last night and it should have his fingerprints on it. I also have a card he gave me and I was going to bring that over to forensics when we're finished here. He bought me dinner a few days ago and used a credit card to pay the check. I plan on going to the restaurant and try to get a copy of the charge slip."

"That sounds like a good start. If you really believe Russians have this transporter device, perhaps some kind of receiver is required. If that's the case, do you have any idea where that might be?"

A bell started ringing in my head. "Yes, when we were following Samantha Clarke she stopped at a warehouse on Industrial Parkway. The receiving unit might be there."

The chief, who was obviously pissed off, said very emphatically, "Take two other guys and check out that warehouse NOW!"

"Yes sir," I said meekly as I left his office.

As I walked back towards my desk, two patrolman walked in. I waved them over to my desk and asked, "Are you guys going off duty now?"

"Yeah, we are. Why?"

"Would you like some overtime?"

They both said "Sure."

"Good. Come with me."

We walked to my car and drove to the warehouse that Samantha led us to. On the way, I explained the situation to the two patrolmen. When we got to the warehouse it looked abandoned. It was the first time I saw it during the day. There were several broken windows and the outside of the building was dirty and adorned with graffiti. We walked to the door and my opinion changed instantly. The door was new and it appeared to be made of steel. It was secured by a deadbolt and a huge padlock. On the door was a sign indicating the building was protected by an alarm company.

I immediately called the chief to let him know the situation. There was no way we could legally break in without a warrant. The chief asked for the address and told me to wait by the door. He said he would have the warrant in ten minutes. True to his word, he called me ten minutes later and told me he had the warrant.

Now we had to figure out how to get in. The lock was too big to cut with a bolt cutter, and even if we got the lock off, we still had to deal with the deadbolt. We decided to try the windows. They were probably six or seven feet above the ground and we didn't have a ladder, so I pulled my car up under one of the broken windows. One of the patrolmen climbed up on the car and looked through the window.

A moment later he said, "This won't work either. There's a wall on the other side of the window."

We needed a vehicle with a battering ram on the front, but the department didn't own one. I thought about it for a few seconds and called a friend of mine at the fire department. I explained the situation and he said he was sure he could take down the door with the "jaws of life".

He arrived with the tool about twenty minutes later. It took him about five minutes to set up and a minute later the door was down. I wasn't surprised when a very loud alarm began to sound. We walked in and once inside the alarm sounded somewhat softer.

I looked around and saw several large racks of electronic equipment. On the floor was a metal disk that appeared to be eight feet in diameter. There were several thick cables that connected the disk to the racks of equipment. There was also some kind of medical scanner. I called the chief and told him what we found. He said he would send a forensics team immediately.

Jim Doyle and one of his assistants arrived a short time later. When Jim walked in he looked around for a minute or so, then he turned to me and asked, "Why is there a CT scanner here?" Then pointing at the metal disk on the floor continued, "And what the hell is this thing?"

I knew he wouldn't believe me, but I answered, "It's a receiving unit for a Russian transporter."

Jim looked at me and said, "Sure it is. I'll just call Mr. Spock and get him over here to explain how it works."

"I know how that sounds, but it's the truth. The Russians have been experimenting on death row inmates by sending them here. The bodies we have been finding in the motel rooms are the result of the experiments."

Jim looked like he was going to say something, but instead he turned around and began dusting everything for fingerprints. His assistant was busy taking pictures.

I told the two patrolmen to stay until they were relieved and went back to the station. When I got back I told the dispatcher to send two guys over to the warehouse to guard the forensics team and relieve the two patrolmen who were there. Then I went to the chief's office.

He saw me and waved me in. I sat down across from him and he said, "I have some news regarding our friend Marvin. His real name is Igor Restovitch. He's a member of an elite Russian group that's similar to our Secret Service.

The guy he killed yesterday isn't in any database, but the medical examiner said he appeared to be from Russia or some other Eastern European country."

"Did you find anything regarding Samantha Clarke?"

"No. There's no record of anybody with that name who has a driver's license, voter's registration, or credit card in the state. We're still waiting for a response from the feds."

"Do you think it's time for me to confront Igor and try to find out what the hell is going on?"

"Yeah, but be careful. Make sure you have backup before you arrange your meeting, and make sure the meeting is in a public place."

"Yes sir, I know the drill. I'll keep you informed."

I walked back to my desk, sat down, and was wondering how I was going to confront Igor when my cellphone rang. It was Marvin, or Igor.

"Hi Marvin, how is the interrogation going?"

"By now I'm sure you realize I'm not Marvin and I don't work for the CIA. But I do want to meet with you to explain what's going on."

"Okay Igor, where do you want to meet? By the way, your English is perfect."

"I know you don't trust me, so let's meet at the park across from City Hall. I know you'll have backup watching us, but I have no intention of harming you. Is four o'clock okay?"

"Yeah, sit on a bench by the fountain. I'll find you."

"I'll be there."

I went over to the chief's office and knocked lightly. He motioned for me to come in. After I sat down I said, "Igor just called me. He's going to meet me at four by the fountain in the park across from City Hall."

"Send three guys in street clothes there at 3:00. Do you think we should arrest Igor?"

I thought about it for a few seconds and said, "Not now, I want to hear what he has to say about a lot of things."

"I understand that, but I'm not taking any chances. I want you to wear a mic so we can listen to your conversation."

"I don't have a problem with that."

"Come back here after the meeting."

"Yes sir."

I left his office and walked over to the dispatcher and told her I needed three people in street clothes to be at my desk by 2:45. Then I went back to my desk to ponder the situation.

At 2:40 two men and a woman walked up to my desk. They were smiling so I smiled back at them and said, "Hi, I hope you're all ready for a very difficult undercover assignment." Their smiles disappeared and they looked at each other. The woman, whose name was Jennifer, said, "Nobody said anything about an undercover assignment. The desk sergeant said you needed some people in street clothes for an hour or so."

"Jennifer relax, the job is easy. At four I'm meeting with a Russian agent by the fountain in the park by City Hall. The chief wants you to keep tabs on me in case the Russian gets aggressive. I don't think that's likely, but he insisted. This should be nothing more than the proverbial 'walk in the park'."

I gave each of them a small earpiece transceiver. Then I said, "I'll be wearing a mic so you will be able to hear our conversation, but I won't be able to hear you."

Jennifer said, "Thanks for clearing that up Frank. I guess we should get going. It'll take us about ten minutes to walk there."

The three of them left and I was trying to figure out what Igor was going to say. By 3:45 I gave up and left the building to go to our meeting. I was going to walk, but once outside I realized I would be unprotected while walking, so I went to my car and made the five-minute drive to the park. I parked in a spot marked "Police Vehicles Only" and walked toward the fountain. I saw Igor, but none of my guards were visible, so I whispered, "If any of you are around, please make yourself visible for a moment."

I saw Jennifer get up and walk to the garbage can to throw something away. I was relieved to see they were there but not very visible. I walked up to Igor and sat down next to him. He looked at me, smiled, and said, "It's good to see you again, my friend."

"Friends don't lie to one another."

"With the exception of telling you I was a CIA agent and Samantha was a spy, everything else I told you was true." He paused for a moment, then said, "Actually, Samantha is a spy so that part is true too. We both work for the Russian government, but we aren't in the KGB or the Secret Police. Our job is resolve problems with potential rebel factions within Russia. The transporter is real, but it wasn't developed by the government. It was developed by a group of disaffected scientists who want to overthrow the government. To do that, they need a lot of money. The transporter is worth billions, and the potential buyers are all Islamic nations who would use the device to cripple Europe and the United States. Even though they don't have true nuclear weapons, they do have the ability to build a 'dirty bomb' and send it anywhere they have set up a receiving station. Every country on Earth is a potential enemy of these Islamic terrorists. That includes Russia and the United States."

"It would appear the device is near the prison where our victims recently resided. Why can't you just go round up the bad guys and end this mess?"

"Because 'near the prison' covers a lot of territory. The device could be anywhere within a hundred miles of the prison. It's not very large, so it's easy to hide. It doesn't require massive amounts of power or generate unusual radiation. There's no way to find it. However, one thing we do know is that the system is two-way. We know the receiving stations are capable of activating the transporter and sending something back to their primary location. If we can figure out how to do that, we can destroy the device. To the best of our knowledge the only receiving station is here, in the warehouse you raided today."

"Why did they build the receiving station here?"

"Have you ever heard of Dr. Raymond Kravitz?"

"Yes, of course. He's the head of the Science and Engineering School at the university. He's in the news all the time, although I haven't heard anything about him for a while. He's an avowed socialist."

"The reason you haven't heard about him recently is because he's not here. He's in Russia working on the transporter. He came back here about a year ago to build the receiving unit. When it was finished he went back to Russia. The guy I killed yesterday was his assistant. His name was Fredrick Kruskov. He must have recognized me and thought his only chance was to kill me before I could kill him. In hindsight, I probably should have shot him in the shoulder, but in dangerous situations we're trained to react first and think later."

"Won't they realize something is wrong when they can't contact him?"

"Yes, I'm sure they will. We probably only have two or three days before they figure out there's a problem."

"What do you need me to do?"

"I need you to keep Fredrick's death a secret and I need you to find your best and brightest engineer to figure out how to activate the transporter from the receiver here. I have a set of plans for both the transporter and the receiver, but they are at least two years old. There have been a lot of changes made to the transporter since these plans were current, but I hope it will be enough."

"You probably guessed that other people are listening to this conversation. Sir, please get over here as soon as possible so we can talk about this."

My cellphone rang almost immediately. It was the chief. He asked me to bring Igor back to the station so we could discuss this in private.

"The chief wants me to bring you back to the station. Is that okay?"

"Yes, I'm willing to do anything to get this problem resolved."

"Good, we'll take my car."

Both of us got up and left. As we walked I asked, "What does Samantha have to do with any of this?"

"Samantha was sent here when we realized Dr. Kravitz was involved. Her job was to find out if any of his close associates were working with him. She made contact with Fredrick and discovered he was still in contact with Dr. Kravitz, so she expressed sympathy for their cause and offered to help. When it became apparent they were going to try sending people through the system, Fredrick was asked to find somebody with medical training who could help him. Samantha went to medical school, but joined our group before she graduated. It pays better than being a doctor in Russia. She had mentioned her medical training to Fredrick before, so he asked her to help him. He needed her and the CT scanner to evaluate the subjects after they were transported."

"Who killed our victims?"

"They were executed right before they were transported here. After they arrived they were scanned, and the scans were sent back to the primary location. I would presume they were also scanned before they were transported and the two scans were compared."

I thought about what Igor said and then I had to ask, "Why did you lie to me in the first place?"

"I thought if I told you I was a Russian agent, you probably would have dismissed everything I told you. I had to get you involved before I would be able to tell you the truth."

"Alright, I'll accept that explanation. But please, no more lies. If what you told me is true, we have to be able to trust each other."

Igor looked at me and simply said, "Okay."

I still had more questions, but decided this wasn't the best time to ask them.

When we arrived at the station we walked directly to the chief's office. He was waiting for us. We walked in and I closed the door before sitting down. Then I said, "Igor, this is Chief Mitchell."

The chief said, "I wish I could say it's a pleasure to meet you, but I can't. I heard your entire conversation including the part in the car on the way here. I already placed a call to the Dean of the Engineering School to ask him for recommendations, but I think we may want to look at people who have more practical experience. So I called one of our Senators and asked him to get me a contact at NASA. We only have one shot at this, so we have to be sure. Do you have the plans with you?"

"No, they're in my hotel room. Samantha is guarding them."

Just at that moment the chief's phone rang. The chief stared at the phone for a moment. He said, "I told the dispatcher not to disturb me unless it was really important."

Then he picked up the phone and said, "Chief Mitchell, how can I help you?"

He said nothing for about a minute then said, "Yes, sir."

He spent the next several minutes giving a synopsis of the situation to whoever he was talking to. Then he said, "Yes, sir. I'll meet him at the airport in an hour," and he hung up the phone.

"That was the Vice President. Apparently, Senator Morgan called him and explained our situation. He told me they're sending their top engineer from the Army Weapons Research Center here. His name is Tim Harris. Mr. Harris is also a pilot and will be arriving in an hour in his jet fighter. Frank, I want you and Igor to go to his hotel and get the plans. Then go to the warehouse. I'll bring Mr. Harris there as quickly as possible."

Igor and I left the station and went to his hotel. I waited in the car while he went up to get the plans. He was gone less than five minutes. We drove to the warehouse and discovered ten police cars and two men with automatic weapons guarding the entrance. They recognized me and waved us in.

I parked near the missing door and Igor and I walked in. There were more guards inside.

Igor said, "I have never been here, but Samantha described it to me. I'm not an engineer, but this looks very complicated. I hope Mr. Harris will be able to figure this out before the people in Russia realize what's happening."

We didn't have to wait very long. The chief and Tim Harris walked in just a few minutes after we arrived. I looked at Tim Harris and could hardly believe what I saw! He looked like he was no more than twenty-five. The chief introduced us to Tim. We shook hands and then Tim asked, "Where are the plans for the transporter?"

Igor handed Tim the plans and Tim asked, "Is there a desk or table around here where I can study this stuff?"

One of the guards said, "At the end of that hallway on the right there's a conference room with a big table and several chairs."

Then Tim said, "I need a cold six pack of Mountain Dew. Would somebody get that for me while I look at these plans?"

The chief looked at one of the guards. The guard said, "I'll take care of that sir," and he left.

Tim went to the conference room with the plans. Igor and I had nothing to do, so we looked around the building and found an office with a desk and a few chairs. All we could do at this point was to wait. A few minutes later the chief joined us. After he sat down I said, "It looks like we're trusting the future of the world to a guy who looks like a teenager!"

"I know he looks young, but he's older than he looks. He graduated from high school at fourteen. By the time he was nineteen he had earned degrees in both electrical and mechanical engineering. He decided to join the Airforce and was trained as a pilot. While still in the Airforce he went back to school and earned doctorates in Electrical and Mechanical Engineering. After that he transferred to the Army Weapons Research Center. He has been designing and building weapons for our armed forces for more than five years. However, what makes him uniquely qualified for this job, is that he is currently designing a transporter for us."

"Did he give you his life's history on the way here from the airport?" I asked.

"When I first saw him, I thought he was too young to have the experience needed to do the job. I don't remember exactly what I said, but it was some stupid remark. After I said it he gave me a synopsis of his background, and it's very impressive."

"How far has he gotten on designing our transporter?"

"I asked, but the project is classified and he couldn't tell me anything. If you still have security clearance, he might tell you."

"I do still have security clearance, but I'm not going to ask. Actually, I don't think anybody should have a transporter. It completely changes the rules of warfare. It has the potential to be the ultimate weapon."

Igor said, "I agree. Nobody should have one, but there's no way to prevent progress. I'm sure people felt the same way about machine guns and airplanes when they were invented. If somebody has a transporter, I don't want it to be some Islamic fanatic."

We continued talking but we were interrupted when Tim walked in and said excitedly, "We have a problem! As soon as I turn on the receiver the guys at the other end will know it. I'm fairly sure I know how to send something to them, but if they are prepared, they may be able to send something to us first. After I turn on the system it will probably take two or three minutes to put the system into 'send' mode. They may be capable of sending a bomb here before I could complete the mode change."

"Tim, do you have any suggestions?" the chief asked.

"Yeah, the first thing I want to do is have a KX device sent here. That's our most powerful conventional weapon. A five-hundred-pound KX device has the explosive power of two tons of TNT. That, I'm sure, will be enough to destroy their facility. We also need to build a containment wall around the receiver deck. The wall will be open at the top so any explosion on the receiver deck would be directed up. We need a thousand concrete blocks, mortar, and people to build the wall here as soon as possible. The wall has to be completed within twelve hours."

"I'll call the mayor. We can probably have a crew and the materials here in less than two hours," the chief said.

Tim said, "I'll have a five-hundred-pound KX bomb and a detonator here in six hours."

Tim and the chief both took out their cellphones and made the calls. An hour and a half later five city workers showed up with a truckload of bags of mortar, a portable cement mixer, and other tools needed to build the wall. Tim explained to them what they had to do and made it clear the wall had to be built as quickly as possible. He looked at the ceiling and told the guys they had to cut a hole above the receiver plate as well.

Two of the guys immediately went to the roof to figure out the best way to cut the hole. While they were on the roof a truck loaded with concrete blocks arrived. Two hours later the hole in the roof was finished. The wall was four feet high, except for a four feet wide opening that was left so the bomb could be placed on the receiver deck. They had to wait until the bomb was in position before they could continue.

Tim went to the conference room to study the transporter plans, but soon came out to tell us the plane with the bomb would arrive in twenty minutes. The chief quickly made arrangements for a truck with a police escort to meet the plane and bring the bomb to the warehouse.

Forty-five minutes later the bomb was wheeled in and placed on the receiver deck. Tim attached the detonator to the bomb and set it for a one-minute delay. The detonator was activated by a small transmitter that Tim placed in his shirt pocket.

I watched him prepare the bomb, and when he was done I asked him, "Is that a safe place for the detonator control? What happens if something accidentally hits the button on the control?"

Tim laughed and said, "Nothing would happen unless the correct four-digit code was set on the controller. That won't happen until I'm ready."

"Good, I don't want to be blown up by accident."

Six hours later the wall was completed. It was twelve inches thick and only six inches from the hole in the roof. It was impressive, but it still didn't make me feel safe. The only thing that would make me feel safe was to be several miles away.

Tim announced he was ready. He had written out the exact instructions to set the device in "send" mode. He told the chief to move everyone out of the building. The chief ordered everyone out, and they all left except for Igor and me. The chief looked at me and said, "Frank, you have to get out of here too. I can't afford to lose my only homicide detective."

I turned to Tim and said, "Would it be helpful if I stayed?"

He thought about it for a few seconds and said, "Yeah, with two people operating the switches, we might be able to reduce the time to change modes by thirty seconds."

"That settles it, I'm staying."

Igor said, "I'm staying too. I started this whole thing and I have to stay until it's finished."

After everybody else was gone, Tim said, "There are thirteen steps to change the mode and they have to be done in sequence. You will perform steps 8, 9, and 10." He spent a minute showing me what to do. Then he walked over to the power switch and asked, "Are you ready?"

"Yes."

"Once I turn on the power I have to wait until the system is ready to accept a command. That will probably take about thirty seconds. I'll perform the first seven steps and say 'start'. Then you will perform your steps and say 'done'. Then I'll do the final three steps."

Tim turned on the power. Lights began to flash everywhere. I watched Tim. He was staring at something on the panel in front of him. I saw a green light come on and he started changing switch settings. Each time he completed a step he yelled the step number. A few seconds after he said "five" he yelled, "Shit, I think they know what we're doing!"

It didn't stop him. He yelled "seven". A moment later he yelled "start."

I immediately started performing my tasks. I was about to do step ten when I saw a bright light reflecting off the ceiling and the equipment starting to make a loud whining sound. It slowed me down for only a fraction of a second. I completed step ten and yelled "done."

The light got brighter and the sound grew louder as Tim performed the last two steps and then he pushed the button on the detonator control. Suddenly there was an explosion inside the cinder block wall. I heard it and felt it. Then, as suddenly as it started, it disappeared.

Tim turned off the power to the device and the room became silent.

"What the hell happened?" I asked.

"They were obviously ready for us. They sent a bomb here too. It actually exploded inside the wall, but their bomb, which was in the process of exploding, along with ours was sent to them. I don't know what happened on their end, but I would guess our plan worked. Igor, perhaps you can check the news in that area and find out if any explosions were reported."

"I can do better than that. I'll call my office in Moscow and let them know what we did and ask them to confirm there was an explosion in that area. I should know in an hour."

Igor made the call, but since he was speaking Russian, I didn't understand anything he said. After he ended the call he said, "They'll call me back as soon as they know anything."

While Igor was on the phone the chief came back. I told him what happened and we were waiting for confirmation from Igor's contacts in Russia. The chief left three people there to guard the warehouse and everybody else left.

I took Igor back to his hotel. He promised to call me as soon as he heard anything. He also said he was leaving the following day to return to Russia. He gave me another card. This one, I presumed, was real. It had his name, an address in Moscow, and a different phone number. He said if I ever find myself in Moscow, I should call him and he would buy me a bottle of vodka.

He called me an hour after I dropped him off at his hotel to tell me an explosion occurred at a medical research facility just outside of Moscow, but there were no details. I thanked him for the information.

The following morning, I turned on the TV to get the news. The big story was about a probable terrorist attack at a medical research facility near Moscow. Twenty-six people were killed in the attack and the building was demolished by two explosions a minute apart.

Now I knew the Russian rebels no longer had a transporter to sell, and I guessed the people who designed it were dead. Tim probably had enough information to complete his design. The immediate threat was gone, but I had a bad feeling it would be back.

When I arrived at the station that morning I found a note from Jill asking me to call her. The first thought I had was that there was another body. I called her and when she answered I asked, "Is there a problem?"

"No, the rumor is that there won't be any more bodies with missing parts. But I have a much more important subject to discuss with you."

"What is it?"

"I have a ten-year college reunion to go to next week and I don't have a date. Would you like to go with me?"

"Yeah, I'd like that very much."

The Antique Car Caper
A Frank Carver Mystery

Jill Tanner and I had our first date after the incident with the Russian transporter. That was three months ago, and we've been living in sin (according to my mother) for the past two months. She moved into my apartment because she had been living with her parents and really wanted to be out on her own. Jill was the county Medical Examiner and I was the only homicide detective in the Norfolk County Police Department.

She called to tell me she would be home about an hour late because of a case she was working on. I was sitting in the living room watching the news, and getting more depressed by the minute, when I heard her opening the door. She walked into the living room, looked at me, and smiled. Then she sat down next to me, kissed me passionately, and said, "We have to talk."

We had a rule that we wouldn't discuss events from work at home, but I had the distinct feeling the rule was about to be broken. "Does this concern the case you're working on? Do you remember our rule?" I asked.

"Yeah, I remember our rule, but if you let me break it I promise I'll make it up to you later this evening."

"Well, okay, but just this once."

"Great, I'm sure you remember the body that was found in the 1937 Ford that was discovered in the abandoned barn on K Street."

"Yes, of course I remember it. It was only four days ago. After the initial examination, you said the guy died from natural causes. Is that no longer true?"

"That's the point. I can't find a cause of death. There's no sign of trauma, and his blood work was normal. There were no toxins detected and the only chemicals in his system were the result of the prescription medications he was taking. By the way, his name was Douglas Baker."

Thinking back to the case that brought us together I asked, "Were all of Mr. Baker's internal organs intact? Was there a small incision at the base of his brain?"

"Look, I'm being serious about this. I need some ideas."

"Did you check his body for needle marks?"

"Of course, Amanda and I looked everywhere. We checked all the obvious spots and we looked between his fingers and toes, in his mouth, under his arms, his crotch, and even between his butt cheeks. There were no needle marks on his body."

"Could he have been killed by something he ingested that his body had already metabolized so there was no trace left to be detected?"

"I thought about that, but those types of products would have resulted in a detectable cause of death. There was no indication of a heart attack, cardiac or respiratory arrest, or a stroke. I can't see any reason why Mr. Baker should be dead. I want to do a full autopsy, but his wife won't allow it. I was hoping you would talk to her about it."

"I can't do that unless you tell me Mr. Baker's death is suspicious. If you do that, I can open an investigation and then you can do your autopsy without permission from his wife."

"I know that. I'll think about it and make my decision tomorrow. Let's go get something to eat. I'm really hungry."

The following morning while I was in the shower Jill came into the bathroom and said, "I've made my decision regarding Mr. Baker. I'll send you an official notice this morning that since there's no obvious cause of death, an investigation into the circumstances of his death is needed."

"Okay, you send that to me. I'll get the chief to open a case file."

"Thanks honey, I love you. I'm leaving now. Do you want to meet for lunch?"

The Antique Car Caper

"Sure, I'll call you. Bye."

By the time I got out of the shower Jill was gone. I got dressed and went to the station. When I arrived at my desk the report regarding Mr. Baker was already there. I filled out a form and took it and the report from Jill to the chief's office. He wasn't there so I left it on his desk.

Twenty minutes later my phone rang. I picked it up and said, "Lieutenant Carver speaking. How can I help you?"

The chief said loudly, "You can find out who the asshole was that killed Doug Baker! He was a friend of mine."

"Yes sir," I responded. "How well did you know him?"

"We've been friends for more than twenty years. We're both antique car buffs. Unlike me, Doug had the money to pursue his hobby. I have to be content to look at antique car magazines or go to car shows."

"Did he own a 1937 Ford?"

"Not that I'm aware of. I know he was found in one, but I don't think he owned it. I'm sure he would have bought it if he had the opportunity."

"How many old cars did he own?"

"I would guess about twenty. If you go see his wife, Dorothy, I'm sure she'll give you anything you need."

"Jill wants to perform an autopsy and his wife refused. Once you approve opening the case, the autopsy will be done as soon as you send her the paperwork. Will that cause a problem with Dorothy?"

"No, I don't think so. Doug was in excellent health and his death was a shock to her. But if she thinks foul play might have been involved, she won't hesitate to help you."

"I'll go see her this afternoon."

"I'll call her and let her know you're going to be there. Keep me informed."

"Of course, sir."

I called Jill and told her the case file was opened and the chief would be sending her the paperwork for the autopsy. I also told her I was going to see Douglas Baker's wife in the afternoon. I asked her to delay the autopsy until after my meeting. She agreed to wait and said she was busy anyway, so we decided to cancel our lunch date.

I arrived at the Baker residence at 1:30. The house was in a neighborhood I had seldom been in. All the houses were very large, had lawns that were obviously maintained by professional gardeners, and probably cost several million dollars. I drove up the circular driveway and stopped by the front door. Before I could ring the bell, the door was opened by a woman who looked like she was in her mid-sixties. Her gray hair was flawlessly combed. She had bright blue green eyes and a perfect smile. She said, "You must be Lieutenant Carver. I'm Dorothy Baker. Please come in."

I followed her in and found myself in the entrance foyer. It was probably twenty feet wide and had a thirty foot ceiling. The walls were adorned with paintings. We turned right and walked into a large room with two leather sofas and four matching recliners. In one corner of the room was a grand piano, and in another was a large ornate wood desk. The walls of the room were covered with dark wood paneling. Dorothy sat on one of the recliners and I sat on a sofa across from her.

I said, "I'm sorry for your loss, Mrs. Baker. If this becomes difficult for you please let me know and I'll come back at another time."

"Chief Mitchell told me that it now appears Douglas didn't die from natural causes." She paused for moment and then said emphatically, "I want you to catch the bastard that killed him. I'll do anything I can to help."

I was somewhat surprised by the harsh tone of her comment. "Do you know why he was in that abandoned barn on K Street?"

"No, the last time I saw Doug he told me he was going to meet somebody who wanted to use some of his cars in an antique auto show that was being held in London later this year. He never gave me the name of the person he was going to meet or told me the location of the meeting."

"Does he often allow his cars to be used in auto shows?"

"He gets requests constantly. Every one of his cars has been meticulously restored. The process was time consuming and very expensive. But, Doug told me that allowing his cars to be displayed was quite profitable. I was never directly involved with the financial aspects of it. I'm sure all the information is on his computer. Please feel free to look at his files."

"Thank you, I'll do that. Did Chief Mitchell tell you we need to do an autopsy to determine how your husband died?"

"Yes, I didn't see any reason to do that before. But now I understand why it must be done. I would like to have the funeral as soon as possible, so please have it done immediately."

"I'll try to get it done today. I'm sure they'll release the body to you as soon as the autopsy is finished. Thank you for your time. If it's alright with you, I'll have a forensic accountant contact you to arrange a time for him to go over your husband's computer files."

"That will be fine. I'll be waiting for his call."

As soon as I got back into my car I called Jill. When she answered I said, "I've just met with Dorothy Baker. She now wants the autopsy done as soon as possible so she can have the funeral for her husband."

"Good, I'll get started on it in an hour. Do you want to observe?"

"Jill, I don't like looking at dead bodies when they are whole. You couldn't measure my desire to see one cut up into little pieces."

She laughed and said, "Coward".

"Okay, if it makes you feel better call me a coward. However, I recently ate lunch and I would like to keep it where it belongs."

"I'll call you when I'm done."

I went back to the station and told the chief about the meeting with Dorothy and my call to Jill. Then I said, "There had to be a reason Doug Baker was killed and I suspect it had something to do with his car collection. Dorothy said we could send a forensic accountant to the house to look at the files on Doug's computer. I think we should do that as soon as possible."

"I agree, but I have to get approval to hire somebody for the job. I'll take care of that this afternoon. We should be able to get someone tomorrow. I think you should be there too."

"No problem, just let me know when I have to be there."

I left the chief's office and went to my desk. I was just sitting there thinking about the case when the phone rang. I answered it and heard Jill say, "I know you don't want to look at body parts, but the autopsy revealed something I think you should see."

"I'll be there in ten minutes."

"I'll be waiting."

The Medical Examiner's office was a five-minute walk from the station. I let the dispatcher know where I was going and left the station. When I arrived, Jill was waiting for me in the lobby. She kissed me lightly on the cheek, took my hand, and pulled me into the lab. There was a body lying on one of the two stainless steel lab tables covered with a sheet. Jill took me over to a counter. On it was a large glass dish that had something in it that kind of looked like a brain.

"What am I looking at?" I asked.

"I know you have seen a human brain before. This one belongs to Mr. Baker. I have never seen anything like this. It looks like his brain was subjected to a very high temperature and cooked inside his skull. But, there's no indication of external trauma or burning anywhere on his head. I can't imagine what kind of weapon could have done this."

"I can. I've seen this type of injury before, but not on a human."

She sounded more than a little irritated when she said, "Please elaborate!"

"When I was in Army Intelligence, I saw a report about a weapon that could 'cook' our enemy's organs inside his body without leaving a mark. I saw pictures of the results after the weapon was used on a pig carcass. I didn't think the weapon ever made it into production."

"Are you saying someone from the US Army killed Mr. Baker with an experimental weapon?"

"I suppose it's possible, but I don't think it's likely. I think a more reasonable scenario would be that somebody stole the plans for the weapon and built a few. Then they were probably sold to the highest bidder."

"That's comforting. I know that's going to make me sleep better tonight," Jill said sarcastically.

"I'm certain that these weapons weren't cheap, so whoever bought them had to have an almost unlimited budget for weapons. I think only the big drug cartels could afford to buy them."

"I'm not a weapons expert, but why would this weapon be an advantage over a gun?"

"It doesn't need external ammunition. As long as the battery is charged the weapon will fire. It has no effect on inanimate objects, so you can fire the weapon almost constantly without destroying anything except a living target. Also, it's silent."

"Can you find out if any of these weapons were ever made or if the plans were ever stolen?"

"Yeah, I'll call a buddy of mine who still works in Army Intelligence and ask him. By the way, I would guess this weapon is secret, so don't discuss this with anybody else."

I went back to my desk and called George Dyer. He still worked for Army Intelligence. We talk a few times a year and last year we went on a fishing trip in the Canadian Rockies. When George answered I said, "Hi George, it's Frank. It's been a while since our last conversation."

"Yeah, the last time was a few months ago when I gave you some info about some CIA agent. Was that helpful?"

"Actually, it proved to be very helpful. I have another question for you. Do you remember the RX Microwave Weapon that…" I never got to finish the sentence.

George interrupted me by yelling, "***STOP!*** This isn't a secure line. I can't discuss anything regarding the RX unless you are here in person or we are speaking on a secure line."

"I'm sorry. I didn't realize the RX required that level of security. There's an Airforce base an hour from here. I'll go there now and call you again when I get there. Will that be okay?"

"Yes, I'll be waiting for your call."

It took me forty-five minutes to get to the Airforce base. I'm in the Army Reserve, so I still have my ID and security clearance. I stopped at the gate and showed the guard my Army Intelligence ID. I told him what I needed and he directed me to the Communications Office.

The guard must have called to let them know I was coming, because when I arrived at the Communications Office they were expecting me. An attractive young woman took me to an enclosed soundproof room with a table and two phones. One was black and the other was red. She asked me if I had any recording devices or cameras because they weren't allowed in the room. I told her all I had was my cell phone, which I took out of my pocket and gave to her.

I walked into the room and closed the door. I picked up the black phone and called George again. When he answered I gave him the number on the red phone and he said he would call me in a minute. When the phone rang I answered by saying, "Hi George."

"We are now on a secure line. Tell me why you want to know about the RX."

"Because I'm working on a murder investigation, and it appears the victim was killed with a weapon that has the same capabilities as the RX."

"I've been waiting for that to happen. I knew it was just a matter of time. The development of the RX continued after you left active duty. They built twenty-five prototypes. During the testing two problems were found. The primary problem was that the weapon wasn't reliable. Sometimes the battery would die after a single burst and sometimes it would last for more than fifty. The other problem was the width of the burst. At fifteen feet it was about two inches wide, which was perfect. However, at twenty feet, the effective width of the burst was almost four feet, and at a distance of thirty feet the effective width increased to an astonishing twelve feet! I'm sure you remember, the RX was supposed to be a stealth weapon that could kill without leaving any evidence. But if you were more than fifteen feet from your target, the intense heat from the weapon would cause the target to explode! Not exactly what we were trying to develop. They tried to fix the problems, but after six months, and millions of dollars, the project was canceled."

"So, what happened to the prototypes?"

"They disappeared. All twenty-five of them were placed in a secure storage facility. Someone with the appropriate clearance must have taken them one at a time. They were small, but probably still too big to remove all of them at the same time. I don't think you ever saw one, but they were made almost entirely of plastic, so the metal detectors at the storage facility wouldn't have been triggered when the weapon was carried out. What happened to your victim?"

"His brain was fried. If I find out who killed our victim, I'll let you know. Perhaps he can tell you where the weapons are."

"It's a nice thought, but I would guess they were sold to multiple buyers."

"You're probably right, but I'll let you know anyway. Thanks for the information."

"You do know you can't discuss this with anyone."

"I know. Thanks again for your help. Maybe we can go fishing again sometime soon."

"That would be great!"

I ended the call. It was nice to know my suspicions about the weapon were confirmed, but I didn't see how that was going to help find our killer. I suddenly thought of something I should have done yesterday. I called Jim Doyle who is in charge of the Forensics Department. He answered on the first ring and I said, "Hi Jim, I need your help with something."

"Of course, you do, that's the only reason anybody ever calls."

"You sound a little down. Do you need a hug?"

"Yeah, but not from you. If you want to send Jill over, that would be okay. Anyway, what do you need?"

"Did your guys get involved with the Douglas Baker case?"

"Not really. We impounded the car, but we never looked for any evidence. I saw the report this morning saying a murder case had been opened up. I'll go check out the car myself and send two guys to the barn, but I wouldn't expect to find anything there."

"Thanks. Please send me the report when your guys are finished."

"Did Jill find a cause of death?"

"Yes, Doug Baker's brain was fried."

"What? Can you explain that?"

"All I can tell you is that something destroyed his brain and caused no external trauma to his head."

The Antique Car Caper

"How is that possible?"

I couldn't tell him the truth so I said, "I'm working on that."

"Good Luck, and don't forget about my hug from Jill."

"I'll discuss it with her tonight."

The day was almost over so I went home to think about what I had discovered so far, which wasn't very much. I walked in, grabbed a beer from the fridge, and sat on the sofa to think about the case. My conclusion was that unless either the accountant or forensics comes up with a lead, this case is dead.

When Jill came home she sat next to me on the sofa and asked, "Did you find out any additional information about the weapon used to kill Mr. Baker?"

"Yes, but it's classified, so please don't ask. All I can do is to confirm the weapon I told you about is capable of inflicting the type of injury that killed him."

"Do you see any reason why the body shouldn't be released to Mrs. Baker?"

"No, I'll call her in the morning and let her know. I'm going to have to tell her how her husband died, and I really don't want to."

"I'm sure you'll think of something. What's for dinner?"

"Whatever you feel like cooking."

"I don't, so let's go out."

"That works for me." Then I added, "The next time you see Jim Doyle, give him a friendly hug."

"Sure, but why."

"When I spoke to him earlier today he sounded a little depressed, so I asked him if he needed a hug. He said he did but not from me, so I told him I would ask you."

The following morning, I got to my desk at 8:00. The Chief was already there so I walked over to ask him about the accountant. When he saw me he smiled and said, "Good morning Frank. Anything new with the Doug Baker case?"

"Jill found the cause of death and it wasn't due to natural causes. His death was caused by severe brain damage."

"But there was no sign of trauma. How is that possible?"

I didn't want to lie so I said, "I wish I could tell you. Anyway, yesterday afternoon I asked Jim Doyle to check out the car and the barn, but I haven't heard anything yet."

"That's a start anyway. The accountant will be here at 1:00. Do you want me to call Dorothy and tell her?"

"No, I'll do it. I have to call her anyway to tell her we found the cause of death."

"Okay, just let me know if you need my help with anything."

I went back to my desk and called Dorothy. I told her we found out what killed Doug and it wasn't due to natural causes. Thankfully, she didn't ask for any details. I also told her I would be bringing the accountant over at 1:30.

The accountant showed up a few minutes early. He looked like an accountant. He was wearing black pants and a blue sport coat with patches on the elbows. He was short, maybe five eight or nine, and a little pudgy. He had thinning black hair and a narrow mustache. His name was Archie Winters. After a brief meeting with the chief, Archie and I went to Dorothy Baker's house.

Like before, she opened the door before I had a chance to ring the bell. I introduced Archie. Then she led us into the room where Doug's computer was located. She handed Archie a note that had the password for the computer and Archie walked over to the computer and got busy.

Dorothy looked at me and said, "I want to thank you for getting Doug's body released so we can schedule the funeral."

"You're welcome. So far, we have no information with regard to a motive for the crime. I had a forensics team go over the car and the barn where your husband was found, but they haven't given me a report yet. I'm hoping that between the forensics people and Archie we will at least come up with a clue as to what happened."

"Please keep me informed."

"Of course."

She said, "I have to plan the funeral. Please excuse me," and left the room.

I sat down on one of the sofas thinking this was going to be a long, boring, afternoon. A few minutes later my cell phone rang. It was Jim Doyle.

"I have some information for you, Frank. We found three sets of unidentified prints on the car. We are running them through the system now. There was no way to trace the owner of the old Ford Mr. Baker was found in. There were no plates on the car, and cars didn't have VIN numbers until 1954. The search of the barn turned up exactly zilch. So, other than the prints, we have nothing."

"Thanks for the update. If you find out who the prints belong to, let me know."

I watched Archie for a while and then remembered I downloaded a book a few days ago and I hadn't started reading it yet. It was something about future world history. I spent the next couple of hours alternating between watching Archie and reading the book.

I was totally engrossed in the book when Archie came over and tapped me on the shoulder. He said, "I found something interesting."

"Okay, what did you find?"

"Mr. Baker had been leasing a few of his cars to companies that put on antique car shows. Apparently, it was very profitable. He made almost $400,000 doing that last year. That seemed a little excessive, so I checked and found that unless the car is extremely rare, they would lease for about $2500 a month. None of Mr. Baker's cars would be considered rare, but he was leasing them for more than $10,000 per month. In one case, his Ford Model T was leased for two months at $30,000 per month!"

"That does seem a little suspicious. Where were these car shows held?"

"None of them were in the US. All of them were in Europe or South America."

"Could he have been smuggling something in the cars?"

"That's what I was thinking, but I have no idea what."

Archie went back to the computer to continue his investigation while I sat on the sofa thinking about the antique car leasing business. I realized I had a few more questions for Dorothy. I didn't want to disturb her while she was planning her husband's funeral, so I waited until she returned. When she walked into the room she sat across from me and said, "I'm glad that's over. The funeral will be on Saturday at 1:00. Will you let Chief Mitchell know?"

"Of course, I know he was one of your husband's friends and I'm sure he'll attend. May I ask you a question?"

"Sure."

"What kind of work did Douglas do?"

"He was a pharmaceutical salesman. He worked for Advanced Laboratories for more than thirty years. When he left he was the Sales Manager for the North American territory. That was five years ago. About three years ago he decided to go back to work. He developed his own sources for the drugs he sold and was able to get back many of his previous clients. I really don't know the details, but apparently it was very profitable."

"Did he have an office somewhere?"

"No, he worked from home. I think there was a warehouse where the drugs were stored. I would guess they were shipped from there too."

"Do you know the location of the warehouse?"

"As I said, I think there was a warehouse. I'm not sure. I overheard some conversations where Doug was telling someone what products to ship and who to ship them to. So, I guessed he was speaking to someone at a warehouse."

"Thank you for that information. How long had Doug been collecting and restoring antique cars?"

"Probably for at least twenty-five years, but he only had a few of them before he retired. Since his retirement, he has purchased a lot of them. We have a big garage under the house. The cars are kept there. It looks like a museum."

"Do you know when he started leasing them for shows?"

"He started that right after he started working again."

"One last question. Was this computer the only one Doug used?"

"Yes, I believe it was."

"Thank you, I appreciate your help with the investigation.

Dorothy said, "You're welcome. Please excuse me again. I have to go make some calls regarding the funeral. When you and Mr. Winter are finished, please let yourselves out."

"We'll do that. I suspect it will be another hour or so. I'll call you tomorrow and let you know what we found."

After Dorothy left, Archie walked over to me and said, "I heard that conversation. Do you believe her?"

"Not completely, I think she's hiding something. I don't understand how a wife could know so little about her husband's business. Was there any information on his computer regarding drug sales?"

"No, the only financial information on it is for his antique car leasing business."

"There must be an office and a warehouse somewhere. I think I'll start calling hospitals and clinics and find out if any of them were Doug's customers. Do you need more time here?"

"No, I made copies of all the pertinent files."

"Okay, let's go."

51

When I got home, Jill was there waiting for me. I was expecting her to ask about the case, so I wasn't surprised when the first thing she said after I walked in was, "Anything new regarding Douglas Baker's murder?"

"Yeah, the accountant who went through Baker's files found some interesting stuff. I'm not sure what it all means yet, but I'm certain our victim was some kind of crook."

"Have you told the chief yet?"

"No, I want more evidence before I tell him about it."

"What did you find?"

"Several separate things I'm sure are somehow tied together. Doug Baker had a collection of restored antique cars. He would lease them regularly to companies that produced auto shows. However, according to his books, he typically received ten times the normal rate on his leases. I also found out he used to be the national sales manager for Advanced Laboratories. I think they are one of the biggest suppliers of pharmaceuticals in the world. He resigned several years ago, and after a while went into business for himself. Apparently, he continued to service some of his old customers. I would like to know how he did that. He had to be getting the drugs he sold from somewhere. His wife, who claimed to be almost totally ignorant regarding his drug sales business, told me he worked from home, but she thought there was a warehouse somewhere that serviced the orders. You're a doctor; does that seem to be a little strange?"

"Well, not exactly. Because of my profession I don't buy drugs, but I know, reimbursements to providers from both the government and insurance companies has been substantially reduced as a result of the Affordable Care Act. I'm sure most providers are looking for bargains wherever they can find them."

I thought about what Jill said for a moment. Then I said, "Would they buy off brand drugs to save money?"

"That depends on what you mean by 'off brand'. They would buy generic drugs that have USP approval, but

I don't think they would buy a non-approved generic version of a name brand drug. That could present a substantial and unacceptable risk to their patients."

"What if they thought they were buying the real thing, but at a big discount."

"I suppose they would consider doing that. But if it was me, I would wonder why I was getting a bargain."

"Thanks Jill, I think you may have just given me the lead I've been looking for. Tomorrow I'm going to call the purchasing managers at every hospital in the state and find out if they were buying drugs from Doug Baker."

"What do you think is going on?"

"I'm not sure yet, but I think I'll be able to answer that question tomorrow."

The following morning, I got a list of the hospitals in the state. At 10:00 I began calling them asking to speak to the purchasing manager. I started with the two local hospitals. The first hospital I called, Timberlake Medical Center, was the largest hospital in the county. After several minutes on hold I spoke to a woman name Grace who did her best to prevent me from speaking to her boss. Finally, I said, "We can do this two ways. You can put me through to your boss, or I will be there in an hour with a search warrant and tear apart your office until I find what I'm looking for. It's your choice."

Grace still wasn't being cooperative, so I said, "This conversation is over. I will be there shortly with the warrant. I will also make sure the hospital administrator knows you're responsible for the police going through your files. Goodbye," and I hung up the phone.

I knew it wouldn't take long. About five minutes after I hung up on Grace my phone rang. I answered the phone, "Lieutenant Carver, homicide."

"Lieutenant Carver, my name is Dr. Gerald Cheever. I'm the administrator for Timberlake Medical Center. I want to apologize for Grace. She's supposed to screen calls, but not from the police. There's no need for a warrant. How can we help you?"

"I'm investigating the murder of Douglas Baker."

Before I could continue Dr. Cheever loudly asked, "Doug was murdered?"

"Yes, he was murdered. I'm trying to find out if your hospital was buying drugs from him."

"Yes, we were. May I ask why?"

"In a moment. First tell me something. Were you buying generics or brand name drugs from Mr. Baker?"

"I believe they were all brand name drugs from Advanced Laboratories, but I'm not sure. You will have to speak to Dean, our purchasing manager, for a list."

"That's what I was trying to do when I ran into a brick wall named Grace. Please have Dean call me as soon as possible."

"Yes Lieutenant, I'll have him call you immediately. Can you tell me why you want to know what drugs we were buying from Doug?"

"I think there's a possibility the brand name drugs you purchased may have been uncertified generics."

"Oh my God!" Dr. Cheever exclaimed, "If that's true, we could be in real trouble. I promise you Dean will provide you with whatever information you need. But don't hesitate to call me directly if you need anything."

"Thank you for your cooperation doctor. I'll be waiting for Dean's call."

About ten minutes later Dean called. He said, "Dr. Cheever told me to call you. He said we may have been buying counterfeit drugs from Doug Baker. Is that correct?"

"Yes, is there any way to verify if the drugs you bought were the real thing?"

"I can tell you the drugs were packaged correctly. After Dr. Cheever told me about the problem I verified that the lot numbers on the packaging corresponded to the drugs we purchased. I think Advanced Laboratories would be able to analyze the drugs and verify if they're genuine."

The Antique Car Caper

"I would like to stop by the hospital and pick up two or three samples of different drugs you purchased from Doug Baker. I'll send them to Advanced Laboratories for analysis and let you know what I find out. Can you do that?"

"I'll have them at the reception desk in ten minutes."

"Thank you for your help with this."

The hospital was a fifteen-minute drive from the station, so I left immediately. When I arrived at the reception desk the package was waiting for me. I opened it and inside were three vials of different medicines, all in their original packaging. It was exactly what I wanted.

When I got back to my desk I spent a few minutes checking out Advanced Laboratories. It was a huge company. They employed about eighty thousand people all over the world and more than fifty thousand in the United States. I called their corporate number and asked to speak to somebody in Customer Relations. A woman named Joanne Green answered the phone.

I said, "Ms. Green, my name is Frank Carver. I'm a homicide investigator for the Norfolk County Police Department. I'm currently investigating the murder of one of your former employees. His name is Douglas Baker. It appears Mr. Baker may have been involved in counterfeiting drugs that Advanced Laboratories produces. I need to speak to somebody about this situation. Can you help me?"

"Yes sir. Please give me a moment to find the correct person for you to speak to."

"That will be fine."

She put me on hold and I spent a few minutes listening to advertisements about all the fantastic new products Advanced Laboratories makes. When she came back on the line she said, "I'll connect you with Dr. Katz now."

I heard a few clicks and a man said, "I'm Dr. Bruce Katz. Ms. Green said you may have found some counterfeit Advanced Laboratories products. Is that correct?"

"Yes, Dr. Katz. I'm investigating the murder of Douglas Baker, and in the process of that investigation I discovered he was selling Advanced Laboratories products. Since he's no longer employed by you, I was concerned that the products he was selling might not be genuine."

"I appreciate your concern and I'm glad you brought it to our attention. If someone is selling counterfeit drugs, it could injure or kill a patient. What can I do to assist you?"

"I have three samples of drugs I received from our local hospital. I would like to send them to you for analysis. Would you be able to determine if they're the real thing?"

"Yes, I'm certain we can do that. But you don't have to send them to me. I'll have a courier pick them up as soon as possible. I'll have them by tomorrow morning and I will have an answer for you by noon. Please tell me where I can have the samples picked up."

I gave Dr. Katz the information he needed. Then I decided I had to tell the chief his friend was a crook. I walked over to his office and knocked lightly on the open door. He looked up from the papers he was reading and said, "Hi Frank, come in. Do you have any news concerning Doug's murder?"

I sat on the chair facing his desk and said, "Yes, but I don't think you're going to like what I have to say."

"Just tell me, Okay?" he said with some irritation in his voice.

I spent the next several minutes telling him what I found. When I was finished he just looked at me for a few seconds and then he said emphatically, "Shit! I can't believe Doug would do that. I've known him for more than twenty years." He paused for a moment and then asked, "How does this tie in to his murder?"

"I don't know yet. At first, I thought the murder was related to his antique car business, but now I feel the murder is a direct result of his drug sales."

"Do we know if anyone died as a result of receiving his phony drugs?"

"No, and I suspect we will probably never know. No drug is one hundred percent effective. If you think the drugs you are administering to your patients are brand name products and the patient dies, why would you blame the drug? I think most doctors would simply feel the patient didn't respond to the drug in the same way other patients did."

"You're probably right. What's the next step in the investigation?"

"I have to find out where the warehouse is, and I have a plan to do that. But I want to wait for confirmation from Advanced Laboratories that the drugs are counterfeit."

"That sounds reasonable. Just keep me informed."

"Yes sir".

The courier showed up an hour later. There was nothing to do now except wait for the test results on the drugs, so I went home.

Jill arrived a few minutes after I did. I brought her up to date on the status of the investigation. I knew I had made some progress but I still didn't know who killed Doug Baker, why they killed him, or how they got the weapon they used.

Those questions kept me from sleeping much that night. I got out of bed at 4:30, took a shower, got dressed, and left without waking up Jill. I stopped for breakfast and arrived at the station a few minutes after seven.

I looked at the news online, but as usual, it was very depressing. Since I was already somewhat depressed by this case, I turned off my computer and started reading my book again. Jill called at 8:00 and we agreed to go to lunch together. I was really getting anxious for the call from Dr. Katz. That call came at 10:15.

Dr. Katz said, "The active ingredients in the drugs appear to be compounded correctly, but the inactive ingredients are not. These drugs are definitely counterfeit. We add different inactive ingredients to every batch of drugs we manufacture. That way if there's a problem with any batch of drugs, we can analyze it and find out what batch it's from. Then, if it's necessary, we can recall the entire batch."

"Since the active ingredients are identical, I would assume these drugs will provide the same benefit to patients as the real drug."

"That's correct. I don't believe any patients are in danger because of these drugs, but obviously we have a financial concern. It can easily cost more than $100,000,000 to bring a drug to market. We need to be the exclusive supplier of that drug in order to recover our investment. If we are unable to do that, we won't have the funds to continue to develop new drugs."

"I understand your concern. Now that I know the drugs are phony, I have an idea how we can find out who, besides Douglas Baker, is involved. I hope that won't only lead me to the murderer, but also put these drug dealers out of business and in prison where they belong."

"If I can be of any assistance in your investigation, please don't hesitate to ask."

"Thank you. I'll keep you informed as the investigation continues."

"I appreciate that."

My next call was to Dean. This time Grace put me through immediately.

"Hi Dean, when you want to order drugs from Doug Baker, how did you do it?"

"It was all done using e-mail. I sent a message and within twenty-four hours I would get a confirmation back from Doug."

"How do you pay for them?"

"The payments are sent by wire transfer."

"So, the bank could be anywhere."

"Yeah, I suppose so."

"I would like you to come to the station and use one of our computers to place a drug order. Our systems are set up so we can trace where the e-mail is going. I'm hoping that

The Antique Car Caper

will help us locate the other people involved in this deception."

"I'll come by around 1:00. Is that okay?"

"Sure, I'll see you then."

I immediately called our computer expert and told him what I wanted to do. He told me there was no guarantee the plan would work, but there was no reason not to try it.

When Dean arrived at the station, one of the duty officers brought him to my desk. We shook hands and introduced ourselves. Then I took him to the room where the computer was set up.

He logged into his e-mail system and sent the message to order the drugs. When he was finished, I told him to save any responses he receives, and when the drugs arrive, to contact me so I can check the package for shipping information. I thanked him for his help and he left the station. I returned to my desk.

I thought I was going to be bored, but there was a shooting at a liquor store during a robbery. One of our upstanding citizens tried to hold up the store by pointing his little 22 revolver at the owner and demanding the contents of the cash register. The owner, who had been robbed several times before, had a 45 under the counter by the cash register. There was also an opening in the counter that was designed so he could shoot through it. The owner asked the potential robber if he was sure he wanted to do this. The robber responded by cocking the hammer on his gun. The owner of the store shot him with his 45. The assailant died at the scene. The entire episode was captured on video by the store's security system.

When I came in the following morning, there was a message on my desk from our computer guy telling me he was unable to trace the e-mail. Another dead end. Then Dean called to tell me he received an e-mail from Doug confirming his order. Obviously, wherever Doug is now, he still has access to e-mail. I told Dean to save the message in case there was any way to trace it. Then I called our computer guy again and told him what happened. He said it was unlikely he would be able to get any useful information from the message, but he would try anyway.

Since tracing the e-mail address was probably not going to yield anything useful, there were only two other possibilities: the shipping location and the payment processing information.

The payments were deposited in a bank somewhere. I had to find out who owned the account.

I called Dean again. When he answered the phone I said, "Dean, there's one more thing I need you to do regarding the drug order."

"Okay. What is it?"

"Refuse to pay by wire. There must be some contact information on the invoice. When it comes contact them and tell them you can only pay by check."

"Do you think it will be easier to trace a check than a wire transfer?"

"I'm not sure, but I hope so. I know one of the vice presidents at Community Bank. I'll ask her about it."

Dean was silent for a moment and then asked, "What do you think would happen if I just refused to pay the bill? Would they turn it over to a collection agency? Would they send some big Mafia enforcer named Guido who will threaten to break my legs if I don't pay?"

"What if you don't pay and they send Guido to kill you instead? Do you want to risk that?"

"I see your point. We'll try it your way. Please let me know what they say at the bank."

"Okay, I'll call you later."

I drove over to the downtown Community Bank branch. When I walked in I saw Marcia Blackburn sitting at her desk. Marcia and I went to high school together. We even dated a few times. She saw me looking at her and waved to me. I walked into her office and said, "Hi Marcia, how are you!"

She stood up and said, "Pregnant!"

The Antique Car Caper

It was obvious when she stood up. I said, "Congratulations, I remember you once telling me you wanted to have a lot of children. Is that still true?"

"I think I'll have to wait and see how difficult it is raising the first one before I make that decision. Anyway, how can I help you?"

"I'm working on a murder case that involves counterfeit drugs. The payments for the drugs are made by wire transfer to an offshore numbered account. I don't think there's any way for me to find out who owns the account. I was wondering if it would be easier to trace if the payment was made by check."

"I don't think that would help find the owner of the account. The only advantage might be using the address where the check was mailed to. It's probably going to be a post office box or something similar, but you could watch and see who picks it up."

I smiled at her and said, "Thanks, I didn't think of that. I hope the mailing address is somewhere in this country, because if it's not, there may be a problem convincing the local police to keep tabs on a mail box."

"I'm glad I could help."

After I left Marcia's office I went back to my car. I sat inside and wondered why I didn't think about where the check would be mailed. I called Dean and told him about the conversation I had with Marcia, and then returned to the station.

Now all I could do was wait. Four days later Dean called to say the drugs had arrived. I told him not to let anybody touch the package and I would be there as quickly as possible to pick it up.

I arrived at the hospital twenty minutes later. When I walked in, Dean was waiting for me. I followed him to the mail room and he showed me the package. It was probably twelve inches square and six inches high. I put on gloves and picked up the package so I could look at it. It was sent using UPS overnight service. There was no address for the sender, but it was sent from Cleveland, Ohio. It wasn't much, but at least it was a start. I put the box in a large evidence bag, thanked Dean for his help, and I left the hospital.

When I got back to the station I contacted UPS, told them who I was, and asked for any information they could provide about the package. The man I spoke to said he was unable to provide information over the phone, but if I went to the local UPS office, they would be happy to help me. The UPS office was only two blocks from the station, so I walked over.

There were two people in line. I waited until the clerk was available. He was a middle-aged man who looked like he was bored beyond belief. He sort of smiled at me and asked, "How can I help you today?"

I showed him my ID and said, "I need any information you can give me regarding the person, or company, who sent this package." I handed him the package. He scanned the barcode, a moment later he said, "The sender is Advanced Pharmaceuticals International. The corporate address is in Sao Paulo, Brazil. There is no indication there are any offices in the United States. This package, along with eleven others, were brought into a UPS store in downtown Cleveland."

"Can you give me the destinations of the other packages?"

"Give me a moment and I'll print everything out for you."

"Thanks," I said as I smiled at him.

When he handed me the print out I said, "You have been very helpful. I really appreciate it."

"This is the most interesting thing I've done for a while. I'm glad I could help. Can you tell me what this is all about?"

"I'm investigating the murder of a drug salesman."

"Well, good luck with your investigation."

I went back to the station and I looked up Advanced Pharmaceuticals International on the internet. On their website, they described themselves as a supplier of low cost brand name drugs. There was a "contact us" page so I selected it and sent them a message requesting that they contact me by phone.

Then I contacted the other hospitals and clinics that were on the list that UPS gave me. None of them were near my location, but I wanted them to know they were buying counterfeit drugs. Of the eleven places I contacted, only three seemed to be concerned. I suspected the other eight already knew the drugs were counterfeit, but really didn't care.

The day was almost over when my phone rang. After I answered a man said, "Lieutenant Carver, my name is Phillip Martinez. I'm the CEO for Advanced Pharmaceuticals International. How can I help you?"

I was surprised by the call, but I responded, without any trace of the excitement I felt. "I'm investigating the murder of Douglas Baker. I believe he was employed by you."

"Yes, he was our US sales manager. His wife, Dorothy, called to tell me the unhappy news."

"I assume you know what you are doing is illegal in the United States. Do you believe Mr. Baker's occupation was a factor in his murder?"

"Of course, I know what we are doing is illegal, but our customers don't seem to care. They have apparently been put under a lot of pressure to reduce costs, and we offer them a safe, low cost, alternative to purchasing brand name drugs. However, I don't believe Doug's employment was a factor in his murder."

"Do you know who will be taking his place?"

"Not yet, we're talking to several people, but I won't tell you who they are. The job pays very well, so we won't have a difficult time finding a replacement. However, as you probably already know, the system is completely automatic. Our current customers won't even realize Doug is gone until they are contacted by his replacement."

"You are being surprisingly candid."

"Why not? Brazil has no extradition treaties with the United States, and I don't plan on returning there. Besides that, other than Advanced Laboratories, nobody is hurt by what we do."

I thought about what he said for a moment and then I asked, "How did Doug's antique car collection fit in."

"Doug didn't want to be paid by check or cash. He preferred to be paid in precious metals. So we would arrange to have his salary converted to gold or platinum and the material would be hidden on one of his cars before it was shipped back to him. I have no idea how he converted the metals to cash, or perhaps he was simply hoarding the stuff somewhere."

"Do you know anything about a 1937 Ford? Doug's body was found in one."

There was hesitation before he answered, "No, sorry I can't help you with that. I have to go now." Then he ended the call.

It was obvious Phillip knew something about the old car, but he didn't want to share it with me. I was wondering if Doug was lured to the barn by the possibility of purchasing the car and then killed there. So, I decided that the following day I was going to try and find out who owned the 1937 Ford.

The obvious place to start was with the chief. I arrived at the station by 7:30. I was surprised to see the chief was already there. I went to his office and knocked lightly on the glass next to the open door. He looked up from the newspaper he was reading, smiled at me, and said, "Come in Frank. How is my best homicide detective doing this morning?"

"I'm fine, sir. I wanted to let you know I spoke to the guy who heads up the counterfeit drug company late yesterday afternoon. He believes what he's doing is altruistic, and to some extent I agree. I think the drug companies have been screwing the American public for

The Antique Car Caper

years. Anyway, after speaking to him, I'm convinced he's not involved in Douglas Baker's murder. I think whoever murdered him was connected with the antique car he was found in."

The chief said, "Since I'm involved with antique cars, you want me to help find the owner of the car. Is that about right?"

"Yeah, can you help?"

"I have been thinking about that since Doug's body was found. I have no idea who owned the car, but I can give you a list of antique car clubs. Perhaps somebody from one of the clubs will know who the owner was. I'll have the list for you in an hour."

"Thank you, sir." Then I went back to my desk.

A short time later the chief walked over and handed me a printout of the antique car clubs in our area. The list included contact names and phone numbers. It was too early to start making calls, so I waited until 10:00. I spent the time checking the websites for the clubs on the list. I wasn't surprised every club had a website, but there was no useful information.

The first few calls yielded no results. The next club on my list was called the Norfolk County Car Collectors. I called and the man who answered the phone said cheerfully, "Good morning, this is Herb King. How can I help you?"

"Mr. King, my name is Frank Carver. I'm a detective in the county police department. I'm investigating a murder. The body was found in an antique Ford. I'm trying to locate the owner of the car and thought that perhaps you might be able to help."

"Was it a two-door model 74 sedan?"

"I have no idea, I really don't know much about old cars. But if it was a two-door model 74 sedan, what does that mean?"

"Matt Breslin sold one about a month ago. It was an unusual sale because the payment was made in gold. He never met the buyer. He was told to leave the car in the lot of a closed gas station."

"Do you have a phone number for Mr. Breslin?"

"I can get it for you. Do you think Matt is involved in the murder?"

"No, but I think whoever bought the car from him is."

"Okay, give me a few minutes and I'll get his number for you."

"Okay, I'll wait."

A few minutes later I had Matt Breslin's phone number. I called him immediately, but he didn't answer. I left a message giving him a very brief synopsis of the situation and asked him to call me as soon as possible.

Less than an hour later my cell phone rang. It was Matt. I answered the phone and said, "Mr. Breslin, thank you for returning my call. Can you give me any information about the person who purchased your 1937 Ford?"

"Not really. I know you spoke to Herb King and he told me what he told you. The only thing I can add was that the buyer was female. She paid me in gold."

"Did she sound young or old? Anything you could tell me will help."

"I'm sorry, I really don't remember."

"Is there anything on the car that would definitely identify it as the one you sold?"

"Yeah, there was a dent in the left front fender above the wheel well."

"Thanks for your help. I'll contact you again if I need anything else."

I called Jim Doyle and asked him if he could check and find out the model number for the car and look for the dent in the fender. He said he would do it as soon as he finished what he was working on.

Jim called an hour later and confirmed the car was a model 74 and had the dent on the fender.

The Antique Car Caper

It was obvious, at least to me, that it was Dorothy who purchased the car. She used it to get her husband to the old barn and killed him. I still didn't know why she wanted her husband dead or how she managed to get a secret army weapon.

Before I confronted Dorothy, I wanted one more piece of evidence. I called Matt Breslin again and asked him what form the gold was in that was used to pay for the car. He told me the payment was made in one ounce gold maple leaf coins from Canada. I thanked him for the information.

Then I left another message for Phillip Martinez asking him if he ever paid Douglas Baker in gold maple leaf coins. He terminated our last conversation rather abruptly so I wasn't sure he would call me back.

While I was waiting for a response I went to talk to the chief. When I got to his office he looked like he was daydreaming about something. I said, "Hi chief, do you have a minute?"

That brought him out of his daze and he said, "Sure, come on in."

I walked in and sat across for him. Then I said, "I'm sorry to tell you this, but you have to know. The evidence now indicates that Dorothy was involved with the murder. I doubt she actually killed him, but I suspect she may have arranged it."

"That's very difficult for me to believe. I've known them for so long and they always seemed to get along. So, tell me what you found out."

I spent a few minutes telling him about my conversations with Phillip and Matt, and I told him I was waiting for a call from Phillip to confirm that at some point Doug was paid with Canadian gold coins.

When I was done the chief looked at me, and with an obvious note of sadness in his voice, said, "The evidence is all circumstantial. If we get a confirmation that Doug was paid with the same type of coins that were used to pay for the car, then we will have to get a warrant to search the house and any safe deposit boxes she has access to. But I can understand why you think Dorothy is involved."

"I'm sorry it turned out this way."

"I am too."

I went back to my desk. Sitting on it was a message from the dispatcher. The message said, "Phillip Martinez called and said the answer to your question is 'Yes, several times'."

I went back to the chief's office. He wasn't there so I left the message from the dispatcher on his desk.

It was almost 5:00 so I went home. Nothing else was going to happen tonight. When I got home, Jill was already there. She was sitting in the living room with a glass of wine. She put down the glass, walked over to me, we hugged, kissed, and went to the bedroom where we spent most of the evening. We never did have dinner.

When I got to the office the next morning the chief was in a foul mood. When I said, "Good morning," he just grunted and walked away. A few minutes later he called in one of the other detectives and spent several minutes yelling at him about some report. When he was finished yelling he left the station. He came back about an hour later, he walked by my desk and threw an envelope on it and said harshly, "You take care of this. I don't want to be involved."

I opened the envelope and inside was a search warrant allowing us to search the Baker house and their safe deposit boxes.

I went to the dispatcher and told her I needed two uniformed officers to go with me when I serve a search warrant. She said she would pull in two people who were on traffic detail. They would be available in about twenty minutes.

It took a few minutes longer, but I really wasn't in a hurry. The three of us went in my car to the Baker residence. Dorothy Baker answered the door smiling and said, "Hello Lieutenant Carver. Can I help you with something?"

The Antique Car Caper

I handed her the envelope and said, "It's a search warrant." Her smile disappeared. She opened the envelope, read the warrant, and asked, "Why are you doing this? Does Chief Mitchell know about this?"

"We know your husband was involved in the sale of counterfeit drugs, and we know his antique cars were used to smuggle gold into the country. We also know a woman bought the car he was killed in and paid for the car in gold coins. That information was sufficient for a judge to issue a warrant."

She turned around and walked back into the room where we had met before. She sat on the sofa, covered her face with her hands, and began to cry. I didn't say anything. A minute or two later she regained her composure and said, "The search won't be necessary. I didn't kill Doug, but I was responsible for his death."

She paused for a few seconds and then continued speaking, "After Doug retired I realized our lifestyle was about to make a dramatic change. For ten years prior to his retirement Doug earned between one and two million dollars every year. We spent almost every penny. We went on lavish vacations, we spent over five million for this house, and we had servants that took care of everything. I didn't have to lift a finger. Doug worked hard, and it was beginning to affect his health. When he retired we had almost a million dollars in the bank, the house was paid for, but our income dropped to almost zero. Then Doug began to buy and restore more antique cars. That's a very expensive hobby. By the end of his first year in retirement our nest egg dropped to under a half million dollars. We fired all of our servants except the gardener, cancelled our upcoming vacations, and Doug promised to stop buying cars."

She hesitated only for a moment and started speaking again, "Everything was okay for a while, and then Doug found a Pierce Arrow he really wanted to buy. We argued and Doug said he would go back to work to earn the money to buy the car. He started making some calls to people he knew, but there was really nothing available that would pay the kind of money he was looking for. Then Phillip Martinez called. He talked to Doug for more than an hour. The following day Doug flew to Brazil. He was gone for almost a week. When he came back he told me he found a job that would pay him more than he was making before and he would be selling Advanced Laboratories products again. Things were great. We had more money than we had before. Until three months ago Doug thought he was selling genuine drugs, but because they were much less expensive to buy in Brazil, he was able to sell them for substantially less than buying the drugs directly from Advanced in the United States. He realized he was involved in drug smuggling, but wasn't concerned until he found out the drugs were made at a company in India. He was concerned because the drugs were counterfeit. Someone might die as a result of receiving phony drugs, and he didn't want that kind of responsibility. He called up Phillip and said he was going to quit. Phillip told him the drugs were identical to the real ones and nobody was going to die. He asked Doug to think about it for a few days, and Doug agreed. I asked him not to quit. I didn't want to start watching every dollar we spent again. Phillip called me the following day and told me that retirement from the company would only last a few days. If Doug insisted on quitting he would be killed. I told Doug about Phillip's warning, but either he didn't believe it or he didn't care."

I interrupted her and asked, "If Phillip arranged for Doug to be killed, how are you responsible?"

"Phillip made me an offer I couldn't refuse. Either I participated in Doug's death or I would join him. I wasn't ready to die, so I agreed. Phillip told me his plan and my part in it. I bought the antique Ford and paid for it with some of Doug's smuggled gold coins so it couldn't be easily traced to me. I put the car in the abandoned barn and called Phillip. I'm not sure exactly how Phillip lured Doug to the barn, and I had no idea how Doug was going to be killed. Phillip did tell me that Doug would appear to have died from natural causes, and that I wasn't to allow an autopsy to be performed. I was somewhat relieved when I was told he died from natural causes. But when you showed up the first time I knew I was going to get caught, and I made up my mind if that happened I would confess."

I thought about it for a while and said, "I'm sorry to do this, but I am placing you under arrest for conspiracy to commit murder. I think you should use some of Doug's gold to hire a really good criminal lawyer."

I took Dorothy back to the station and put her into one of the interrogation rooms. Then I went to the chief's office. I told him about Dorothy's confession and he said he would handle it.

I went back to my desk and called George Dyer. When he answered I told him I would call him back from a secure phone in an hour. I left the station and drove to the Airforce base again and I ended up in the same room I was in before. I called George from the black phone and less than a minute later the red phone rang.

"Hi George, I have some information for you."

"Great! Tell me what you have."

"There is a company in San Paulo, Brazil that has been selling counterfeit drugs here. The name of the company is Advanced Pharmaceuticals International. It's run by a guy named Phillip Martinez. My murder victim, Douglas Baker, was their US sales manager. Apparently, once you join the company, it's for life. When Doug Baker tried to resign, they killed him with one of your missing weapons."

"I suppose you would like me to put Mr. Martinez out of business."

"Yeah, that's what I was thinking. He believes that since we have no extradition treaty with Brazil, he is untouchable. But, I'm sure you have the resources to touch him."

"I believe I do. Just leave everything to me."

"Thanks George, please let me know how it turns out."

"No problem. How about if we go on another fishing trip before winter starts."

"I'd like that, but I'll have to ask Jill about it."

"Aha! There is now a woman in your life. It's about time too. Why don't you bring her along?"

"Okay, I'll ask her tonight."

I did discuss the fishing trip with Jill that evening. She said she didn't like to fish, but would be happy to get away for a while. I also told her George was going to take care of Advanced Pharmaceuticals International.

Three months later Dorothy Baker was acquitted. Apparently, she took my advice and hired a good lawyer.

George, Jill, and I went on our fishing trip during Dorothy's trial. George told us Phillip Martinez and Advanced Pharmaceuticals International would no longer be a problem. They even managed to recover two of the RX weapons. Phillip Martinez said, under duress, he bought them from an arms dealer based in Afghanistan, but refused to provide any additional information. He was arrested by Brazilian authorities and is now serving a lengthy term in one of Brazil's many awful prisons.

Although the relationship between Dorothy and the chief had become strained, after the trial was over their friendship was renewed. The chief felt Dorothy was trapped and she deserved to be given a break, and he said so at her trial. As a token of their friendship, Dorothy wanted to give the chief her 1937 Ford, but he insisted on paying for it. After a lot of haggling, they agreed on a purchase price of $100.

The Armchair Prophesy
A Frank Carver Mystery

Joshua Brewster was, without a doubt, the richest person in Norfolk County and one of the richest people in the country. He dropped out of high school and joined the army. When he was discharged, he got a job working in a railroad yard unloading boxcars. He saved most of the money he earned and started investing it. Over the years he made his fortune by constantly switching his investments between stocks, precious metals, and real estate. He had an uncanny ability to know which of those three things would produce the greatest profit at any given time. Some people thought he was psychic. He was seventy-four years old when his maid found him in his library on a warm August morning. He looked comfortable; like he had fallen asleep in his favorite armchair, but he was dead.

I was sure Mr. Brewster died of natural causes. The maid said he suffered from congestive heart failure and emphysema. The county had just passed a rule requiring an autopsy unless death occurs while under direct medical supervision. Since he died in his own house, I called Jill Tanner, the County Medical Examiner, and my live-in girlfriend.

I'm the only homicide detective in the county and I get called in every time somebody dies at home. There was nothing unusual about Mr. Brewster's death except that when he died he had a note clutched tightly in his right hand. The note, which he apparently had written shortly before he died, said, "There will be three deaths in the next thirty days. Each of the victims will be wealthy, and their deaths will occur under unusual circumstances."

He had signed and dated the note. I planned to give the note to our forensics people to verify the handwriting, but I was certain it was written by Mr. Brewster. I was looking at the note again when Jill walked in.

When she saw me she smiled and said, "Hi Frank." Then she walked over and kissed me lightly on the cheek. "I guess you need me to determine the cause of death, right?" she asked.

"Yeah, Mr. Brewster wasn't very healthy, but you know the rules; an autopsy is required."

"The ambulance will be here in a few minutes. I'll have them bring the body to my lab. Did he have any relatives?"

"No. According to the maid, his wife died several years ago and they didn't have any children. I suppose there might be a brother or sister somewhere. Nobody as rich as this guy, dies without a will. I'll look through his papers and see if he has an attorney. Perhaps he left instructions for the disposition of his body."

"You know, after the autopsy, I can only hold the body for ten days."

"I promise I'll speak to his attorney as soon as I find out who it is."

Mr. Brewster's library was quite large. I guessed it was thirty feet wide and almost fifty feet long. The walls were covered with book shelves and paintings. A large ornate wooden desk was at the far end of the room. I walked over to it and began to go through the papers on the desk. There wasn't much there, just two utility bills and an American Express bill. I looked at the American Express bill. Mr. Brewster charged almost fifteen thousand dollars in the previous month. That was a big chunk of my annual salary. I looked in a file cabinet next to his desk for anything that would help me find the name of his attorney. It didn't take long before I found copies of some real estate transactions that were sent from the office of Janet Sanders.

I've never met Ms. Sanders, but she is one of the more prominent attorneys in the area. The reason I never met her is that she doesn't handle criminal cases. I called her office. When the receptionist answered I said, "Good morning. I'm Lieutenant Carver with the Newport Police Department. Is Ms. Sanders available?"

"May I tell her what this is about, Lieutenant Carver?"

"Yes, it concerns the death of Joshua Brewster."

"Oh my God! Mr. Brewster is dead! He had an appointment with Janet this afternoon," she exclaimed.

"I believe Mr. Brewster passed away in his sleep last night. I really need to speak with Ms. Sanders."

"Yes sir. I'll get her for you. I'm going to put you on hold for just a moment."

"Okay."

A few moments later he heard a woman say, "Lieutenant Carver, I'm Janet Sanders. How can I help you?"

"Last night Joshua Brewster died. I found some paperwork from your office in his files. I was hoping you were his attorney and had a copy of his will."

"This is an unbelievable coincidence. He didn't have a will until a few days ago. He had been a client for more than ten years, but he didn't ask about a will until two weeks ago. I wonder if he knew he was going to die."

"According to his maid he was quite ill. I haven't spoken to his doctor yet, but I suspect his death wouldn't have been a surprise."

"I don't know anything about his health, but he appeared to be relatively healthy for a man in his seventies. I never discussed it with him, but I heard a rumor he was psychic and used his abilities to make a fortune."

"Are you saying he knew he was going to die?"

"I think it's a possibility."

"Well, I don't believe in all that crap. The maid told me he had no relatives. Who benefits from his death?"

"Lieutenant Carver, the will is very complex. Will you come by my office at 2:00 so I can explain it to you?"

"I'll be there."

I purposely didn't mention the note. It was in a clear evidence bag, so I used Mr. Brewster's copier to make several copies of it.

I arrived at the attorney's office right on time. They were waiting for me. As soon as the receptionist saw me she asked, "Are you Lieutenant Carver?"

I suppose I must look like a cop. Anyway, I answered, "Yup."

"Please follow me sir."

A few moments later I was seated across from Janet Sanders. The receptionist left, closing the door on her way out. Janet said, "Good afternoon Lieutenant."

"Good afternoon Ms. Sanders."

"Mr. Brewster left an estate valued at about twenty billion dollars. However, all but one billion is tied up in the ownership of various corporations. The ownership of his corporate assets will be given back to the corporations. It will be up to the boards to determine what to do with the stock. If he had any relatives, he never mentioned them to me. He left substantial amounts to several of his favorite charities, and left his maid, who had worked for him for almost twenty years, five million dollars and his house."

"Wow! I'm sure she'll be happy with that."

Ms. Sanders ignored my remark and continued, "Those bequests were in cash. Mr. Brewster also owned substantial amounts of gold, silver, and platinum. He estimated the value at five hundred million dollars. He requested the precious metals be sold and the proceeds from the sale be split evenly between five people. These people are already very rich, although not in Mr. Brewster's class. There are three things that are really unusual here. First, Mr. Brewster, to the best of my knowledge, didn't know any of them, the money won't be distributed until one year after Mr. Brewster's death, and if any of them die before the year is up, the money will be split between the survivors."

"That is a bit unusual, isn't it?"

"More than a bit."

The Armchair Prophesy

"I wonder if what you just told me is related to this," I said as I handed her a copy of the note.

She read the note and asked, "Where did you find this?"

"It was in Mr. Brewster's right hand. Does that look like his handwriting?"

She looked down at the file, then back at the note, and responded, "I'm not an expert, but it sure looks like his writing."

"Can you give me a copy of the will?"

"I can, but it won't be official until the probate court approves it."

"Is there any chance they won't approve it?"

"No, it's unusual but perfectly legal."

"Thank you for your time, Ms. Sanders."

She said, "You're welcome, Lieutenant." Then she picked up her phone, pressed one button, and said something I couldn't hear.

A few seconds later the receptionist came back. Ms. Sanders handed her Mr. Brewster's will and said, "April will make a copy of the will for you. If I can be of further service, please let me know."

I followed April out of the office and back to the reception area. April told me to wait there and she would be back in a few minutes with a copy of the will.

As soon as I had the copy in my hand, I went back to the station. I wanted to read the will, find out something about the five people who were about to inherit a huge sum of money, and then discuss it with the Chief.

I spent a few hours researching the five people who were the big beneficiaries in Mr. Brewster's will. When I was finished with my research, I went to the Chief's office. He wasn't there so I left a message on his desk telling him I wanted to discuss the details of Joshua Brewster's will and the note he left for us.

The Chief returned just before 5:00. I was about to go home when I saw him walk toward his office. A minute later my phone rang. The Chief said now would be a good time to talk, so I told him I would be there in a minute. I picked up the file and walked to his office.

When he saw me, he smiled and waved for me to come in. Then he asked, "Why do we need to discuss Joshua Brewster? Didn't he die from natural causes?"

"I don't have Jill's report yet, but I suspect you are correct about the cause of death. What you aren't aware of is the note we found in his hand." I handed the Chief a copy of the note.

After he read it he said, "The note is interesting, but no crime has been committed. Why do you want to get involved?"

"I spoke to his attorney this afternoon. There was something unusual in his will. He apparently had a substantial stash of gold, silver, and platinum. Mr. Brewster estimated the value at five hundred million dollars. The will directs his executor to sell the metals and divide up the proceeds to five different people. However, the money will be paid out one year after his death and will be split evenly between any of the five who are still alive. I think he expected them to kill each other to get a bigger share of the money. Also, his attorney believes Brewster didn't know any of them personally."

"That's interesting, but we still can't get involved until a crime has been committed. Do you know anything about the five lucky people?"

"Yeah, I spent some time researching them. All of them are very wealthy already, although I would guess that even if you are rich, you can always use an extra hundred million dollars. Of the five, only one lives in this area, Ben Masters. He owns Masters Chevrolet, Masters Ford, Masters Nissan, and Masters Toyota, and a few other businesses in town."

"I've met him several times at big charity functions. He seems like a very nice guy. Does he know he just inherited a hundred million dollars?"

The Armchair Prophesy

"I don't know, but I plan to ask him tomorrow. I also want to speak to Mr. Brewster's doctor."

"I guess that's okay, but if something new happens, it takes priority. What do you know about the other four?"

"John Leonard lives in New York City. He's a hedge fund manager. Apparently, he has a net worth of about one hundred fifty million dollars. He lives in a penthouse on 5th Avenue he purchased a few years ago for twenty million. The only other winner in the Brewster lottery who lives in the United States is Joanne Rice. She lives in San Francisco, also in a very expensive condo. She inherited her money when her parents died. She also inherited a substantial portion of several of America's largest corporations including United Airlines, Chevron, DuPont, and Verizon."

"Where do the last two live?"

"Fredrick Parkes is a citizen of France and has a home just outside of Paris, but he's seldom there. He spends almost all of his time on his yacht. Actually, it's probably too big to call a yacht. According to my source, it's the largest privately owned ship on Earth. It's almost four hundred feet long, has a crew of thirty-five people, and has two helicopter landing pads on the deck. However, there's no information about how he acquired his money or how much he has. The last person on the list is Peter Lundov. He's our mystery man. All I can find out about him is that he's rich and lives in Moscow."

"I wonder if our friend, Igor, could help us find out more about him."

"I have Igor's card. I'll call him tomorrow. I'm wondering if we should warn these people about Mr. Brewster's prophesy."

"I think a warning is premature. If any of them meet an untimely end in the next week or so, then a warning would be appropriate. After you speak to Ben Masters, perhaps we'll have a better idea about what's going on."

"I hope so. I'm going home now. Goodnight Chief."

"Goodnight Frank."

By the time I got home Jill was already there making dinner. She kissed me and handed me a glass of wine saying, "Dinner will be ready in about a half hour. Also, I thought you should know the autopsy revealed that Joshua Brewster died as the result of a brain aneurism. His death would have been instantaneous. Unless he had a premonition he was about to die, it would've been impossible for him to write the note prior to his death. I'm beginning to think he really was psychic. Also, he probably only had another month or two. His heart and lungs were in bad shape."

I filled Jill in on what I found out about his will. She thought about what I told her for a moment and said, "You need to find out if he has any relationship with those people. There has to be a reason why he left them that much money. What happens if all of them die before the anniversary of his death?"

"That's a good question. I have a copy of the will but haven't read it yet. I'll do that in the morning."

"Do you think he was trying to get them to kill each other?"

"That seems like a possibility, but if that was what he was trying to do, there has to be a reason."

"I agree. I'm sure you'll figure it out," she paused for a few seconds. Then she smiled at me and said, "I want to ask you something but I don't want you to get upset."

"I promise I won't get upset. Just ask your question."

"We've been living together for almost five months and we love each other. Can we set a date to get married?"

"You've been talking to your mother again, haven't you?"

"Yes, but this time I agree with her. After all, if we do love each other, and we've been happy together for the past five months, why not set a date to get married?"

I knew this was coming and I was prepared with the answer. "Okay, let's get married on your next birthday. That way it will be easy to remember and I'll only have to buy you one gift."

The Armchair Prophesy

"You do know sometimes you act like a real asshole! Okay, I accept. We are getting married on November 14th."

"I really do love you."

"I know. This will make my mother very happy. I'm not sure how she'll feel about the date, but I'm not going to worry about it. I know she wants me to have a big wedding, and now she has plenty of time to plan it."

The following morning, I arrived at the station by 6:30. I wanted to call Igor and Moscow is seven hours ahead of us. I called the number on Igor's card. The phone rang several times before a machine answered the call. The message was in Russian, so I didn't understand any of it. After the beep I left a brief message for Igor and asked him to return my call.

The chief came in at 7:30. I stopped him as he walked past my desk and told him why Mr. Brewster died. When I was finished he asked, "If he died instantly, how did he write the note?"

"That was my question too. Jill thinks he may have actually been psychic, but I don't believe in that stuff."

"Neither do I," the Chief replied. Then he went to his office.

Later that morning I called Ben Masters. It took a while to get through to him, but when I did he seemed very pleasant.

"This is Ben Masters. How can I help you?"

"Good morning Mr. Masters. My name is Frank Carver. I'm a homicide detective with the Norfolk County Police Department. I'm investigating the death of Joshua Brewster. I would like to ask you a few questions."

"I've heard of Joshua Brewster, but I never met him. I don't understand why you would want to ask me questions."

"Because you're mentioned in his will and he left you a very substantial sum of money."

"How much did he leave me?"

"About one hundred million dollars."

"What! Is this some kind of sick joke?" He exclaimed.

"No, Mr. Masters, this isn't a joke. I'm sure Janet Sanders will be contacting you shortly. If you would like to meet in person, I'll bring you a copy of the will."

"My office is at 145 Main Street. Can you be here in a half hour?"

"That's only four blocks from the station. I can be there in ten minutes."

"Okay, I'll see you in ten minutes."

I left the station and walked over to Ben Masters' office. I walked into the reception area and showed my ID to the girl manning the desk and told her I had an appointment with Mr. Masters. She picked up her phone, pressed a few buttons, and said, "Lieutenant Carver is here to see you, sir."

She hung up the phone and said, "Mr. Masters will be with you in a few minutes."

I sat on one of the chairs in the reception area thinking he was going to keep me waiting for a while, but the door opened less than a minute after I sat down. I recognized him immediately since I had probably seen him in hundreds of car commercials. He walked over to me, stretched out his hand in my direction, and said, "I'm Ben Masters, it's a pleasure to meet you, Lieutenant Carver. Please come with me."

We shook hands briefly and I got up and followed him to his office. He sat behind a big desk and said, "Please have a seat, Lieutenant."

After I sat he said, "After your call I called Janet Sanders and she confirmed what you told me."

"Did she tell you the stipulations in the will?"

"No, just the amount, which I still can't believe. What are the stipulations?"

"You're one of five people who will inherit the proceeds from the sale of Mr. Brewster's cache of precious metals. He estimated the value at five hundred million dollars just before he died. The money will be paid out on

The Armchair Prophesy

the first anniversary of his death. At that time, the funds will be split evenly by those of you who are still alive."

"It sounds like Mr. Brewster wanted us to kill each other. Who are the other people?"

I gave him a copy of the will with the area he was concerned with highlighted, "Here, you can read it for yourself."

He read the will, thought about what he read, and said, "I have no idea who these other people are. Do you know anything about them?"

"Only that they are all rich. There is one more thing you should know concerning Mr. Brewster," I gave him a copy of the note and continued, "This is a copy of a note found in Mr. Brewster's right hand. I don't know if it refers to you and the others, or if it's just a load of crap."

He read the note and said, "Lieutenant Carver, if your mission was to frighten me, you have succeeded. What do you suggest I do now?"

"I don't think you should do anything. This may all have been Brewster's idea of a joke. If something happens to anyone in the group, I'll let you know. At that point it may be prudent to take some action to protect yourself. Thank you for your time, Mr. Masters."

I got up and left the office. Mr. Masters didn't say a word. When I got back to the station I went right to Chief Mitchell's office. He looked up from his computer and asked, "What happened with Ben Masters?"

"He had no idea he inherited any money from Joshua Brewster and said he knew nothing about the others. I think he agrees with me that the whole thing is a plot to get them to kill each other, and he's scared."

"I don't blame him. If he's killed, the others will each get another twenty-five million. People have been killed for a lot less."

"I would like to do a little more research on the lucky five. Is that okay with you?"

"Yeah, until something else comes up."

"Thanks Chief," I said. I returned to my desk to start a more thorough search for information on the five inheritors. I also decided to include Joshua Brewster in my search. I was hoping something would turn up that connected them.

Igor hadn't returned my call, so I called him again and left another message. Then I decided to run criminal checks on Ben Masters, John Leonard, and Joanne Rice. I wasn't expecting to find anything, but it was a start. I also sent a request to Interpol for information on Fredrick Parkes and Peter Lundov.

Looking through what little information I had, I suddenly realized one thing they all had in common. They were all about the same age. Joanne Rice was the youngest at fifty-four, and Peter Lundov was the oldest at fifty-six. I suspected that meant something, but I had no idea what.

I decided to read the entire will hoping to find a clue. I also promised Jill I would find out what happens if all five of them are dead at the time the money is supposed to be distributed. The will was almost twenty pages of the most boring legal stuff I have ever read. I only found three interesting things. In the event of the deaths of all five recipients, the executor was supposed to donate the money to any of the charities that were listed in the will, and to compensate the executor for their time, the executor would be paid five hundred thousand dollars. The executor was Janet Sanders. The last thing I thought was unusual was that Mr. Brewster's memorial service was to be scheduled no sooner than forty-five days after his death.

When I returned from lunch there was a fax on my desk from Interpol. Fredrick Parkes had no criminal record. Peter Lundov had been arrested several times in several different places around Europe, but all of it was minor stuff that had to do with excessive alcohol use.

An hour later I received the reports on John Leonard, Joanne Rice, and Ben Masters. I finally found a connection. All three were students at UCLA. They were all arrested during some kind of protest thirty-five years ago. There were no details other than the fact they pleaded guilty to a disorderly conduct charge. They were each fined fifty dollars and released.

I wondered what they protested and what they did that got them arrested. I decided the best way to find out was to ask Ben Masters. I called him, but he was out. I asked the receptionist to have him call me when he returned.

Then I placed a call to UCLA to find out if Fredrick Parkes and Peter Lundov were also students. I spoke to several people, but none of them would give me any information unless the request was made in writing. I was told that after they received the request they would respond within thirty days. I was also told that the request must be made on official letterhead, the signatures had to be notarized, and the request had to be sent by certified mail. I didn't understand their reluctance to give me any information. I wasn't asking for anything personal. All I wanted to know was if they were ever students at UCLA. It appeared they had no desire to cooperate with the police unless forced to do so.

I decided to take a different approach. I thought about calling my congressman, but that would probably be a waste of time since he's a liberal and a moron. So I called my friend George Dyer who works in Army Intelligence and said, "Hi George, it's Frank."

"I bet you need help with something."

"Yeah, I do. I currently find myself in a position of investigating a crime that hasn't happened yet."

"I probably shouldn't ask, but can you explain that?"

I spent a few minutes filling him on what happened. When I was finished he said, "What do you need from me?"

"I need to know if Fredrick Parkes and Peter Lundov were students at UCLA thirty-five years ago. I called UCLA to ask and was told to submit my request in writing and they would answer it within thirty days. I really can't wait that long for an answer."

"Okay, send me an e-mail with the names and the approximate dates. I should be able to get an answer for you by tomorrow. You know, someday I may call you for help, so you better be prepared."

"George, I'm now forever in your debt. Anything I have is yours for the asking, except Jill."

"I knew there was a catch."

"By the way, Jill and I are getting married on November 14th. We just decided this a few days ago. Please plan on coming. I'll even pay for your transportation and hotel."

"I wouldn't miss it, and it won't cost you a dime. I'm really very happy for both of you."

"Thanks for your help. I'll send that e-mail in the next few minutes."

If Fredrick and Peter were at UCLA, and I was fairly sure they were, then all five were connected. It was almost 5:00 and Ben Masters hadn't returned my call, so I called him again. The receptionist told me he had an appointment at 2:00 and should have been back by now. She said she would leave a note on his desk to call me. She also mentioned that Mr. Masters was one of the few people in the world who didn't carry a cell phone all the time, and his phone was on his desk.

I went home, but Jill wasn't there. I called her and she told me she was on the way home and would be there in about ten minutes. I sat on the sofa and turned on the news. I really wasn't watching until they interrupted the woman reading the news.

A business jet lost its front landing gear when the pilot lowered it on approach to the airport. The plane was severely damaged but the pilot, who was the only one on board, was okay. However, the landing gear hit the windshield of a car and the driver was killed. They said the police were withholding the name of the driver until his family was notified. I thought about that for a while and decided it was probably the most unusual death I had heard about in a long time.

Then I remembered Joshua Brewster's note warning the deaths would be unusual. If the person who died was Ben Masters, the prophesy was coming true. But there was still no crime. It had to be an accident.

I was actually shaking when I called the station. When the dispatcher answered I said, "Hi, it's Frank. I'm almost afraid to ask, but can you tell me who died in the car that was struck by the airplane landing gear?"

"Yeah, it was that guy who owns all the car dealerships in town, Ben Masters."

"Oh shit! I knew it. Thanks." Then I hung up the phone.

Now that Ben Masters was dead, I had no way of finding out what happened thirty-five years ago. Jill walked in and looked at me and said, "You look like you just lost your best friend. Did somebody die?"

"Yeah, Ben Masters was killed when a part fell off of an airplane and hit his car."

"Is this a joke?"

"I wish it was. I found out this afternoon that three of the five people mentioned in Brewster's will attended UCLA at the same time, and they were all arrested in some kind of protest march. Ben Masters was probably my only source for information about it. The other thing that concerns me is that Brewster's prophesy may be coming true. You must admit that being killed by a part falling off of a plane is an unusual way to die."

"I agree, it's unusual, but it could still be a coincidence. Did the other two attend UCLA too?"

"I don't know yet. I called the school and they basically refused to help, so I called George. He said he would have the information for me tomorrow afternoon. I also told him about the wedding. Have you discussed it with your mother yet?"

"She was thrilled with everything but the date. She said nobody gets married on a Wednesday. However, she wants us to come over during the weekend to discuss the plans. I told her we would be there on Saturday."

"That's okay with me. We should probably bring her a list of who we want to invite."

"Good idea. We can discuss it over dinner. Let's do Italian tonight."

When I got out of bed the next morning I turned on the local news. The lead story was the death of Ben Masters. I watched it for a while. When I realized I wasn't really paying any attention to the TV, I turned it off. I took a shower, got dressed, ate a bowl of cereal, and left.

I got to the station at 8:00. The Chief was in his office so I went over and briefed him on the events of the previous day. When I was finished he said, "You should try to contact John Leonard and Joanne Rice. It's a longshot, but they may want to help when they find out Ben Masters is dead. By the way, there has still not been a crime committed unless the pilot of the plane purposely dropped his front landing gear on Ben Masters' car."

"I don't think that's likely. I'll try contacting Leonard and Rice, but I'll bet they have an army of people screening their calls."

"Probably true, but do it anyway."

"I will."

I decided to try John Leonard first. I called his office and ended up speaking to his executive assistant, Tom, who said Mr. Leonard was very busy. But he did promise to give him a message. So I told Tom to tell him someone was targeting people involved in a protest march he participated in thirty-five years ago at UCLA, and one person had died already. I thought about mentioning Joshua Brewster, but decided against it. I hoped that if nothing else, it might make him curious enough to return my call.

Apparently, my plan worked. An hour later, one of the clerks came by my desk and gave me a message. There

The Armchair Prophesy

was a phone number and the message said, "Call this number at 10:30 and you will have five minutes to speak with John Leonard."

I had to wait twenty minutes before I could make the call. When I did the man who answered said, "This is John Leonard. Am I speaking with Lieutenant Carver?"

"Yes sir. Do you remember the protest march at UCLA thirty-five years ago? I thought you might, because you were arrested and charged with disorderly conduct."

"Lieutenant Carver, I spent very little time at UCLA sober. I don't remember any protest march or getting arrested."

"Do the names Ben Masters, Joanne Rice, Fredrick Parkes, or Peter Lundov mean anything to you?"

"No, I don't think so."

"How about Joshua Brewster?"

"Are you really a cop or is this some kind scam?" he yelled.

"I am a homicide detective with the Norfolk County Police Department. The other four people I mentioned were also beneficiaries in Mr. Brewster's will. I know you, Joanne Rice, and Ben Masters were all students at UCLA at the same time and all three of you were arrested in the protest. Ben Masters was killed yesterday. Many people thought Mr. Brewster made his fortune because he was psychic. When he died he had a note in his hand that said three rich people will die in unusual circumstances in the next thirty days. Now, one of you is dead."

"When Brewster's attorney contacted me all she told me was that I had inherited approximately one hundred million dollars, but the money wouldn't be paid out for a year."

"She never mentioned the other recipients?"

"No, she did not."

"The will stipulated that on the first anniversary of Mr. Brewster's death, five hundred million dollars would be split up between any of the five recipients who were still alive."

"Okay, this is really creepy. I'm going to call Brewster's attorney and tell her I don't want to be involved. That's a lot of money, but it isn't worth getting killed for. I'm curious, how did Ben Masters die."

"The front landing gear from a plane fell on his car."

"I guess that would be considered unusual."

"I agree. Thank you for your time, Mr. Leonard. If you somehow manage to recall anything about your days at UCLA, please call me."

I wondered why Janet Sanders didn't tell him about the other people mentioned in the will. My next call would be to Joanne Rice, but it was too early to call San Francisco. While I was deep in thought my phone rang. I picked it up and said, "Lieutenant Carver."

"Hi Frank, I have some information for you."

"I hope its good news, George."

"I'll let you decide that. Fredrick Parkes and Peter Lundov were students at UCLA as well. All five of them were arrested, along with a bunch of others. The records are a little sketchy. I couldn't even find out what they were protesting. However, during my research I discovered a woman named Melissa Brewster died during the protest. Apparently, the protesters were blocking traffic and she was riding a bicycle. She hit one of the protesters with her bike, fell down, and hit her head on the curb. She died instantly. It was considered an accident, so nobody was charged. You should also know Melissa wasn't a student, she was a courier."

"She must be related to Joshua Brewster. That's got to be the connection. I guess now I have to check Brewster's past too. Thanks George."

"You're welcome."

I knew Joshua Brewster grew up in Norfolk County and worked in the railroad yards here when he was discharged from the army. Then he became extremely

The Armchair Prophesy

wealthy. But that left a lot of gaps. The first thing I did was run a check on his criminal record. Then I checked his driving record, credit report, and requested whatever information social security had.

The credit report came back first. There was nothing in it older than twenty years and his credit report was perfect. While I was thinking about it I realized I should also be checking on Melissa Brewster. In order to do that, I needed her social security number. My first check with social security was useless. There were more than a hundred people with social security cards named Melissa Brewster.

It took almost two hours before I was fairly sure I found the right one. The one I found changed her name from Melissa Cole to Melissa Brewster thirty-six years ago. Presumably Ms. Cole changed her name to Brewster because she got married. Her last record of earnings was from Reliable Parcel Service, and that was thirty-five years ago.

Then I checked with LA County to see if there was a marriage certificate issued in that appropriate time frame. There wasn't any. I checked with some of the other counties in the area and received the same result. I thought maybe Melissa and Joshua eloped, so I called Clark County, Nevada. Sure enough, ten months prior to her death, Melissa and Joshua got married in Las Vegas.

This was all beginning to make sense now. Joshua felt the five people named in his will were responsible for his first wife's death. I could even see how setting them against each other would be a way of getting revenge, although he wouldn't be alive to enjoy it. But the note was still puzzling. Why did he write it? Did he do it to scare them? Then I had another thought; did he arrange for the landing gear to fall on Ben Masters' car? Is that even possible?

I had to speak to an airplane mechanic. There was a maintenance facility at the airport so I called them. A man named Tim answered the phone.

"Tim, I'm Lieutenant Carver. I'm a homicide detective with the Norfolk County Police Department. I have a question regarding the incident that occurred yesterday afternoon."

"Yeah, that was really strange."

"I'm not a mechanic in any sense of the word, but it seems to me it would be very unlikely for the landing gear to fall off."

"Unlikely is the wrong word. It's virtually impossible for the landing gear to fall off. The gear is attached to the frame of the plane with more than a dozen bolts. Unless the bolts were intentionally removed or loosened, it's impossible."

"I'm sure the plane is still there. Can you check it for me?"

"No, the plane is being held by the National Transportation Safety Board for analysis. You need to call them."

"I'll do that. Thanks for the information, Tim."

It took at least a half hour and five calls before I got to the right person at the NTSB. However, he refused to give me any specific information about the condition of the plane. He did say the information would be made public in ninety days. The level of bureaucracy in this country is truly astounding! I was determined to do this myself without calling George.

I called the manager at the airport to find out what he could tell me about the plane. He told me who manufactured the plane, the model number of the plane, and that the plane was owned by Brewster Holdings.

To say I was surprised by that last piece of information would be a substantial understatement. I asked him if he knew the name of the pilot. That answer was also surprising. The flight plan was filed by a pilot named Joe Goldman, but it wasn't Joe Goldman flying the plane. Joe Goldman was thirty-seven years old, about six feet tall, black hair, and weighed about 195 pounds. The pilot of the plane

The Armchair Prophesy

was in his late fifties, was several inches shorter than six feet, very thin, and bald. The pilot was unhurt during the crash and has since disappeared.

I immediately called the NTSB again and told them I needed to send a forensics team to the plane to check for fingerprints. I was surprised when they said it would be okay, but someone from the NTSB had to be there while the forensics team was working on the plane. I said that was fine, and we agreed to meet at the hanger where the plane was taken at 10:00 the next morning.

I called Jim Doyle, the manager of the forensics department, and he agreed to have someone there at 10:00. I went to see the Chief to tell him what I found out. When I was done he said, "Okay, the death of Ben Masters is now a homicide. You are free to spend whatever time you need to resolve this."

I went back to my desk and called Brewster Holdings. I asked for the personnel manager and was connected with Betty Richards. I told her who I was, explained the situation, and asked if she had contact information for Joe Goldman. She told me Joe worked on an "as needed" basis. But, he hadn't submitted any time for several weeks. She also gave me his cell number.

I called Joe and he answered on the first ring. After he answered I said, "Hello Mr. Goldman, my name is Frank Carver. I'm a homicide detective with the Norfolk County Police Department. Did you file a flight plan for a flight here last week?"

"No, I already told this to the NTSB. Do you mind telling me what's going on?"

"Apparently, whoever was flying the plane dropped the front landing gear on a car during his landing approach. The driver of the car was killed."

"What! Are you telling me the pilot intentionally dropped the landing gear like it was a bomb on a car?" he asked forcefully.

"That's what I'm trying to find out. Do you think it's possible to do that?"

He didn't answer right away. When he did he said, "I suppose it's possible, but you would have to be incredibly skilled or lucky. Do you know who the pilot was?"

"I have a description but no name. Tomorrow we're going to check the plane for fingerprints. The guy was in his late fifties, short, thin, and bald. He was unhurt in the crash and has disappeared. Do you have any guess who that might be?"

"No, not a clue. Do you know how badly the plane was damaged?"

"No, I haven't seen it yet."

I had a suspicion Joshua may have hired the guy who was flying the plane, and he had to be paid. So I ordered copies of his financial records. His criminal record came back a little while later. It was clean. His driving record was too. Just before the end of the day I received the report from social security. Apparently, Joshua lived in California for a while. He held several jobs in the LA area around the time Melissa died. There was a gap of a few months and then he moved back here and began working at the railroad yard. He worked there for a few years and that was the end of his employment information. The last entry in the report was thirty-three years ago.

It was the end of the day so I went home. It was Friday, so I was hoping for a relaxing weekend. Jill arrived at home just a few minutes after I did. We sat in the living room, each of us with a glass of wine, and we talked about the Joshua Brewster case for an hour. Jill asked, "Why was Ben Masters on the road near the airport? How did Joshua lure him there?"

"Those are questions I plan to get answers for on Monday. I would like to forget about the case for the weekend."

The Armchair Prophesy

"We have more important things to worry about anyway. We're going to my parent's house for dinner tomorrow and we're going to start planning the wedding."

"I had actually forgotten about that. Let's work on the list of who we want to invite now."

Jill and I had a quick dinner and then spent a couple of hours figuring out who we wanted to invite to the wedding. The list was long because we planned on inviting most of the people we worked with. We ended up with a list of fifty-four names.

We were getting ready for bed when my cell phone rang. I didn't recognize the number so I hesitated for a few seconds before answering it. "Hello, this is Frank Carver."

"Hi Frank, it's Igor. How are you?"

"I'm fine, Igor. I'm really glad you called."

"Are you planning on coming to Moscow to get your free bottle of vodka?"

"Not in the immediate future. I'm working on a murder case and there's a Russian involved. I was hoping you could get some information about him for me."

"I'll do what I can. What's his name?"

"His name is Peter Lundov. Do you know anything about him?"

There was a brief pause and then Igor said, "I know one thing about him. He's dead."

"He's dead! What happened?"

"He was driving his car behind a truck that was carrying several four thousand kilo spools of wire cable. The chain holding one of the spools broke, it rolled off the back of the truck and struck the front of Peter's car. He was driving at about one hundred twenty kph. That's about seventy-five mph. The car was completely demolished."

"That makes him victim number two."

"Who was the first victim?"

I spent the next few minutes giving Igor the details of the case. When I was finished Igor asked, "So, do you think he was murdered?"

"Yeah, I do. Was there any information about the truck driver?"

"I don't remember reading anything about him. Would you like me to try and find out something?"

"That would be helpful, but if he's anything like the pilot, I'll bet he's disappeared."

"That actually happens regularly in Russia when people get involved in accidents."

"Well, if you do find out anything, please let me know."

"I'll do that."

Jill only heard my half of the conversation, but she obviously knew Peter Lundov was dead. She asked, "Did the guy die under unusual circumstances?"

"He died when he drove his car into a huge spool of wire that fell off of a truck."

"I think that qualifies as unusual. I wonder if it's just a coincidence both your victims died when something struck their cars."

"We'll probably have to wait for victim number three."

When I arrived at the station on Monday morning, I went to the Chief's office immediately. I spent some time bringing him up to speed on the case. Then I went back to my desk and placed a call to John Leonard. I ended up speaking to Tom again. So, I told him to let Mr. Leonard know a second person mentioned in Joshua Brewster's will died.

On Friday I had planned on calling Joanne Rice, but I got sidetracked and never did it. I wanted to make sure I called her so I set a reminder on my phone to make the call in the early afternoon. Then I went over to Ben Masters' office. I asked the receptionist if Mr. Masters had an assistant. She said Mr. Masters' son, Sean, was almost a partner in the business. I asked if he was in and she said he was out planning the funeral. I told her it was important that he call me as soon as possible.

The Armchair Prophesy

By the time I returned to my desk I had copies of Joshua Brewster's bank statements for the last twelve months. I looked through the statements quickly, looking for anything unusual. It appeared he maintained a balance of about two million dollars. I was sure that was sufficient for him to have a free checking account. It looked like his monthly expenses were about thirty-five thousand dollars. Every other month there was a transfer from another account for one hundred thousand dollars. Everything looked normal until about three weeks ago. There was a wire transfer for three hundred fifty thousand dollars. I called the bank to ask about it and was told the transfer was requested by Mr. Brewster in person, and the funds were transferred to a numbered account in Switzerland.

I called Janet Sanders about the funds transfer but she said she knew nothing about it. As soon as I hung up the phone it rang again. It was Sean Masters.

"Thank you for returning my call. I'm sorry to disturb you at a time like this, but there is some indication your father's death may not have been accidental."

Sean, who was obviously stressed yelled, "He was murdered?"

"That's a possibility. Do you know why he was on that road near the airport?"

"Yes, we were looking for a place to build a warehouse and a body shop. We had been trying to buy that land for a while, but the owner wanted too much money for it. Dad received a call that morning from his real estate agent. She told him the price for the land had been reduced, but to get the reduced price the sale had to close within fifteen days, and it had to be a cash transaction. Dad told her he would go look at the property that afternoon and give her his decision the next morning."

"Did he tell her what time he was going to go look at the lot?"

"Not to my knowledge. What makes you think dad was murdered?"

"Your father was one of five people who inherited a substantial sum of money from Joshua Brewster. Two of them are dead. Your father was the first."

"I don't understand. Why would inheriting money make him a target for murder?"

"The will stipulated the money would be paid out on the one year anniversary of Mr. Brewster's death. The funds would be split up among any of the five recipients who were still alive at that time."

"How much money was involved?"

"The total amount of the bequest was five hundred million dollars."

"Wow! That's a lot of money. So, you think one of the people who will inherit the money is killing off the others to increase their share?"

"Actually, I don't think that at all. I think Joshua Brewster planned the murders before he died to avenge his first wife's death."

"Dad was responsible for the death of Brewster's first wife?"

"Not directly. He was involved in some kind of protest thirty-five years ago and Melissa Brewster died accidentally during the protest. I need the name of your real estate agent. Do you have it?"

"Not with me. I'll look it up when I get back to the office and I'll call you."

"Thank you for your help, Mr. Masters."

"You're welcome, Lieutenant."

I was sitting at my desk daydreaming when my phone started to play music. It was my reminder to call Joanne Rice. I called her office, introduced myself, and told the girl who answered the phone it was very important that I speak to Ms. Rice as soon as possible. She was polite, but told me I would have to speak to Ms. Rice's Executive Assistant, Cynthia, first. I said that was okay. A few moments later a female voice said, "This is Cynthia Webber. How can I help you?"

The Armchair Prophesy

"Ms. Webber, my name is Frank Carver. I'm a homicide detective and I'm currently investigating the death of a man who stood to inherit a substantial amount of money from the estate of Joshua Brewster. Ms. Rice also inherited a substantial amount of money from Mr. Brewster. I believe her life may be in danger. It's imperative I speak with her as soon as possible."

"Would you hold on for a moment, sir?"

"Yes, of course."

About two minutes had passed when I heard another female voice say, "This is Joanne Rice. You told my assistant my life may be in danger. Can you please elaborate?"

I spent a few minutes telling her everything I had found out since the investigation started. When I was finished she said, "I remember that night as if it was yesterday, although I don't remember Ben Masters or John Leonard. We were protesting a fifty percent increase in tuition that was going to be phased in over three years. They were increasing other fees too. There were hundreds of us who were really upset. I heard that a young woman had fallen off her bicycle and died, but I never knew her name."

"Your family had a lot of money. I'm sure you wouldn't have been affected by an increase in tuition. Why were you protesting?"

"I didn't want my friends to know my family was rich. I was actually embarrassed by it, so I kept my family's wealth a secret."

"Until this situation is resolved, I would suggest you invest in some extra security and don't go anywhere alone."

"Thank you for your concern. I really do appreciate your call. I dated Peter Lundov for a while. I liked him a lot. His family was also wealthy, so I was able to be myself when I was with him. He went back to Moscow the following year and I never saw him again. I think I'll go to Moscow and pay my last respects. Thank you again for calling."

"You're welcome. If you do decide to go to Moscow, please make sure you're well protected."

I was very impressed by Joanne Rice. She seemed like a very nice person. I hoped she wasn't next on the killer's list.

A few minutes after my conversation with Joanne Rice ended, Sean Masters called and gave me the name and phone number of the real estate agent working with his father. Her name was Lee Bishop, and I called her immediately.

After she answered I introduced myself and said, "I'm investigating the deaths of Joshua Brewster and Ben Masters. I have some questions for you."

"I thought Joshua Brewster died from natural causes and Ben Masters' death was an accident."

"Joshua Brewster's death was due to natural causes. However, it appears he may have engineered the deaths of five people he believed were responsible for his first wife's death. Ben Masters was one of those people. Can you tell me why Ben Masters was at that location near the airport?"

"He was there because he was interested in purchasing a piece of vacant land for his business. I was contacted that morning and told to reduce the purchase price by forty percent if the deal could close within fifteen days. I spoke to Mr. Masters about the price reduction and he said he would look at the lot again that afternoon and call me with his decision."

"Did he tell you what time he was going to look at the lot?"

"He said it would be late in the afternoon."

"Did you give that information to anybody else?"

"Yes, someone from the company that owns the lot called and asked if lowering the price generated any interest. I told him that Mr. Masters was very interested and was planning on looking at the lot again late that afternoon."

"Who owns the lot?"

"Advanced Electronic Systems."

"Who was your contact at that company?"

"Adam Hobbes."

"Do you know if Advanced Electronic Systems has any connection to Joshua Brewster?"

"I don't think so, but I'm not sure."

"Thank you, Ms. Bishop. I'll contact you again if I need anything else."

It took only a few keystrokes on my computer to find out that Advanced Electronic Systems was owned by Brewster Holdings. My next call was to Adam Hobbes. When he answered his phone, I introduced myself and explained the case to him. He sounded very concerned when he asked, "How can I help you, Lieutenant?"

"Who told you to lower the price on the lot near the airport by forty percent?"

"I received an e-mail that morning. The message contained a list of at least ten vacant land properties that were owned by various Brewster Holding companies. The message said the asking prices for all of the lots should be reduced by forty percent if the sale could close within fifteen days. I still have a copy of the message. Would you like me to send it to you?"

"Yes, that might be helpful. You called Lee Bishop and asked her if lowering the price generated any interest in the lot. I know what she told you. Did you communicate that information to anybody else?"

"I sent a message to the Property Manager at Brewster Holdings by replying to the message I received that morning. That was part of the instructions in the original e-mail."

"Do you remember the name on the message?"

"I thought that was strange, because there was no name, just the title, 'Property Manager'."

"Do you know the name of the Property Manager at Brewster Holdings?"

"Yeah, his name is Burt Dingle."

"Thank you, Mr. Hobbes, you have been very helpful."

I suspected Mr. Dingle would be totally unaware he sent out a message that morning regarding the vacant lots. I called him and my suspicion proved to be correct. He was actually quite upset about the situation.

I was thinking about the wire transfer to the numbered account. It had to be the payment to the killer. Was it the full payment or was it a partial payment and the balance would be paid when the job was complete? Brewster was a business man and I couldn't believe he would pay in full for a job in advance. If it was a partial payment, what would trigger the final payment? How would it be paid? If I could figure out the answers to those questions, it could give me the identity of the killer.

I called Brewster's bank again and asked if any additional wire transfers were scheduled. The woman I spoke to told me that no additional transfers were scheduled, but a wire transfer could be generated by their online banking system. I asked her if she could notify me if any wire transfer was generated for Mr. Brewster's account. She said that could be done and she would delay the transfer for one day. If needed, the transfer could be cancelled.

Brewster had to have multiple accounts because the amount of money in his checking account was insufficient to cover the bequests made in the will. I called Janet Sanders to ask her about it. I had a brief conversation with the receptionist and she transferred the call to Ms. Sanders. When she answered the phone she said, "Good afternoon Lieutenant. Have you figured out what's going on yet?"

"Yes, I'm sure Mr. Brewster knew he was going to die. He wanted to avenge his first wife's death, so he left the five people he felt were responsible large sums of money, paid somebody to kill three of them, and assumed that one of the two remaining beneficiaries would kill the other one. I'm guessing the killer would probably kill whoever was still living before the anniversary of Brewster's death."

The Armchair Prophesy

"That's an interesting theory, but how would you prove it?"

"I have to find out who the killer is, and I think you can help."

"Okay, how can I help?"

"Brewster must have had more accounts than the one at the local bank. Do you know anything about other accounts?"

"He had an account at a bank in Grand Cayman. As executor I have control of both of his accounts. The funds in the local account will be given to his maid. I'll make up any shortfall by giving her money from the account in Grand Cayman."

"I think the three hundred fifty thousand dollar wire transfer was a partial payment to the killer, and the balance would be paid when the job was finished. I'm sure you're not involved in this plot, but I'm wondering if Brewster gave instructions to somebody at the bank in Grand Cayman concerning the final payment."

"I suppose it's possible. I'll send you the contact information for the bank. I don't want to be involved in this situation."

"I understand. Thanks for your cooperation."

Ten minutes later I received a message from her with the information I needed. I called the bank and was directed to Dustin Smythe, the president of the bank. I gave all the information concerning the case to his assistant, so when the call was connected, he said, "This is Dustin Smythe, how can I be of service lieutenant?"

"I need to know if any arrangements were made to transfer a substantial amount of money from Joshua Brewster's account to an account in Switzerland at some future date."

"Mr. Brewster contacted me several weeks ago regarding a transfer of half a million dollars. The transfer would be made after I received two phone calls. The first call was from someone named 'White' who would tell me the project had started. The second call would be from someone named 'Green' who would tell me the project had been completed. If the calls hadn't been received by the anniversary of his death, the money was to be given to his executor."

"Isn't that a rather unusual request?"

"It's unusual, but I've had much stranger requests than that. Someday I may write a book about it."

"I assume you haven't heard from Mr. White yet."

"Correct, although I'm not sure if it's a man or woman who will contact me."

"For now I'll assume it's a man. Will you let me know when you hear from Mr. White?"

"I can do that, but I am bound by our laws to comply with Mr. Brewster's wishes."

"I understand, but this money will be the final payment in a 'murder for hire' scheme. It'll be the only chance I have to identify the killer."

"I will help you in any way I can, so long as that help doesn't conflict with our laws."

"Can you tell me the name of the bank the funds are going to be transferred to?"

"Yes, but that probably won't help you much. If it was me, I would have the funds transferred several times to different numbered accounts. That would make it impossible to trace."

"I suppose you're right, but I still want to try. I'll contact Interpol and let them know what's going on. Maybe they'll have some ideas."

"I'll call you when I hear from Mr. White, and again when I hear from Mr. Green."

"Thank you for your help."

"You're welcome. I hope you catch the murderer."

"Me too."

It was the end of the day, so I decided to go home and see Jill. I was pretty depressed and I was hoping she could cheer me up. When I walked into our apartment, Jill was standing in the kitchen, nude, with two glasses of wine. "Hi honey, I missed you. I thought I would surprise you. Did it work?"

I smiled and said, "Yes, it's definitely the best thing that has happened to me all day." Then I walked over to her, put my arms around her, and kissed her passionately.

That was the precise moment my phone rang. It was the dispatcher. She told me a couple in their early sixties were having a screaming match that ended when the wife shot and killed her husband.

"Sorry, but duty calls. I'm sure your phone will ring in a minute or two."

"This really sucks! I had our whole evening planned."

"Get dressed. We can go to the crime scene together."

We didn't get back home again until 1:00 in the morning. We both fell asleep immediately.

The next morning, when I got to the station, I sat at my desk with a cup of coffee trying to figure out how I could lay a trap for the killer. My phone rang. "This is Lieutenant Carver, Homicide."

"Lieutenant, this is John Leonard. I think someone tried to kill me last night. I asked Tom to get my car and drive it around to the front entrance of the building. As Tom was getting into the car someone shot him. He's in the hospital, but they say he's going to be okay. I spoke to him briefly this morning. He told me that as he opened the car door he heard a loud pop and the window in the door suddenly had a big hole in it. A few moments later there was another shot. This one struck Tom in the shoulder. At almost the same moment, several people who were in the parking lot ran over to help him. I think those people may have saved Tom's life."

"You're probably right. The killer didn't want to shoot everybody. But, he's going to try again. This may be a perfect opportunity to catch the killer. Has the story been publicized yet?"

"Shootings in New York aren't exactly uncommon. Unless someone important is killed, nobody cares."

"This may work to our advantage. Please stay out of sight for a while. If you can, get out of the city. I'm going to ask the police to make a public statement that you were wounded in an attempted murder last night and you're recovering in the hospital. I'm hoping the killer will try to kill you again while he thinks you're recovering."

"I don't want to put Tom in any danger."

"Don't worry. I'll make sure they move Tom to a different hospital as soon as possible. Please call me back in an hour."

"Okay."

I immediately called a contact we had at the NYPD. I explained everything and he agreed this might be the perfect opportunity to catch the killer. He set the plan in motion and told me he would call me back shortly. After the call ended I went to the chief's office and filled him in on what was going on. He was very pleased and told me I did a great job. Since he was in a good mood, I figured it might be a good time to ask him if I could go to New York to work with the police there. He looked at me, smiled, and said, "No, we can't afford it."

I was going to argue, but decided against it. I just went back to my desk. Twenty minutes later John Leonard called back. He told me the police had contacted him, told him the plan, and asked him to leave the city until this thing was over. He told me he had a friend who owned a ranch in Montana that was on the Canadian border. He was going there and will stay there until it was safe for him to return.

A few minutes later my NYPD contact called to tell me the police had scheduled a news conference for later that morning. They were going to announce that John Leonard was shot the evening before and was in stable condition after several hours in surgery. Tom was doing okay and had

The Armchair Prophesy

already been moved to another hospital. Just in case the killer was watching the hospital, they put a blond wig on Tom and covered his face with an oxygen mask when they moved him. He said Tom's mother wouldn't have recognized him. An undercover cop took Tom's place in bed, and two cops dressed as doctors were roving around the floor. Then he gave me the bad news. They could only keep up the charade for four days.

I thanked him for everything they were doing and reminded him that since the killer committed a murder here, we wanted him first.

At 2:45 am my cell phone rang. I said, "It's the middle of the night. I hope this is important."

"This is Sergeant McDonald with the NYPD. We caught your killer. At 2:00 am he made his move. He was wearing a lab coat, had a stethoscope around his neck, and a badge that identified him as Bruce Phillips, Registered Nurse. There was an IV bottle next to the bed and a tube snaked down from the bottle and under the blanket, but the cop in the bed was holding the tube in his hand. The guy in the bed was wide awake, but he had to keep his eyes closed and breathing shallow. When he felt the IV tube move, he pushed the button on a small transmitter he was holding in his left hand. In less than twenty seconds Officer Simmons and I were in the room with our guns drawn."

The killer gave up without a fight. He refused to give us any information. He gave us a card with the number of his lawyer on it and asked us to call him. All he said was, "I knew I should never have taken this job."

After his lawyer showed up he gave us his client's name, Stanley Driscoll. However, Interpol identified him as Daniel Kurtz. He was wanted for murder in almost every country in Europe. Apparently, he had been killing people for a living for more than twenty-five years.

I expected him to fight extradition to my jurisdiction, but he didn't. When he was brought in I wanted to ask him some questions. We were seated in one of the interview rooms. I said, "Tell me about your deal with Joshua Brewster."

"I guess at this point it really isn't going to matter. I'd rather be in prison here than in some hell hole in Europe. Brewster never wanted to meet me in person. We did everything over the phone. He told me he was going to die in three weeks and he gave me a list of five names and told me to kill any three of the five people on the list. I asked him if he had a preference. He told me he already knew who I was going to kill, so there was no reason for him to tell me. He also said one of the murder attempts was going to fail. But by the first anniversary of his death they would all be dead except for Parkes. He told me I had to kill Parkes before the anniversary of his death if I wanted to get the remainder of the money. He said after I killed Parkes, I should call the manager of a bank in Grand Cayman, identify myself as Mr. Green, and tell him the job is finished. I don't understand how he could possibly know what was going to happen, but he obviously did."

"I was told he was psychic. That was how he made all his money. Somehow, he was able to predict the future. When he died we found a note in his hand that said three rich people were going to die in unusual circumstances. But from what you told me, he knew that was wrong. I wonder why he did that."

We talked for a while longer. Aside from the fact he was a cold-blooded killer, he seemed like a really nice guy. He told me he grew up near LA. After he graduated college he joined the Air Force. When he left the service, he moved to Europe and got involved with some bad guys and ended up as a professional hit man. I asked him where he went to college. He said UCLA.

By the time the anniversary of Joshua Brewster's death occurred, Joanne Rice was the only survivor. John Leonard died when the car he was driving was broadsided by a garbage truck. The truck driver claimed his brakes failed. After the accident it was determined that the brake line came loose and all the brake fluid leaked out. Fredrick Parkes was electrocuted while taking a shower on his ship. Because it occurred in international waters, no investigation was ever performed, so the details of his death are unknown.

Joanne Rice used the money to set up the Joanne Rice foundation. Their primary goal was to provide housing and education in some of the poorest countries in the world. Unlike many of the other charities with the same goal, the Joanne Rice foundation never gave any money to the governments of the countries where they were providing aid. Instead, managers were sent to oversee every project and they reported directly to Ms. Rice.

Daniel Kurtz was convicted of first degree murder and received a life sentence. He will be eligible for parole when he is eighty-four. I found out that he was also arrested during the UCLA protest.

There were still some unanswered questions, and they are likely to remain that way. We don't know how Joshua Brewster knew he was going to die that evening. We don't really understand why he left that note or how he knew Daniel Kurtz would fail in the attempt to kill the third person on his list. I presume Mr. White's job was to notify the bank when all the beneficiaries were dead, with the exception of Fredrick Parkes. But we have no idea who he is. I think, despite my negative feeling regarding psychics, the rumors that Joshua was psychic were true. There is simply no other possible explanation. But I suspect he didn't completely trust his ability to predict the future, so he hired Daniel Kurtz. Or maybe Joshua hired Daniel because he knew Daniel was going to get caught.

Frank Carver Mysteries

The Halloween Incident
A Frank Carver Mystery

It was a week before Halloween, and like every Halloween, the Abrams family was determined to win the "Best Decorated House" award again. They spent two weeks building a cemetery in their front yard. There were ten graves, all in various states of disrepair, including one with an open coffin lying next to the headstone. That night, while the family slept, they had no idea that someone was going to enhance their decorations.

I got the call early on Saturday morning. A body was found at 2235 Pine Court Drive. I woke Jill up because I knew her phone would ring in a minute or two. I'm the only homicide detective in Norfolk County and Jill Tanner, my live-in girlfriend, is the county medical examiner.

I showered and dressed quickly. While Jill was in the shower she received a call summoning her to the same address. When we arrived two squad cars were on site. The Halloween display in the yard was the most gruesome one I have ever seen.

As Jill and I got out of my car, Mike Stevens, the local beat cop, walked up to us and said, "You guys are going to love this. Apparently, somebody decided to improve the display by adding a real body."

Jill and I followed Mike into the yard. We went over to the open coffin which contained the body of a man. Jill put on gloves and bent down to examine the body. A few moments later a man walked out of the front door of the house and came over to us. He looked at me and said, "Good morning, I'm Gordon Abrams. Are you in charge here?"

"Yes sir. I'm Lieutenant Carver. Are you the one who found the body?"

"Yeah, I was taking my dog for a walk. As soon as we stepped into the yard he started barking and pulled me over to the coffin. It was quite a shock to see the body there."

"Do you have any idea who the victim is?"

"No, I've never seen him before. I was wondering, would it be possible to leave the body there until after the judging tonight? It really makes the display more realistic."

I couldn't believe he asked me that question. I know I've only been a homicide cop for a year, but that had to be the dumbest, most insensitive question I have ever heard. "No, I'm really sorry, but we won't be able to help you perk up your display."

He said, "Thanks anyway," and walked back to his house.

Jill stood up and said, "I'm not sure, but it looks like our victim died as a result of asphyxiation. His lips and tongue are blue, but there is no evidence he was strangled." Then she turned to Mike and asked, "Did you call for an ambulance?"

"Yeah, but apparently there was a bad accident on the interstate, so they said it would probably be an hour before they could get one here to pick up the body."

"Please have them bring the body to my lab. Did you check him for identification?"

"I did, but all of his pockets were empty."

I called Jim Doyle, the guy in charge of forensics. I told him about the crime scene and asked him to send somebody over to check the area. The ambulance arrived earlier than expected, and Jill walked over to speak to them.

When she was finished we walked back to the car. Once we were inside she said, "It's a light day so I should be able to do the autopsy as soon as the body arrives," then she asked, "Are you getting nervous yet?"

I knew she was talking about our wedding, which would occur in less than three weeks. "No, I'm not nervous about the wedding. I'm looking forward to it."

"Good, I'm looking forward to it also. I'm anxious to begin our honeymoon. I've never been to Hawaii."

The Halloween Incident

"I hope I can resolve this case before we go. I don't want to leave with an unsolved murder to worry about."

I dropped Jill off at her office and drove to the station. I filled out some paperwork to open a murder investigation and took it to the chief. He's not normally there on Saturdays, but he always comes in when there's a murder. He looked at it for a minute, signed it, and said, "You better solve this one fast."

"I know. Jill and I were discussing it on the way here. It's not in the report, but I thought you might be interested to know that the guy who found the body asked me if I could leave it there until tomorrow because he wanted it to be part of his Halloween display."

"Do you think he killed the guy in order make his display more realistic?" the chief asked with a laugh in his voice.

"I'll have to think about that."

I had nothing to do until I heard from either Jill or Jim Doyle, so I sat at my desk and used my computer to catch up with the news. I was really getting bored when Jill called. She said, "I'm not finished with the autopsy yet, but I wanted to let you know our victim did die from asphyxiation. However, it was the result of being exposed to a powerful nerve toxin. I don't know how he came in contact with it, or what the toxin is, but I wanted you to know what I found so far."

"What are the chances you'll be able to identify the toxin?"

"Not very good. Most of these toxins are metabolized by the body very quickly."

"I understand, but nerve toxins aren't a normal homicide weapon. If I can find out what was used, it may be very helpful."

"I know. I'll call you as soon as I have anything to tell you."

"I know you will. Thanks."

After I hung up the phone I was thinking that since I've been working in homicide, we've had Russians transported here with missing body parts, a guy was found with his brain cooked by a top-secret military weapon, and a psychic who managed to cause the death of four people after he died. Norfolk County seemed an unlikely place for all these weird incidents to occur.

An hour after my conversation with Jill, I got a call from Jim Doyle. He told me our victim's name is Owen Carson. He was able to identify him from his fingerprints. He lived on a farm in the northern part of the county, just west of Springdale.

I looked up Owen Carson on my computer. He had no criminal history. It appeared the reason his fingerprints were on file was because he had a permit to carry a concealed weapon. I looked him up in the local phone book. I thought about calling his family and decided it would be better to tell them in person. I didn't want to go alone, so I went to the dispatcher and told her I needed a female officer to go with me. Fifteen minutes later a young officer named Bonnie Griffin came to my desk. She said, "Hi Frank, what can I help you with?"

"Hi Bonnie. There was a murder last night and I want to go the family's home. I wanted a woman with me."

"I'll help any way I can. Who was murdered?"

"A man named Owen Carson."

"That's not a name I'm familiar with which makes this easier."

"Maybe, but it's never really easy. Let's go."

We arrived at the house twenty-five minutes later. The house was set back at least two hundred feet from the road. There were animal paddocks set up all over the property, but there were no animals. The house looked big, and although it was old, it was very well maintained. In addition to the house, there was a large barn and several other smaller buildings. I stopped the car in the circular

The Halloween Incident

driveway in front of the house and walked up to the front door.

I rang the doorbell and a few seconds later a woman opened the door and said, "May I help you?"

"Is this the Carson residence?"

"Yes, it is."

"I'm Lieutenant Carver with the Norfolk County Police Department and this is officer Griffin. Are you related to Owen Carson?"

She stammered when she answered, "Yes, I'm his wife. Has something happened to Owen?"

"May we come in?"

"Yes, of course."

We followed her into the living room, and after we all sat down, Mrs. Carson asked, "Please tell me what this is all about."

I looked into her eyes and said softly, "I wish there was an easy way to tell you this. I'm sorry to inform you that your husband has been murdered."

She screamed, "Oh my God! Owen's been murdered? What happened?"

She began crying so I asked, "Is there someone we can call for you? If you prefer, we can do this later."

She took some time to compose herself and then said, "It's okay. Can you tell me what happened?"

"This is probably going to seem a little strange. Your husband appears to have been exposed to some kind of nerve toxin. His body was put into an open coffin in a Halloween display. I know your husband had a permit to carry a gun. Do you know why he felt he needed protection?"

"No, I didn't know he had a gun or a permit. Owen was a real estate agent. I don't think that's a dangerous profession."

"When was the last time you saw him?"

"It was yesterday morning. He told me he was going to Chicago for a meeting and would be gone for two days."

"Was yesterday the first time he mentioned the trip?"

"No, he had been talking about it for at least two weeks."

"Do you know what time his plane was supposed to leave?"

"No, but I know he ordered the tickets online, so I'm sure the information is on his computer."

"Where is his computer?"

"He has a laptop he carries with him and a desktop on his desk in the den."

"I assume he drove himself to the airport. What kind of car does he have?"

"It's a black Chrysler 300."

"What did Owen do before he became a real estate agent?"

"I really don't know. Owen and I have been married for less than two years. I met him when I was trying to sell my mother's house after she died. Owen never wanted to talk about his past, and I decided not to press him."

"So, it certainly is possible his murder could have been the result of something that happened before you met him. What made you buy this place?"

"Owen and I both love animals. We bought this place thinking that at some point in the future we would raise horses. However, after we moved in, we discovered the animals in the forest surrounding this place come here almost every evening to graze in the fields. We have between fifty and a hundred deer here. Owen and I have spent countless hours watching them. He was such a gentle person. I just can't imagine him involved in anything illegal or violent."

"I'm going to have to dig into Owen's past. Do you want me to tell you what I find?"

"Yes Lieutenant, I do want to know."

"I have to ask you for one more thing. Can you come to the Medical Examiner's Office on Tuesday to identify the body? That will give the Medical Examiner time to complete the autopsy. If it's difficult for you, I would be happy to pick you up."

"Thank you, lieutenant. I'll accept your offer. Can you pick me up at 10:30 Tuesday morning?"

"Of course. I don't think we have any more questions for you. Can we call someone for you? This is probably not a good time to be alone."

"I'll call my neighbor and ask her to come over for a while. I appreciate your concern."

I said, "Once again, I'm truly sorry for your loss. Thank you for your cooperation. I'll see you Tuesday morning."

Then Bonnie and I left and drove back to the station. On the way back Bonnie said, "Everyone at the station is looking forward to your wedding. I hope you are too."

"Jill asked me the same question this morning. Yes, I'm looking forward to the wedding and the honeymoon afterwards. I have to get this case solved before the fourteenth."

When I got back to the station I started running a check on Owen Carson. While I was waiting for some information to come back I got the license number for his car from DMV and sent out a statewide notice to look for it.

I had a suspicion I knew what was going on. Two hours later my suspicion was confirmed. Owen Carson didn't exist until three years ago. His background had been carefully fabricated, but I knew it was phony a few minutes after I looked at it. Owen Carson was in the Witness Protection Program. Now I had to find out why.

I went to the chief's office to bring him up to date on what was happening with the case, but I discovered he went home for the weekend. I also wanted to ask him if we had a contact at the Justice Department. I decided it could wait till Monday and went home.

I arrived at the station at 8:00 on Monday morning. The chief was there so I went into his office and brought him up to speed on the murder. Then I asked him about a contact at the Justice Department. He told me I was on my own regarding the Justice Department and wished me good luck. This wasn't an encouraging sign.

I went back to my desk and started the task of discussing Owen Carson with the Justice Department. After four calls and forty-five minutes I was connected with Mark Bishop.

"Mr. Bishop, my name is Frank Carver. I'm a homicide detective with the Norfolk County Police Department. I'm investigating the murder of Owen Carson. A background check on Mr. Carson, coupled with the manner of his death, made me feel he was in the Witness Protection Program. Can you confirm he was in the program and perhaps tell me why? He obviously no longer needs protection."

"I'm sorry Mr. Carver, but I can't discuss anything concerning people in the program, even if they are no longer alive. That information is classified. But I'm curious, what makes you think your murder victim was in the program?"

"I spent a few years working in Army Intelligence. I can spot a phony background fairly quickly. It was obvious Owen Carson didn't exist until three years ago."

"You mentioned the manner of his death was unusual. How did he die?"

"He was exposed to a very potent nerve toxin. So far, our Medical Examiner hasn't been able to determine how the toxin was administered or what toxin was used."

"I'm sure you realize if you develop a chemical or biological weapon that will be used to kill an individual, you want to make it as difficult as possible to identify and determine the method of exposure. That's what makes these types of weapons effective."

"That seems to be a rather cold-blooded thing to say. I'd like to think our government doesn't develop or utilize chemical or biological weapons."

"You are free to think anything you like. While we were talking I brought up your record. Since you are still in the reserve I must warn you, pursuing this investigation could violate your oath and put you in prison."

"Wow! Owen Carson is that important. You must realize I have no choice. I have to pursue this investigation. My job is to find the person who killed Mr. Carson, regardless of the consequences."

"That is your choice. Goodbye Mr. Carver."

After that conversation I was absolutely positive my theory about him being in the Witness Protection Program was correct. I told the chief about my conversation with Mark Bishop, including his warning about going to prison. The chief sighed and told me to go home and spend the evening with Jill and forget about the case for tonight. I took his advice.

The following morning, I decided to pick up Mrs. Carson instead of going to the office. I stopped in front of her house at about 10:25. I walked to the front door and found it was open. I slowly opened the door and looked around. I didn't see anything so I yelled, "Mrs. Carson, it's Frank Carver. I'm here to pick you up."

There was no response so I yelled again. I took my gun out and began to look around. Everything looked fine on the first floor so I walked upstairs. When I got to the top of the stairs I saw her lying on the floor. I went over to her and checked for a pulse. She was dead. Her lips looked blue. I suspected she was killed with the same stuff that was used to kill her husband.

I called the station and told the dispatcher what I found. I asked her to send an ambulance, a forensics team, and notify Jill about the murder. I checked the rest of the house while I was waiting. I found nothing unusual.

The ambulance arrived first. They verified Mrs. Carson was dead. Now we had to wait for Jill to arrive. It was a short wait. She walked in, put on gloves, and began her examination of the body. Then she turned to me and said, "I'm sure you already guessed she was killed with the same toxin that killed her husband."

"You're right. I don't suppose you made any progress identifying it?"

"I wish I had. I know what the toxin does, but I have no idea what it is. I'm fairly certain it was inhaled, because we couldn't find any puncture marks on her husband, but we'll check her too."

"I'm going back to the station. I'll see you later."

When I got back to my desk I called Jim Doyle and asked him to let me know as soon as his people were finished at the Carson residence. I intended to go over every inch of it. I was sure there had to be something in the house that would enable me to figure out who Owen Carson was before he became Owen Carson.

I got a call from Jim two hours later to tell me they were finished at the Carson house. It was getting close to 5:00, so I called Jill to make her an offer she couldn't refuse.

Amanda answered the phone. I said, "Hi Amanda, is Jill available?"

"Yeah Frank, I'll get her for you."

A minute later Jill said, "Hi honey, are you working late or something?"

"Well, kind of. I want to go back to the Carson house and go through it thoroughly. I'm certain there's something there that will tell us Owen Carson's previous identity. If you help me I'll take you to that new steak house that just opened for dinner when we are done."

"Okay, but we have to limit the search to two hours. Is that okay?"

"Sure, I'll pick you up at 5:15."

"Okay, bye."

When I pulled up in front of her office she was already waiting for me. She got in, kissed me on the cheek, and turned on some soft music. After I started driving she asked, "So what are we looking for?"

"I was hoping that maybe he saved letters from old girl friends, report cards from school, maybe he kept a diary. Anything that has a name on it could be helpful. Even if it

The Halloween Incident

isn't his name, it could still be somebody who could identify him."

We arrived at the Carson house a few minutes before 6:00. Jill looked at her watch and said, "We stop and go to dinner at 8:00, right?"

"Yes, dear. We'll leave at 8:00."

For the next hour and a half we opened every drawer, looked at every scrap of paper, and opened every book in the house. There was nothing. I was in the master bedroom closet and looked up. There was a pull-down attic ladder on the ceiling. I pulled it down and walked slowly up the ladder. I took out my pocket flashlight and looked around. A foot in front of me was a switch. I turned it on and instantly the attic was flooded with light. There were at least a dozen fluorescent light fixtures mounted on the ceiling. The floor was finished, and the walls and ceiling were insulated. There was a desk, three file cabinets, and a table with a printer on it. There were also several small book cases.

I went back down the ladder to find Jill. She was sitting in the living room relaxing. When she saw me she asked, "Are we done? Can we leave now? I'm hungry."

"We can leave, get dinner, and then come back. I found an office in the attic above the master bedroom. I want to go through that stuff, but if you want to go to dinner we can do that now."

"Okay, let's go and come back. I'm kind of curious why he set up an office in the attic when there are two empty bedrooms on the second floor."

"Me too."

Jill and I went to dinner and then drove back to the house. As I approached the house I noticed a car parked across the street. The house is in a sparsely populated area. The closest neighbor is at least a quarter of a mile away. I parked in the driveway and looked at the car across the street again. It just didn't belong there. We went inside the house and I locked the door. Then I called the station and asked them to send some backup. Jill was watching the car and I took out my gun just in case I needed it.

A few minutes went by and I heard a siren approaching. The squad car stopped in front of the suspicious car. There were two officers in the car. One approached the car with his gun drawn. The other man waited in the car. The door to the car opened and a man stepped out. He immediately raised his hands.

I walked out of the house and over to the car. The man was still standing with his hands up. When I was ten feet from him he said, "Good evening Lieutenant Carver. We recently spoke on the phone. I'm Mark Bishop."

This was certainly an unexpected development. Then I looked at him and said, "Please reach slowly into your pocket and give me your identification."

The officer kept the gun trained on him. He handed me his government ID. It looked real enough so I handed it back to him and said with some irritation in my voice, "You were somewhat rude when we spoke on the phone and you threatened me. So, tell me why you're here."

"Because I need your help. Can I put my hands down?"

"Yes," then I turned to the patrolman and said, "Thanks for the quick response Jeff. I'm sure I can handle it from here."

Jeff holstered his gun and walked back to the car. Before he got there, he said, "Frank, we're going to patrol this area for a while. If you need us we'll come back."

"Thanks Jeff."

Jeff got in the car and drove away. I said, "Please come in the house Mr. Bishop."

As we walked into the living room Mr. Bishop said, "Hello, you must be Frank's fiancé. It's nice to meet you, Jill. I'm Mark Bishop. Please call me Mark."

Jill said, "It's nice to meet you too, Mark."

I said, "Okay Mark, you've obviously been checking up on me. Do you want to tell me what this is all about?"

The Halloween Incident

"You're right, I have been checking up on you. I apologize for being rude to you during our phone conversation. I should have realized I could trust you as soon as I noticed you were in Army Intelligence. Anyway, I did a little more checking on you, and I even spoke to your friend George Dyer. When he told me the level of security clearance you have, I knew I could trust you, so I came here just in time to find out Elizabeth Carson was also murdered. I think we can help each other."

I asked, "Who is Owen Carson?"

"Owen has been in the witness protection system for three years, as you guessed. Prior to becoming Owen Carson his name was Michael Finch. Michael was a genius with money. Somehow, he came to the attention of the Humbolt drug cartel. They aren't big in the United States, but they are the largest supplier of illicit drugs to Eastern Europe. Michael was hired to launder money for them, and he did it very well. In the span of two years he was able to launder more than two billion dollars. We might never have caught him if someone hadn't hacked Michael's secure e-mail. We don't know who that hacker was, but he sent us some information concerning the amount of gold and platinum Michael was buying. We kept a close watch on Michael and pounced on him when he was in the middle of trading gold bars worth about three hundred million dollars for a hotel in Dubai."

"We made him an offer he couldn't refuse. If he helped us put the cartel out of business, we wouldn't prosecute him. He gave us some very useful information, but before we could act on it, somebody tried to kill him. Someone in the Justice Department leaked the information concerning Michael to the cartel. Michael got scared and said he wouldn't testify at a trial or provide us with any more information until we could absolutely guarantee his safety. So, Michael became Owen Carson, complete with a degree in accounting and a CPA certification. We gave him some minor plastic surgery to change his appearance, gave him $50,000, and brought him here."

"So, the cartel found him despite your best efforts to hide him?"

"That's the point. Only five people knew about Owen Carson, and I can assure you none of them gave the information to the cartel."

"So somehow Owen must have screwed up."

"Exactly, I think Owen may have been hiding something and maybe he tried to blackmail the cartel with it. I'm sure he thought they wouldn't be able to find him."

"Just before Jill and I left to go to dinner, I discovered an office in the attic. We came back here to check it out. Let's go see what he was hiding."

We all climbed up the ladder and into the attic. It soon became obvious we hit the jackpot. There were records of hundreds of transactions, and every transaction included account numbers. This information was more than enough to bury the Humbolt cartel. Since the government now had the account numbers, they would be able to seize their assets. This was great news for Mark, but I wasn't sure how it would help me find the murderer.

I thought about it for a few minutes while Mark continued to look through the files. I knew what I wanted to do, but I wasn't sure Mark would agree. I said, "Mark, I know the information we found will put the cartel out of business, and that resolves your problem. However, I still have to find the killer. I think the best way to do that is to use the information in these files to draw him out."

"How do you propose to do that?"

"Do you have any way to leak information to the cartel?"

"We have a low-level contact. I think he could do that for us. What do you want us to leak?"

"Before you announce you have all this information, let the cartel know the investigation by the local police into

The Halloween Incident

the two murders turned up some files in the house that are suspicious, and I'm working on them at home."

"I'm sure you realize you are putting yourself in danger. These people won't hesitate to kill you."

"I realize that, in fact I'm counting on it. If they think they can kill me and get access to the files, I'm sure they will try to do it. I just have to be prepared."

"Don't forget they use nerve gas. They could toss something through your window and you would die almost instantly."

"I know from my work in Army Intelligence that nobody develops a biological weapon unless they have an antidote or something that would protect the person using the weapon from harm. I think knowing what the weapon is could provide us with the edge we need."

"I'll have somebody here in the morning who can work with Jill to identify the weapon. I'll have to discuss the delay with my superiors, but I'm sure I can convince them to delay any action for three or four days. You can't stay in your apartment because that would put Jill in danger. I think you should either stay here or in a hotel."

Jill, who had been quite for a while, said rather emphatically, "Hey guys, don't talk about me like I'm not here. I think I have a say in this plan too. I don't want to risk either my life or Frank's to catch a killer."

"Jill, I'm a cop. I risk my life every day."

"Yes, but you don't purposely set yourself up as a target."

"I promise I'll take every precaution to protect myself."

"This is bullshit! We're supposed to get married in less than three weeks. If I can't stop you from doing something this stupid then the wedding is off and I'll move back home with my parents."

Mark said, "Jill is right. We have to find a way of trapping the killer without putting anyone in excessive danger."

Jill said, "Thank you, Mark. I'm sure we can think of some way to do that."

I sighed loudly and said, "I suppose you're right. Let's try to come up with another plan to draw out the killer."

A few minutes went by and Jill asked, "Where does the police department keep old files?"

"In a warehouse on Kennedy Street."

"Supposing we pretend to move the files there and then discretely place several armed people there to wait for the killer to make his move."

"That may work! How about if we leak that the files were found, but they were encrypted, and the police believe they will be able to decrypt the files in a few days?" I suggested.

"That could force them to react quickly. Is there any place in the warehouse where we could hide a few officers?"

"I've only been there once, so I really don't know. We can go over there in the morning. But what do we do with the files here?"

"I think we have to assume this place is being watched. Let's get a truck here tomorrow morning and pretend to fill it, but the boxes will be empty. The truck can take the boxes to the warehouse. That will help confirm the story that we'll leak to the cartel. I think we can just leave the files here."

"Somebody still has to stay here to protect the files on the off chance the cartel decides to check out the house."

"Okay, but not you," Jill said loudly.

Mark said, "I'll stay here for a few days."

I asked, "Are you armed?"

"No, I don't normally carry a weapon."

"I'll have a patrol car sent over with someone who is armed to stay here with you."

"Okay, I appreciate that."

I called the station, and after the dispatcher answered I said, "Hi, it's Frank. I need you to send somebody to the

The Halloween Incident

Carson house to spend the night with an agent from the Justice Department."

"Okay, anybody in particular you would like?"

"I want somebody who is good with his gun and not afraid to use it if necessary. Tell him to make it as obvious as possible that he is here. I want him to use his lights and siren as he approaches the house."

"Dean Fowler is available. Would he be okay?"

"Yeah, Dean would be perfect. I'll stay here until he arrives. Also, leave a message for the chief to call me as soon as he gets in tomorrow morning."

"Okay Frank, I'll take care of it. Dean should be there in about twenty minutes."

I said, "Thanks," and disconnected the call. I turned toward Mark and said, "They are sending over Dean Fowler. He wins the marksmanship contest every year. He's perfect for this assignment and should be here in twenty minutes."

"Thanks, I have to get my bag out of the car." Then Mark walked out to get it. He came back a minute later, closed and locked the front door, and said, "We're being watched. There's somebody up in a tree in the field across the street. They are about two hundred yards from here. I saw the light from the moon reflect off of a pair of binoculars."

"I expected to be watched, but I hope they aren't eavesdropping on our conversation."

"Yeah, I was thinking about that. I guess we'll just have to wait and see if they take the bait."

Dean showed up a few minutes later. Between the siren and the flashing lights, everyone in the whole area knew he was here. I opened the door before he rang the bell. After he walked in I said, "Dean, this is Mark Bishop. He's an agent with the Justice Department. I need you to stay here tonight and protect him and some very valuable evidence that's up in the attic. The house is being watched by someone in a tree in the empty lot across the street."

Dean said, "I'll be right back." Then he walked outside. Less than a minute later he came back in carrying an automatic rifle and a box of ammunition. He sat down at the dining room table, loaded the big gun, and said, "I like to be prepared."

Mark said, "Good, I feel safe just knowing you're here."

Then I asked, "Dean, would you like to have a patrol car drive by every half hour?"

"I think that would be a good idea, but vary the time."

"Okay, I'll take care of it. Jill and I are going to leave now. Don't hesitate to call if anything happens."

"Okay Frank, have a good evening."

Jill and I left. I asked her to drive so I could call the station and arrange for the patrol car to keep a watch on the house. She started to drive back downtown and I said, "Just go home. I'll drop you off in the morning."

When we got home, Jill put her arms around me, kissed me, and said, "Thank you."

"What are you thanking me for?"

"For not risking your life and our future."

We each had a glass of wine and went to bed.

The next morning, I woke up and looked at the clock; it was 5:30. I didn't hear from Dean so I assumed everything was alright, but I called him anyway. He told me that everything was fine. The night was quiet and Mark tried to stay awake but kept drifting off. I told him I would be there in less than an hour to relieve him.

I woke Jill up and told her we had to leave in twenty minutes. She said some very impolite things to me, but got out of bed anyway. We both managed to get showered and dressed in twenty-five minutes. I dropped her off at her office and managed to get to the Carson house about five minutes late.

I rang the bell and Dean opened the door, looked at me and asked, "Where are the donuts and coffee?"

"I think they're still at Dunkin Donuts," I said as I walked in.

The Halloween Incident

Mark was sitting on a recliner in the living room. He looked like he was half asleep, but he seemed to wake up after he saw me. He said, "Good morning, I spent some time on the phone last night. Our contact with the cartel is going to tell them the story this morning. I hope we're prepared to make it look like we're moving the stuff out.

"I have to talk to the chief, but it won't be a problem. I left a message for him to call me this morning."

"Okay, I'll take your word for it. What do we do about breakfast? I'm kind of hungry."

"Yeah, Dean was upset that I didn't bring donuts and coffee."

"Well, that does sound good right now."

At that moment my phone rang; it was the chief. I answered by saying, "Good morning, sir."

"How is my favorite homicide detective today?"

"I'm fine sir, but I need something done immediately." I spent the next few minutes bringing him up to date on what was going on and telling I needed a small truck loaded with empty boxes here as soon as possible.

"The truck will be there by 9:00. I like the plan. Is there anything else you need?"

"Yeah, we need breakfast. Ask the guys driving the truck to pick up donuts and coffee on the way here."

I heard the chief laugh and then he said, "I'll take care of it."

After the call was over I looked at Mark and Dean and said, "The truck will be here by 9:00, and they will be bringing breakfast."

At 8:30 Jill called to tell me Dr. Brooke, an expert on nerve toxins, just arrived at her office. She said she would call me as soon as they made any progress identifying the toxin. After she hung up I thanked Mark for sending someone to help Jill.

The truck arrived a few minutes before 9:00. I opened the garage door and told the driver to back the truck in. After he did that I closed the garage door so our spy couldn't see what was going on. I wasn't sure he was still there, but I wanted to put on a good show just in case.

After a delicious, but very fattening, breakfast, we started the show. There was a window on the landing between the first and second floors. We took turns walking by the window carrying unassembled boxes. Once all the boxes were upstairs, we assembled them, waited about fifteen minutes, and took turns carrying the assembled boxes down, one at a time. We put the empty boxes into the truck, and once they were all loaded, the two drivers left to go to the warehouse. Dean left to go home and get some sleep.

After the others left, Mark said, "There's a team coming here early this afternoon to scan all the documents in the office. It will probably take about two hours. I can't take any chances with the files."

"I understand, but I wonder if that will confuse the guy watching the house."

"I don't think so. When they drive up I'll go out and greet them and hug and kiss one of them."

"I hope the one you kiss is a girl."

"One of the members of the team is my younger sister, Tara."

"Okay, now I understand. I'm sure that will be an effective cover."

A little while later Jill called. After I answered she said, "Dr. Brooke has identified what killed Owen and his wife. It's not a nerve toxin, although the end results are the same. A few seconds after the toxin is inhaled it causes fluid to quickly build up in the victim's lungs and the muscles around the lungs to constrict. In less than thirty seconds they are unable to breathe. After death, when the chest muscles relax, the fluid drains out of the lungs. The toxin leaves minute traces of potassium chloride, which we found in Owen's lungs."

"I've never heard of anything like that. Does Dr. Brooke know where it comes from?"

The Halloween Incident

"Yes, he believes it was developed by Iran about two years ago. Iran has been offering it for sale for the past several months."

"So, I would guess the cartel is one of their customers."

"I'm sure that's true. However, there's an inoculation that will protect you from the effects of the toxin for two or three months. Twenty doses will be here tomorrow morning."

"Good, Mark and I both need to be inoculated as soon as possible. So should the people working at the warehouse."

"I know. Dr. Brooke said he would be at the station to give the shots by 10:30 tomorrow morning."

"I hope our guy doesn't decide to do anything tonight. I'll call the chief and let him know about the toxin. Thanks Jill, I'll see you later."

I called the chief immediately and told him about the toxin. The people at the warehouse, as well as those of us working at the Carson's house, are vulnerable until we receive the shots.

The chief said he had to make a few calls and would get back to me in about a half hour. While I was waiting for the chief to call me back I started to explain the situation to Mark, but he stopped me and said he had listened to my half of the conversation, so an explanation wasn't necessary. Then he said rather emphatically, "This really sucks!"

"I agree, but I'm sure the chief will come up with something."

Twenty minutes later my phone rang. It was the chief. He said there is another way to protect yourself from the toxin. You have to increase your oxygen intake. He said he's sending over four portable oxygen concentrators, and everybody in the house should be using one until they are inoculated.

The car with the oxygen concentrators arrived first. An officer brought the boxes into the house and he left.

Twenty minutes later Mark received a call on his cell phone. I couldn't hear anything he said except, "Okay, I'll see you in a few minutes."

When the call was over he said, "That was Tara. They'll be here in five minutes."

When they arrived, Mark went out to greet them. The driver got out of the car, put her arms around Mark, and kissed him. The man in the passenger seat got out of the car and retrieved a large suitcase from the trunk. Then the three of them walked into the house.

Mark introduced me to Tara, and the man with her introduced himself as Jimmy. We put on our oxygen concentrators and we all went upstairs, this time avoiding being seen through the window.

As soon as we were in the attic, Jimmy set up the scanner and began scanning the files. The file images were saved on the computer that the scanner was connected to, and they were also uploaded to a secure system at the Justice Department.

Since I wasn't needed, I went back down to the living room to relax. The next thing I knew Mark was shaking me and said, "Okay Frank, it's time to wake up."

I opened my eyes, looked at Mark, and thought about saying something unpleasant, but decided against it. Tara and Jimmy said goodbye and Mark walked back to their car with them. When he came back in he said, "I'm glad that's over. I feel better knowing the files are safe."

It was almost 5:00 and Dean was scheduled to take over. At 5:10 I called him. When he answered I asked, "What happened? You were supposed to be here at 5:00."

"I'm in my car, about a block west of the house. I've been watching the guy watching the house for the past fifteen minutes. I saw him make a couple of phone calls."

"I'm going to call the station and see if they can get the phone company to tell us who the guy is, presuming he's using his own phone."

The Halloween Incident

I hung up with Dean and called the station telling them what I wanted. A few minutes later the dispatcher called back. She said, "The phone is a prepaid unit and was purchased by Donald J. Duck, which I suspect, isn't his real name. However, they did say they could shut off service to the phone with a court order. The chief is taking care of that now."

"Thanks for the update. Please keep me informed."

"Of course, Frank."

A half hour later the dispatcher called again to tell me Mr. Duck's phone was no longer functioning. Then I called Dean and told him the guy in tree was using Donald Duck's phone, and the phone company cut off service. He said he was going to go to the house now, but he would continue watching him. He also told me he brought a pair of night vision binoculars to make his surveillance easier.

When Dean arrived, we gave him an oxygen concentrator and told him what was going on. I also said I had a feeling something was going to happen tonight. Then I left to go home and have dinner with Jill.

Just after Jill and I finished dinner, the chief called to tell me they were shorthanded at the warehouse. He wanted three officers there and one of them called in sick. So, he asked to me to go there and stay until my replacement shows up at 11:00.

I told Jill I needed to go to the warehouse and stay there until 11:00. She told me that if I get killed there, she will never forgive me for screwing up her wedding. I kissed her goodbye and left.

I was at the warehouse for about two hours when the perimeter alarm sounded. We all looked at the video monitors. There was a man there carrying a suitcase. I said, "I'll handle this."

I walked outside quietly. When I saw the guy who set off the alarm, I yelled, "Hi, Mickey. Are you lost?"

"Sergeant Carver, what a pleasant surprise."

"I'm a lieutenant now. What's in the suitcase?"

"Would you believe it if I said I didn't know?"

"Put the suitcase down and tell me why you're here."

Mickey put down the suitcase and said, "Somebody paid me a thousand dollars to put the case on the ground next to the door. Then he gave me a number to call when I was finished."

I reached into my shirt pocket and took out the note that had Donald Duck's phone number on it. Then I said, "Is the number 207-555-0641?"

"Yeah, how did you know?"

"That doesn't matter. However, Mr. Duck's number is no longer in service."

"Huh? Who's Mr. Duck? The guy told me his name was Jim Smith."

"Okay, did Mr. Smith give you any other instructions?"

"Yeah, he said if I want to continue living, don't open the case."

"Do you know how Mr. Smith got your name?"

"He said he saw my website."

"Mickey, I'm going to give you a break this time. Get in your car and go home. Don't call that number. I will know if you do."

Mickey said, "Thank you, lieutenant." Then he walked back to his car, got in, and drove away quickly.

I called the station and told the dispatcher to contact the state police and tell them to send the bomb squad here immediately. I also told her we needed to form a quarter mile perimeter around the building. Then I went inside and told everybody to get out of the building.

The chief called me about five minutes later and I briefed him on the situation. He said he would be here in twenty minutes.

The bomb squad showed up in a big van fifteen minutes later. One of them walked over to me and asked, "Are you in charge here?"

The Halloween Incident

"Yes, I'm Lieutenant Carver. I believe there's a very large bomb in that suitcase which can be remotely detonated."

"Get your people out of the area. We'll take care of this."

"I've already sent everyone else away. I'll leave this in your capable hands."

I drove outside the perimeter and parked next to one of the squad cars. The chief showed up five minutes later. He walked over and asked, "Is the bomb squad here?"

"They showed up ten minutes ago."

"Tell me why you let Mickey go."

"He really didn't commit a crime. He was just delivering a suitcase. But I wonder if he's in danger now. He was supposed to call his contact after the bomb was placed. When the guy doesn't get the call he is expecting, he may come after Mickey."

"That's definitely a possibility. Maybe we can use Mickey to get to the killer."

"That might be a good idea. But I think we need to arrest Mr. Duck. I don't think he's the killer, but I suspect he has a way of contacting him."

"I agree. I'll send some cars over to pick him up."

"Dean is watching him with some night vision binoculars. I'm sure he can tell you right where the guy is."

"Perfect."

Then we heard the siren on the bomb squad van and watched it as it drove by us. I guessed he was going at least sixty. Then I said, "I think we can call off the blockade."

"I'll take care of it. Go home and say 'hi' to Jill for me."

"Yes sir."

When I got home, Jill was watching the news. She turned off the TV and said, "Thank you for not ruining the wedding."

"Somebody tried to blow up the whole building."

"Are you serious?"

"Yeah, a guy I arrested several times for petty crap was hired to put a suitcase with a bomb in it by the door to the warehouse. The bomb squad picked it up."

"We have a bomb squad?"

"No, but the state police do."

"Let's go to bed. I'm tired."

The following morning, I arrived at the station at 7:00. As soon as I walked in the desk sergeant said, "They tried to arrest the guy in the tree who was keeping a watch on the Carson house. He apparently had a high-power rifle with a scope and he took a few shots at the guys who were there. They returned fire and he was wounded. Then he fell out of the tree he was hiding in and died as the result of the fall."

This wasn't good news. I was hoping to use him to help us get to the real killer. Now I was going to have to come up with a new plan. I asked, "Was he carrying any other weapons besides the rifle?"

"Yeah, he had a bag with him. Inside the bag were two things that looked like small hand grenades."

"Those things are deadly. Where are they now?"

"I would guess they are in the chief's office."

I walked over to the chief's office. He was already there. He looked up at me and motioned for me to come in. I walked in and saw the bag on the chief's desk. Then I said, "Those things that look like hand grenades are probably filled with the chemical weapon used to kill the Carsons."

"I know that. I'm not touching them. I called Dr. Brooke and asked her to look at them. She should be here in a few minutes. Also, the bomb squad called and told me the suitcase they picked up last night had enough explosive in it to level the entire building."

"Wow! I guess we're lucky we caught Mickey when we did. Do we know anything about Mr. Duck?"

"He was carrying a French passport. It said his name was John Millray. The passport was a fake. At first, I thought he might be our killer, but he arrived in the country on

Sunday, after Owen Carson was killed. We ran his prints and photo through the systems and there were no hits, so I just had the information sent to Interpol."

"If he was here on Sunday he could have killed Mrs. Carson."

"I don't think so. The devices are packed in a molded foam case and there were only two spaces in it."

I thought about the situation for a few seconds and I had a *"eureka"* moment. "Sir, there have to be two guys here. The same guy couldn't have stayed in the tree for two days. He had to eat, sleep, and go to the bathroom. I think it's unlikely he did those things in the tree."

"You're right. We never found Owen Carson's car. I'll bet the guy in the tree was driving it. We have to find it. Also, let's get some of our people to take his picture to every motel and hotel in the area. He had to be staying someplace."

"I'll take care of this," I said as I left the chief's office. When I got back to my desk I called the dispatcher and told her I needed two people with cars to canvas the local hotels. I also told her to broadcast the information about Owen Simpson's car to our people. Then I called the State Police and asked them to help us find the car.

Fifteen minutes later two uniformed officers were dispatched to check the local hotels and motels. The State Police also issued an APB for Owen Simpson's car. Now, all I could do was wait.

If this was a normal murder case, the killer would have left a long time ago, but I was sure our guy wouldn't leave without at least trying to destroy the evidence regarding the cartel.

Dr. Brooke showed up a little later. She looked at the devices we found and confirmed they were gas grenades. She inoculated me and then she and I went to the Carson house and she inoculated Mark and Dean. After that, we went to the warehouse. Until the murderer is caught, the warehouse staff had been increased to three people per shift. Dr. Brooke gave injections to the three people on duty, and then she set up six syringes for the remaining people and showed one of the officers how to administer them. She asked me to take her back to Jill's office. I did that and thanked her for her assistance as she was getting out of the car.

Late that afternoon the canvas of the hotels and motels in the area discovered our guy and Owen Carson's car. He was at the Forest View Motel. The motel was located at the busiest exit off the interstate in the county, and that was a problem. The Forest View was always near capacity, and I was sure our guy had more gas grenades. He could kill a lot of innocent people before we could take him into custody. We had to find a way to lure him away from the motel.

I sent an unmarked car to keep watch on the motel and Owen Carson's car. I didn't want him to know he had been found. The officer who discovered he was there told the desk clerk that if anybody asked why the police were there he was to tell them they were looking for a missing child who disappeared from a nearby restaurant. That story was also released to the news media just in case the guy watched the local news.

I met with the chief and we decided the best place to confront the killer was at the warehouse. It was located in an industrial area. There were no residences within a quarter mile, so if he launched a grenade at us the public wouldn't be affected. But we had to figure out how to make him go there.

I suggested, "Sir, what if we leaked that the FBI was going to pick up the evidence at the warehouse tomorrow morning and the Feds were taking over the case. That would force him to do something this evening."

"I wonder if the cartel would be able to act that quickly. It might take a day for them to react."

"But if we give him another twenty-four hours he could round up a few more guys to help him. That would make the confrontation more dangerous."

The Halloween Incident

"I see your point. Okay, let's try it your way."

"I'll call Mark and have him forward the information to his contact."

"Okay, but I want you at the warehouse tonight, and I want you armed with more than your pistol. In fact, I want everybody there wearing body armor."

I replied, "I understand sir. I'll make sure everyone is appropriately armed and protected," as I left his office.

When I got to my desk I called Mark.

"Hi Mark. I wanted to let you know we found our guy at a motel by the interstate. We can't approach him there, so we want your help to force him to go to warehouse."

"What do you want me to do?"

"Tell your contact in the cartel that the FBI is taking over the case and they will be picking up the evidence at the warehouse tomorrow morning."

"That should force him to take some action this evening."

"That's what we're hoping."

"I'll take care of it immediately."

"Thanks Mark."

Then I called Jill. "Hi Jill. I wanted to let you know we're going to try and close this case tonight. I'm going to spend the night at the warehouse. I promise I'll be careful and won't get myself killed."

She was more understanding than I thought she would be. She said, "Okay, I realize this is part of your job. But I'm not going to sleep tonight until I know this thing is over."

"I promise I'll call you after we catch the guy."

"You better!"

"I love you. Please don't worry. I'll be wearing body armor and have a bigger gun. Everything will be fine."

She said, "I love you too. Please forgive me, but I will be worried about you until I know this is over. Bye."

"Goodbye Jill."

I gathered the equipment we would need to defend the warehouse from attack. I had four suits of body armor, three machine pistols that were capable of firing five rounds per second, ten magazines for the pistols, an AR-15 rifle, and fifty rounds of ammunition for it. I loaded the stuff in my car and drove to the warehouse.

When I got there, I explained the situation to the three men who were on duty. All of them received their inoculations. I gave each of them a suit of body armor and a loaded machine pistol. Three of us went outside and moved a large dumpster near the door. I told them I would take the first watch outside.

I was on watch outside for a little over an hour when my phone rang. It was Mitch Jenkins. I said, "Hi Mitch, what's going on."

"I'm on stakeout watching Carson's car. Our guy just took a small case from the trunk and got into a car with two other guys. I would presume they're heading in your direction."

"Thanks for the update Mitch. Please call the station and let them know what happened. We're ready for them here."

I went inside and yelled, "The bad guys are on the way. They will be here in about twenty minutes."

I heard one of the officers yell back, "We're ready."

There's almost no traffic on the street in front of the warehouse at night, so I heard the car coming before I saw it. It stopped even with the door to the warehouse. I was watching from behind the dumpster. The back window of the car went down. A rocket propelled grenade poked out of the window. I dropped to the ground and took my gun out of its holster immediately. The grenade struck the front door. The explosion was almost deafening. When the smoke cleared, I could see the door was damaged, but still closed.

I heard somebody from the car yell, "Shit! The door is still there. They know we're here. Let's get out of here!"

The Halloween Incident

Another voice, this time with a strong accent, yelled back, "I paid you guys to do a job and we're going to do it. I don't care if we have to chop down the door with an ax. We have to get in. If you're not interested in assisting me, I'll kill you myself. Is that clear?"

I could hear them talking but I couldn't understand what they were saying. Then I saw the grenade launcher poke out of the back window again. This time it looked like it was aimed at the second-floor window. A moment later the window was demolished. Then I saw it again. This time it was loaded with one of the gas grenades. I heard it launch with a soft pop and I saw it fly into the broken window.

So far, the bad guys had no idea I was behind the dumpster. I was laying on the ground in the shadow of the dumpster when they approached the door. I heard one of the bad guys ask, "Are you sure the cops inside are dead?"

The guy with the accent said, "Yes, I'm sure. But we probably only have ten minutes to get in and blow this place into little pieces. Then I watched them wheel an acetylene torch up to the door. They ignited it and began to cut out the door lock. The torch was very bright. Then two things happened. The light from the torch exposed my position, and one of the guys turned away from the door and saw me. He screamed something I didn't understand, but I saw him point his gun at me. Mine was already out. I was in an awkward position, but my gun was pointed in the right general direction. I fired before he did. The bullet struck the acetylene tank. It exploded instantly spewing burning gas and sending shrapnel in all directions. It looked like the bad guys were killed instantly. I had a big chunk of metal imbedded in my right thigh.

The pain in my leg was intense, but a funny thought struck me. The door wasn't locked. The torch and the grenade were unnecessary. They could have simply opened the door and walked in.

I don't remember much after that. When I woke up I was in a hospital emergency room. They must have given me something for the pain because my leg didn't hurt. One of the nurses said they were prepping me for surgery. I remember being wheeled out of the room.

The next time I woke up I was in the recovery room. Jill was there. She looked at me, smiled, and said, "Welcome to the world of the living. The surgeon said your leg is fine, but it will take a while to heal. The muscles in your thigh were severed. I'm sorry to tell you that you will have to be wheeled down the aisle for the wedding. I suspect our honeymoon may not be exactly what we were looking forward to."

"Were the guys in the warehouse okay?"

"You were the only casualty on our side. The three guys who attacked the warehouse are all dead."

About an hour later the doctor came in, checked the wound on my thigh, and told me I should stay off the leg completely until my appointment with him the following week. I wasn't sure how I would be able to do that, but told him I would. Jill and I both thanked him as he was leaving the room.

I was discharged from the hospital shortly after the doctor left. I thought we were going back to my apartment, but instead Jill drove in the wrong direction. I asked her, "Did you forget where we live?"

"We don't live there anymore. I have a big surprise for you."

"Can you tell me where we're going?"

"I can, but I won't. You'll figure it out soon enough. Just relax."

A few minutes later I realized she was driving to the Carson house. When she stopped by the front door I asked, "We live here now?"

"Yeah, the Justice Department bought this house for Owen. Mark arranged for us to stay here while we complete the paperwork to buy the house from them. They made me an offer I really couldn't refuse."

The Halloween Incident

The chief and Mark walked out of the house and helped me out of the car placing me in a wheel chair. The chief wheeled me into the house. After we were inside Mark said, "The Justice Department wanted to thank you for the help you provided in this case. The assets of the Humbolt Cartel have been seized. They are, at least for now, out of business."

"I'm glad to hear that. It serves them right for messing up my honeymoon."

The others laughed. Then Jill said, "I think our honeymoon will be just fine."

The wedding took place as scheduled. Jill's mother had rented a large hall that was currently set up for the ceremony. In attendance were all the members of the police force that weren't on duty and the entire staff of the Medical Examiner's Office, which were only four others besides Jill. There were more than one hundred fifty people there who watched as Jill rolled me down the aisle. The ceremony was brief, as soon as Jill rolled me out of the room, more than a dozen workers managed to change the room over so it could be used for the reception in less than ten minutes. There was a small band playing music. I obviously couldn't dance, so Jill wheeled me around in time with music. Everyone, including me, had a great time.

The following morning, I had my second appointment with the surgeon. After inspecting the incision and checking the strength in my leg said I should be able to walk with a cane now, but I would need at least a month of physical therapy. Jill said she would take care of it, and she would enjoy torturing me a little.

The following day we left for Hawaii. After we got into our room at the hotel Jill looked at me and said, "You know, it's going to be nice working with a patient who is still alive for a change. I have some very adventurous types of therapy I want to try out on you."

Frank Carver Mysteries

The Fireman
A Frank Carver Mystery

Jill and I were sound asleep in the Embassy Suites hotel on Waikiki when my cell phone rang. I looked at the display on the phone and saw the call was from George Dyer. He was at our wedding last week, so he knew we were on our honeymoon. I hit the button on the screen to accept the call and said, "George, I hope this is really important. Jill and I didn't get to bed until after 2:00."

"Frank, I'm really sorry to disturb you so early in the morning on your honeymoon, but this is important. I need your help with something."

"Okay George, how can I help you?"

"Are you familiar with the Schofield Barracks?"

"I know it's an Army base here, but that's all I know about it."

"In the past two weeks there have been two mysterious deaths there. Two men were found in their homes on the base with their bodies burned almost beyond recognition. There was no indication of a fire where the bodies were found, in fact, their clothes were only slightly burned. Also, the smoke alarms in the homes weren't triggered."

"Is this another case involving a weapon that I can't mention?"

"No, although the effects of that weapon are somewhat similar, that weapon requires that the killer be in very close proximity to his target. These two victims were alone, at home, with the doors locked from the inside."

"Okay, this is obviously an unusual case, but how does it involve me?"

"I want you to investigate the deaths. I have to know what killed these guys, and I think you're the best person to handle this case."

"George, I'm on my honeymoon and I can barely walk. The wound in my leg is still healing. Can this wait for a couple of weeks?"

"You know it can't. Since you're still in the reserve, I've already reactivated you and gave you a temporary promotion to Colonel. That will make you the highest ranking officer on the base."

"Okay George, I assume you'll be sending me orders and an ID that shows I'm active."

"It went out by Federal Express yesterday. I've also contacted the base commander, Captain Harkin, to let him know you'll be investigating the deaths and I asked him to assign someone to act as your assistant."

"Jill won't be happy about this."

"Actually, I'm not happy about messing up your honeymoon either. But I really need you for this. Do you want me to call her?"

"No, I'll tell her when she wakes up."

As soon as the called ended Jill sat up in bed and said, "Tell me what?"

"George called to tell me I'm in the Army again."

"What? Why would they do that?"

"There have been two strange deaths at an Army base here and George wants me to investigate them. George has done a lot of favors for me and I have to do this. Besides, it gives us a reason to spend more time here."

"Right now I'm too tired to argue with you about this. I'll just scream at you later."

"Thank you for being so understanding."

I got up, showered, and got dressed. Jill had apparently gone back to sleep. I was watching the news when my phone rang. It was a local number, so I answered with "Hello."

The caller said, "Good morning. Am I speaking to Colonel Carver?"

It took a moment to realize I was no longer a Lieutenant. I answered, "Yes, this is Colonel Carver."

The Fireman

"Sir, my name is Mike Ortiz. I'm a Sergeant with the Schofield Barracks MP. I've been assigned to assist you in the investigation of the deaths of Sergeant Gerald Lender and Corporal Kevin Truman."

"Sergeant Ortiz, I was injured recently and I'm unable to drive. Can you come to my hotel and pick me up tomorrow morning? I'm staying at the Embassy Suites on Waikiki."

"Yes sir. That's a very nice hotel. What time would you like me to be there?"

"Come at about ten o'clock. Bring the case files with you so I can review them before we go to the base. Call me when you get here and I'll come down to meet you."

"Yes sir. I'll see you tomorrow morning."

Jill didn't keep her promise about screaming at me. Instead she said practically nothing to me all morning. We went down to the restaurant to get breakfast, and after we sat down she finally said, "I think George has a lot of nerve interrupting our honeymoon."

"I do realize this honeymoon hasn't been what we were hoping for. We both know my leg is limiting our activities. I promise that when I am healed we'll have a *real* honeymoon."

"Okay, I know this wasn't something you volunteered for. So, how did these guys die?"

"They were severely burned, but nothing else in the rooms where they were found showed any signs of fire damage."

"That's really weird. Have the bodies been examined by a pathologist?"

"No, not yet. The base commander assigned an assistant to me. He's going to be here tomorrow morning with the files. Do you want to examine the bodies?"

"Yeah, why not. If you're tied up with the investigation it will give me something to do."

"By the way, I'm now Colonel Carver. I got a promotion."

"Congratulations! Did you get a raise?"

"I have no idea."

I was able to walk reasonably well using a cane, so we spent a few hours looking through the tourist shops. By one o'clock my leg was starting to hurt again, so we went back to the hotel. When we got to our room there was a FedEx envelope on the desk. I opened it and found a new ID and my orders to investigate the two deaths.

We relaxed in our room for a while, and then Jill decided it was time for my physical therapy. She spent the next thirty minutes finding new ways to inflict pain on me. When she finished torturing me, we put on bathing suits and spent the rest of the afternoon at the beach.

The next morning, we got up early and went down to the restaurant in the hotel for breakfast. Then we went back to the room to wait for Sergeant Ortiz. The phone in our room rang at precisely 10:00. I answered it and told Sergeant Ortiz to come up to the room.

Our room had a small table with four chairs. When Sergeant Ortiz arrived, I shook his hand and said, "Good morning Sergeant. Please come in."

"Thank you, sir."

He sat down at the table with Jill. I joined them and said, "Sergeant, this is my wife, Jill. We were married less than two weeks ago and we're here on our honeymoon. I want to explain my position to you. I worked in Army Intelligence for a few years. I left active duty three years ago, but remained in the reserve. When I left active duty, I was a lieutenant. I'm currently a homicide detective for the Norfolk County Police Department. I was hurt three weeks ago when three guys attacked a police warehouse. I'm still walking with a cane. Yesterday I was notified that I have been reactivated with the rank of colonel, and ordered to investigate the deaths at Schofield Barracks."

"Why would they activate you instead of sending over somebody from the mainland?"

The Fireman

"I think there are two reasons. First, I was already here, and second, because in the past year I've solved several very unusual cases. From the preliminary information I have, this case appears to be unusual as well. Also, you should be aware that Jill is a pathologist and the Norfolk County Medical Examiner."

"Okay, now I think I understand sir."

"Sergeant, since we will be working together for a while, when we aren't on the base, please call me Frank and I'll call you Mike. Is that okay?"

"Yes sir, uh, I mean, yes Frank."

"Are those the files on the two deaths?"

He pushed them over to me, "Yes, but there's not much information there."

I reviewed the files and found that Mike was correct. There was almost no information in the files. No postmortem examination was done. There were some fairly gruesome pictures. It was obvious from looking at the pictures that both men were burned the same way. But the most unusual thing about the pictures was that you could see burned flesh underneath unburnt clothing. I asked Mike, "Where are the bodies now?"

"We have no facility on the base to conduct an examination, so they are currently at the morgue in Honolulu. Do you want to go look at them?"

Before I could answer Jill said, "Yes, I would like to do an autopsy on both victims. Who would have the authority to allow me to do that?"

Pointing at me Mike said, "He would. He's now the highest ranking officer assigned to the base."

I looked at Mike and asked, "What can you tell me about the victims?"

"I don't like to speak ill regarding the dead, but both of these guys were bad dudes. It was known all over the base that Sergeant Lender was the guy to go to if you wanted drugs. We tried on several occasions to catch him in the act of selling, but we failed every time. Corporal Truman was your basic loan shark. He would lend people all the money they wanted, and the interest rate was only twenty percent, per week. However, if they failed to pay, the borrower would end up in the hospital. Neither of them will be missed by the general population at the base."

"Obviously these guys weren't well liked. Do you think it's possible they were murdered?"

"Only if there's a way to murder someone by magic. Both of them were found in their base apartments. The doors were locked with deadbolts on the inside. The windows were closed and locked as well."

"That makes our task more difficult, but not impossible."

Mike looked at me with a very perplexed look on his face and said, "Huh?"

"I worked on a case about a year ago that involved finding dead bodies inside locked motel rooms. I really can't discuss it because the information is classified. Let's go to the morgue and take a look at our victims."

The trip to the morgue took about forty minutes. We used that time to get to know each other a little better.

We arrived at the morgue and Mike introduced Jill and me to Dr. Barnes, the Chief Medical Examiner. Then we all went to view the victims. Dr. Barnes led us to a room that had what looked like nine oversize file drawers built into a wall. He walked over to one of them and opened it. Inside was a body covered with a sheet. He pulled the sheet back and said, "Meet Sergeant Lender. He was the first victim. We didn't do a postmortem examination, but we did scan him. It appears he was burned from the inside. Corporal Truman died the same way. I have no idea how this could happen. I've heard of cases involving spontaneous human combustion, but I never believed it could happen until I saw these victims. I think the strangest part of these deaths is that the victim's clothing was barely scorched."

Jill asked, "Do you have a problem with me doing an autopsy on them?"

"No, in fact I'd be happy to assist you since I'm not busy today."

"Thank you, Dr. Barnes. I would appreciate your assistance."

"Please call me Tony."

Jill said, "Okay Tony," then turning toward me she said, "This is going to take five or six hours. Why don't you go to the base with Mike and then back to the hotel? I'll call you when we're finished."

"That sounds reasonable." Then I kissed her goodbye and Mike and I left.

Mike said the trip to the base would take almost an hour. On the way there I gave him the details of how I got injured. When I was finished he said, "I think that was a very lucky shot. If you hit the guy instead of the acetylene tank, you might be dead now because the other guys would have shot you."

"I suppose that was a possibility. But I never really thought about it that way."

When we arrived at the base, Mike took me to Captain Harkin's office. We walked in and Captain Harkin looked up from his desk. He stood and said, "Good afternoon Sergeant. Is this Colonel Carver?"

"Yes sir."

I leaned the cane against the desk, extended my hand, and said, "Captain Harkin, it's a pleasure to meet you."

Captain Harkin grasped my hand firmly and said, "It's a pleasure to meet you too, Colonel. I want to assure you that you will have my full cooperation during this investigation."

He looked at my cane but didn't say anything. So, I said, "I was injured in an explosion at the end of my last case."

He nodded, sat down again, and asked, "How can I help you?"

"I want to look at the rooms where the victims were found. I thought you should know my wife is a pathologist.

She is currently at the morgue doing an autopsy on the victims. Dr. Barnes is assisting her."

"I know this is none of my business, but why is your wife here?"

"We were married last week and we're here on our honeymoon."

"They interrupted your honeymoon for this investigation?"

"Yes, they did. Sergeant Ortiz has given me a little background on the victims. I would assume neither of them were well liked."

"That's a very reasonable conclusion. These men were barely tolerated. I don't think either of them had any friends. I suspect a lot of the people on the base were at least somewhat pleased they're no longer with us."

"Do you think anybody from the base could be responsible for their deaths?"

"I don't think I can answer that until I find out how they were killed."

"That seems fair. I'll let you know the results of the autopsies as soon as I get the information. I'd like to look at the rooms where the men died now."

"Sergeant Ortiz will take you there, Colonel."

"Thank you for your time this afternoon, Captain."

Mike and I left the Base Commander's office and walked back to Mike's car. A few minutes later we were parked in front of a four-story apartment building. I followed Mike in as he walked to the stairway. As he started to walk up I said, "Mike, I'm not quite ready to do stairs yet. Is there an elevator?"

"Yes Frank, I'm sorry. I forgot about your leg." He led me to an elevator and we went up to the third floor. We walked about a hundred feet along a hallway and stopped in front of a door. Mike reached into his pocket, removed a key, and said, "This is a master key; it unlocks all the apartments." Then he opened the door and walked in.

The Fireman

I followed him into the apartment and asked, "Did a forensics team go over this place?"

"Yeah, as soon as the body was removed. There were only two sets of prints. One belonged to the victim, and the other belonged to a woman he paid to clean the apartment for him. When she tried to open the door, she realized it was locked from the inside. She knocked on the door, and when Sergeant Lender didn't answer, she tried calling him. When he didn't answer his phone, she called us. Two of my people broke down the door and found the body on the floor in front of the sofa. As you can see, the carpet is slightly discolored where the body was found."

"I don't suppose the woman who cleaned his apartment also worked for Corporal Truman?"

"No, she had heard of him, but never met him."

"Okay, there's nothing to see here. Is the scene at Corporal Truman's apartment the same?"

"Yes, Corporal Truman's apartment is a little bigger, and it's on the first floor. But his door was also locked from the inside, and all the windows were closed and locked as well."

"Did forensics check the Corporal's apartment?"

"Yes, the only prints they found were his."

"Okay, this is getting us exactly nowhere. I believe both of our victims were murdered. But, I have no idea how. I hope Jill and Dr. Barnes find something that will help us with the investigation."

"I agree, Frank. I don't think there's anything else to see here. Would you like me to take you back to your hotel now?"

"Sure, when we get there I'll buy you some of those fancy overpriced drinks from the hotel bar."

"That sounds great! Let's go."

An hour later we were both sitting at a table in the hotel bar drinking something that Mike ordered. I didn't know what it was, but it tasted good. While we were sitting there my phone rang; it was Jill."

She said, "Hi honey. I have some interesting news for you."

"I'm listening."

"Both bodies exhibited several similarities. The burns were initiated in their right thighs. That area had the most severe burns on both victims. In fact, the center section of the femur was turned to ash. In case you don't know, the femur is the bone that connects the hip to the knee. Also, the right front pocket on the pants they were wearing when they died was burned to a much greater extent than any other parts of their clothing."

"What do you think that means?"

"I think something they were carrying in their right front pants pocket was responsible for their deaths. We also found something very unusual in that pocket. There were traces of iridium. Iridium isn't exactly something you would expect to find in somebody's pockets. Somehow it must be connected to the deaths."

"So, both victims had something in their right front pockets that contained iridium and that was responsible for their deaths?"

"Yes, that's exactly what I'm saying."

"I think we need to find somebody who knows a lot more about iridium than we do."

"I agree. Anyway, Tony and I are finished here. He's going to drive me back to the hotel."

"Great! When you get here, you two can join Mike and me in the bar. He ordered drinks for us that are really wonderful."

"Okay, we'll be there in about a half hour."

After I ended the call Mike asked, "What is iridium?"

"I don't know much about it. I know it's a very dense metallic element, and it's not very common. I was hoping you might know somebody who could tell us how it's used."

"I have a friend who's an electrical engineer. He also teaches at the university. I'll ask him about it tonight."

The Fireman

"Thanks. Jill and Dr. Barnes will be here soon. I want you to order the same drinks for them."

"Okay."

The four of us spent a very pleasant evening. Jill and I got back to our room at about 8:30. She spent a half hour torturing me with physical therapy. Then we watched an old movie on TV before we went to bed. I fell asleep thinking about what someone could make with iridium.

Mike called the following morning to tell me he would pick me up at ten o'clock and that we had an appointment with his engineering friend, Tim Knight, at eleven.

We arrived at Tim's office a few minutes early. He was in his office meeting with one of his students. When the student left, Mike and I walked in. Mike said, "Hi Tim, I'd like you to meet Colonel Carver."

Tim and I shook hands and he said, "It's a pleasure to meet you, Colonel. Mike said you wanted to know something about iridium."

"Yes, I hope you can help us. There have been two deaths at Schofield Barracks. Both victims were burned to death by a device that contained it."

"I remember reading something about a design for a high-power oscillator that used iridium. But I don't see how you could use an oscillator to kill somebody."

I thought about what he said for a few seconds. Then I asked, "Is it possible to use a high-powered oscillator to cause something to vibrate so rapidly that the friction between the molecules could cause it to ignite?"

Tim rubbed his chin while he was thinking about my question. Then he said, "I believe it is. I read an article recently that talked about using a precision oscillator to heat cancer cells inside a tumor to a point that the cells would die."

"So, it might be possible to cause the bones in the victim's legs to burn."

"Yes, I suppose that's possible."

"How big would such an oscillator have to be?"

"After the design has been completed, it could probably be reduced to one inch square and a half inch high. The biggest parts would be the transducer that produces the output and the battery."

"That's pretty small. I wonder what could be made that size that our victims would want to put in their pockets."

Mike said, "Some kind of 'good luck' charm."

Tim said, "How about something that looks like a coin?"

"Those are both good suggestions, but what we really need to know is, who is smart enough to build something like that. It has to be somebody on the base, or somebody who has a friend or relative on the base. Mike, you mentioned that if anyone failed to pay Corporal Truman, they often found themselves in the hospital. Has that happened recently?"

"Yeah, it has. I don't remember the name, but about six months ago another corporal was hurt very badly in a 'hit and run' accident. He was hurt so severely the doctors weren't sure he would ever walk again. He was sent back to the mainland to recover. I don't know what happened to him. But, he did say he was late paying some money back to Corporal Truman, and that Truman had told him if he didn't pay in forty-eight hours he would be in trouble."

"Corporal Truman really sounds like a wonderful person. Can you find out if the corporal who was injured has any friends or relatives in Hawaii?"

"Sure, I'll have that for you tomorrow."

Turning to Tim I said, "Thank you for your help. I think you have pointed us in the right direction."

Mike took me back to the hotel. When he dropped me off he said, "I'll get the information you asked for and call you tomorrow morning."

"Thanks Mike. I'll be waiting for your call."

When I went to bed that night, I was sure we were on the right track, but the call I received from Mike the following morning derailed everything.

The Fireman

Mike called me at 8:30 and said, "I have some interesting news for you. Last night there was another murder. The body was burned in an identical fashion as our first two victims."

"Was the victim another bad guy?"

"The worst, he sold cocaine and heroin through a network of teenagers to kids all over Honolulu. He had been arrested seven times in the past year, but the charges were always dropped for lack of evidence."

"Did he have any connection to the two guys who were killed on the base?"

"Not as far as I know. The only possible connection is that he may have been the source for Sergeant Lender's inventory. By the way, the name of the man who was hurt in the hit and run was Robert Kidder. I spoke to him last night. He is still unable to walk, but the doctor's think that after two more surgeries he should be able to regain that ability. He spends a lot of time at the Veteran's Hospital in LA, and he is currently living about a mile from there. He wasn't exactly broken-hearted about the two victims. It appears Lender got him hooked and he borrowed money from Truman to pay for his drugs. He has a younger sister. She's a freshman in a junior college in San Diego. She's living with her aunt and uncle. I really don't think he or his family are the key to these murders."

"You're probably right. I guess we have to start over again. Are we going to be able to work with the Honolulu police on these murders or are we on our own?"

"They want to work with us. They were aware of the deaths on the base, and apparently Dr. Barnes was on duty last night when the body was brought in. Before you ask, he found traces of iridium in the victim's right front pocket."

"I think we should meet with whoever is handling the case for the police. Pick me up in an hour and we'll go over there."

"I've already set up the meeting. I'll see you in an hour."

While I was waiting for Mike, I called George and told him how the case was going. The conversation was short because there wasn't much to tell him yet. I told him about the third murder, and promised I would call him again as soon as there was something to talk about.

Mike and I drove to police headquarters. When we arrived, Mike gave the woman at the front desk his business card and told her we had an appointment with Lieutenant Chan. She told us to sit down and she would find him for us.

A few minutes later a middle-aged Asian man, who looked like he could rip the New York City phone book in half without any difficulty, walked up to us. He said cheerfully, "Good morning Sergeant. I'm Lieutenant Chan."

Mike replied, "Good morning lieutenant; this is Colonel Carver. He's in charge of our investigation."

"It's a pleasure to meet you, sir. Please follow me."

He led us to a conference room. After we were seated Lieutenant Chan asked, "Have you made any progress on this case?"

I answered, "Not enough. I'm certain both of our victims were murdered. They were killed by a device that was in their right front pants pocket. We believe the device is a high-powered oscillator that caused the victims' femurs to vibrate with enough intensity that they ignited inside their bodies."

"I would not have thought that was possible. How did you come to that conclusion?"

"We found traces of iridium in the right front pocket of the pants the victims were wearing when they were killed. Mike and I met with an engineer at the university who told us that iridium is now being used in high power oscillators."

"Did he think it was possible to use a high-power oscillator to kill somebody?"

"Yes, he did. But we have no idea what the device is, where it came from, or why the victims were carrying it."

"If your theory is correct, perhaps we can find something in Bruce Martin's house. He's the latest victim.

The Fireman

I'm curious, Colonel; were the men who died on the base criminals too?"

Mike answered, "Nothing was ever proved, but we believe one was a drug dealer and the other one was a loan shark."

Lieutenant Chan nodded his head and said, "Let's go search Mr. Martin's house."

Mike and I followed him to his car. It's amazing how much faster you can get through the Honolulu traffic in a police car. The trip probably would have taken Mike forty-five minutes, but it took us less than twenty.

The house we arrived at was enormous. I would estimate it was more than ten thousand square feet. It was three floors high, all brick and stone construction. The grounds were surrounded by an eight-foot high wrought iron fence. There was a uniformed police officer guarding the door. As we approached the door, the officer said, "Good morning, sir. As you requested, nobody has been allowed in the house, although a man claiming to be Mr. Martin's attorney was very insistent. I told him he would need a court order to be allowed in. He called me a few names I won't repeat, and then left."

"Good job. If he comes back with a court order, call me immediately, but don't let him into the house without my permission."

"Yes sir."

We walked in and I discovered the house was more amazing on the inside than it was outside. The entryway led into a huge atrium that contained a large round swimming pool. There was a circular bar with stools around it in the center of the pool. Outside of the pool were dozens of full grown palm trees. Interspersed with the trees were groups of lounge chairs and tables. The pool area was obviously air conditioned because there was no humidity or smell from the pool chemicals. The ceiling was at least forty feet high.

The house was built around the pool. There were dozens of bedrooms and I could see a large dining room and kitchen. I turned to Lieutenant Chan and asked, "I don't think I've ever been in a house this big. It looks more like a hotel or resort. Where do we start looking?"

"I've only been here once before, and that was when we found the body. It was in his bedroom. Let's start there."

Mike and I followed him as he walked to an area on the other side of the pool. We went into a bedroom that was probably twice the size of the apartment Jill and I shared before we bought our house. In addition to a very ornate king size bed, the room contained a large matching dresser, a large desk, three pieces of exercise equipment, several chairs, and mounted on a wall was what looked like a one-hundred-inch TV. There were three sofas arranged in a semi-circle around the TV.

"His body was on the floor in front of the TV. This would probably be a good place to start our search." Then he handed us gloves and said, "Forensics has already been through this place, but I don't want to destroy any evidence they might have missed."

We all put on gloves. Mike said, "I'll look on the desk."

I walked over to the dresser and began looking in the drawers. Most of the drawers had items of clothing, but one drawer contained more than a dozen very expensive watches. I recognized one of them. It was a diamond studded Rolex with an eighteen-carat gold case that cost about forty thousand dollars. I was gawking at the watches when Mike yelled, "I found something."

I walked over to the desk and Mike handed me a small padded envelope. Inside was a letter. By the time I was finished reading the letter Lieutenant Chan had joined us by the desk. I handed it to him. After he read it he said, "Well, now we know what killed them."

The letter said Mr. Martin had been specifically chosen to test a new type of activity monitor. The device was designed to monitor not only his physical activity during the day, but it could also monitor heart rate, respirations, and blood oxygen levels. At the end of the day the device would automatically connect with his cell phone and send the information to their office. The information would be used to generate a report that would be sent to his phone as a text message. The normal cost for the device was three thousand dollars, and the monitoring service was an additional two hundred dollars per month. If he followed the instructions and wore the device every day for a month, they would provide free monitoring for life, updated devices at no charge as they became available, and a check for five thousand dollars to compensate him for his help. It looked like an offer even someone who was very rich wouldn't pass up.

Lieutenant Chan looked at the envelope. It had no return address and was mailed from a post office in Los Angeles. "Unless the killer left his fingerprints on the envelope, this isn't going to be very helpful."

Then I asked, "Did your people find his cell phone? If he was receiving text messages, the sender's phone number should be there. I realize the number is probably attached to a burner phone, but it might give us a location."

"I know we found Martin's phone. It was in his hand when he died. I'll get my tech people to go over it immediately."

"Would you also check with the other police departments and find out if there have been any similar cases?"

"Yeah, I'll do that as soon as I get back to my office. I'm going to stay here and search the house for anything that might be connected to his illegal drug business. I'll have the officer by the front door drive you back to the station."

"Thank you. Please call me immediately if you find out anything related to my case."

"It will probably be tomorrow morning before I hear anything. I'll call then."

We walked to the front door. Lieutenant Chan told the officer to drive us back to the station, and then he walked back inside the house.

That evening Jill, Mike, and I went to a local restaurant that Mike suggested. It was located in a less traveled area on Oahu and was primarily used by locals who were trying to escape the tourists. The place overlooked the ocean and the views were spectacular. So was the food. Even the prices were reasonable. It was a wonderful evening.

The following morning, Lieutenant Chan called and said, "Good morning Colonel Carver. I hope I'm not disturbing you."

"No, you're not disturbing me in the least. Do you have any information for me?"

"Yes. The phone used by the killer was a burner. My guess is his real name isn't James Bond. In any case, the calls were made from La Jolla. That is just north of San Diego. I also found out there were two other people killed in the same manner as our victims. They were both known drug dealers. The first murder occurred about two months ago in Chicago. The other one occurred two weeks later in Los Angeles."

"So, I guess our killer targets drug dealers with the exception of Corporal Truman. That fact reinforces my belief that somebody from the base is involved."

"That appears to be a reasonable conclusion. Do you have a course of action in mind?"

"I think I'll need a list of Corporal Truman's customers. I'm sure Mike can get me that information. Then we'll check to see if any of them were injured because they were unable to make a payment on their loans."

"Please keep me informed. I'll contact the police in Chicago and Los Angeles and find out what they know about their cases."

"That sounds like a good idea. I'll call you tomorrow afternoon and we can compare notes."

The Fireman

I called Mike immediately and told him what Lieutenant Chan told me. Then I asked him, "Can you get me a list of Corporal Truman's customers?"

"That might be difficult. We have his computer, but the files are encrypted. The computer was sent to Army Intelligence in the hope they would be able to decrypt the files. As far as I know, there has been no progress."

"I have a contact there. He's the one who assigned me to this case. I'll call him and find out the status. Is there a base newspaper?"

"Yeah, I'll put something in tomorrow's edition asking about Truman's customers. That might get us some results."

"Okay, I'll call George now."

There's a six-hour time difference between Honolulu and Washington, so I called George as soon as I hung up with Mike.

After he answered I said, "Hi George, I need your help with this case."

"Does that mean you've made some progress?"

"Maybe, in addition to the murders here there was also one in LA and one in Chicago. All of the victims were drug dealers except for Corporal Truman. I need a list of his customers, but the files on his computer are encrypted."

"So, send me the computer and I'll get somebody working on it immediately."

"You already have it."

"I wasn't aware of that. Do you know who sent it?"

"Yes, it was sent by the man assisting me with the case. His name is Sergeant Mike Ortiz."

"I'll find out who has the computer and I'll assign my best code guy to decrypt the files."

"Thanks George."

"You're welcome. I don't think I told you this, but the government is paying for all of your expenses while you're working on the case."

'Thanks again. I appreciate that. Please call me as soon as any progress has been made with the computer."

"You know I will."

I suddenly found myself with at least one day off. I was waiting for information from Mike, George, and Lieutenant Chan. My leg was much better and Jill and I spent most of the morning in our room enjoying each other's company. After a leisurely lunch by the pool, we wandered around looking in the tourist shops again. We bought a few souvenirs before getting back to the hotel around 3:00. I called Lieutenant Chan to find out if he had discovered any additional information from the LA or Chicago police. He said we knew more about the cases than they did, and they didn't appear anxious to get involved.

Jill and I went up to our room, put on bathing suits, and spent the next several hours relaxing on the beach. I actually forgot about the case for a while.

Early the next morning my phone rang. It was George. He told me they had decrypted the files on Corporal Truman's computer. He promised to e-mail a report to me in three or four hours. He also said he was surprised at the amount of money that was involved. It appeared Truman had more than six hundred thousand dollars in receivables.

I called Mike immediately and told him I would have Truman's client list in a few hours. I also asked him to check into Truman's bank accounts. He told me he already did that. He said Truman had both a checking and savings account at the credit union on the base. Between the two accounts he had about fourteen thousand dollars and the balance hadn't changed very much over the past year.

I told him I would send the client list to him as soon as I got it. I also asked him to think about how a guy with fourteen thousand dollars in the bank is able to lend more than six hundred thousand dollars. He said that perhaps Corporal Truman had other accounts and he would look into it this morning.

The Fireman

This case was getting more complex by the minute. But I was still certain that Truman was the key.

Apparently, my phone conversations had disturbed Jill. She got out of bed, walked slowly over to where I was sitting, and kissed me. Then she asked, "Anything new?"

"Yeah, Corporal Truman had fourteen thousand dollars in the bank, but he had over six hundred thousand dollars in receivables. How does that happen?"

"Maybe he charged very high interest rates."

"He did, but I don't think the rates he was charging, as high as they were, would generate that much income. I think he must have had another account somewhere. Mike is checking it out now."

Around noon I received the e-mail from George that had the list of Truman's clients attached. I forwarded it to Mike and then I looked over the list. Most of the loans were around five hundred dollars, there were twenty-two loans that were more than a thousand dollars, and three of those loans were over a hundred thousand dollars. One of those people who owed over a hundred thousand dollars was our hit and run victim, Robert Kidder.

It was hard for me to believe that Robert Kidder could have bought more than $100,000 worth of drugs from Sergeant Lender. The loan was obviously for something else.

I think it was time somebody had a talk with Mr. Kidder. But I wasn't sure who that should be. I decided to call Mike and ask for suggestions.

When Mike answered his phone I said, "Hi Mike, did you get my e-mail?"

"Yes, but I didn't have time to look at it yet. I got involved in a domestic dispute. Did you find something?"

"The client list contained three people whose debts exceeded a hundred thousand dollars. One of those people is Robert Kidder. I think we need to run a very thorough check on him and somebody needs to have a 'face to face' conversation with him."

"Robert Kidder was earning about eighteen thousand dollars a year. Who would lend him that much money?"

"That was my question exactly. Did you find anything else regarding Truman's finances?"

"Only that, if he had another account, it was in a different name. I'm going to go over to his apartment this afternoon and tear it apart. There must be something there we missed."

"Do you have any suggestions regarding who should have a conversation with Kidder?"

"No, but I'll bet your friend at Army Intelligence has some suggestions."

"I'll call him now."

My conversation with George was brief. He said since I was the person most familiar with the case, Mike and I should go there tomorrow and surprise Mr. Kidder.

We took a night flight over to LA and arrived at 8:00 in the morning. We rented a car, and by ten o'clock we were parked in front of Kidder's apartment building.

We rang the bell and the main entrance door to the building unlocked a moment later. Kidder's apartment was on the first floor. When we arrived, the door to his apartment was slightly ajar. We walked in and I called out, "Mr. Kidder!"

A man who appeared to be in his late twenties rolled into the room in a wheel chair. He looked at me and asked, in a very nasty voice, "Who the hell are you?"

"I'm Colonel Carver and this is Sergeant Ortiz."

"I recognize Sergeant Ortiz. Why are you guys here?"

"We're investigating the deaths of Corporal Truman and Sergeant Lender. We managed to get a list of people who borrowed money from Corporal Truman. Your name was on the list."

Kidder's voice was a little shaky when he said, "I told Sergeant Ortiz that I borrowed money from Truman to pay Lender for drugs."

The Fireman

"How much money did you owe him?"

He hesitated for a moment and then said softly, "I'm not sure. I guess about eight or nine hundred dollars."

"Do you want to rethink that answer?"

"No, I think that's pretty accurate."

"According to Corporal Truman's files, you owed him about one hundred seventeen thousand dollars."

The look on his face said it all. He hesitated again before he said, "I guess there is no point in lying to you. I'm sure you would find out fairly quickly. The Corporal Truman that was killed in Hawaii wasn't the original Corporal Truman. Brian Truman and I were classmates in high school in Kansas City. When I was transferred to Hawaii I discovered there was a Corporal Brian Truman on the base. I went to see him and realized almost immediately that, although he looked like the Brian Truman I knew, it wasn't him. I had access to the personnel records so I looked up his records and verified he should have been the man I knew."

"So, what did you do?"

"I was going to confront him, but before I could do that I found out he was a loan shark, and the people who missed a payment often ended up in the hospital. The Brian Truman I knew was a very friendly, outgoing guy. He volunteered at the local animal shelter, and used to go around the neighborhood trying to find homes for the animals in the shelter. He was a very nice guy. The Brian Truman at the base was, to put it bluntly, an asshole."

Kidder hesitated for a few seconds and then continued, "Anyway, I have a friend who works at the Olathe, Kansas police department. I scanned a picture of Brian that was in our high school yearbook and I sent it to him and asked him if he could tell me who it was. A day later I received a message from him telling me that the guy in the picture was Sean O'Keefe, and he was wanted for murder. He killed a guy during a carjacking. Apparently, Sean worked for a nationwide carjacking syndicate."

"So, you did something really stupid, didn't you?"

"Yeah, I told him I knew who he really was, and for a hundred thousand dollars I would go away and keep my mouth shut. I was really surprised when he said he would get me the money. It was way too easy. He said it would be in the form of a loan, but I would never have to pay it back. He gave me a promissory note to sign, and I signed it. He said he would have the money for me in thirty days."

"I'll bet you never got the money."

"That would be a safe bet. When I left my apartment a few weeks later a car came out of nowhere and ran me over. I think the driver might have tried for a second pass, but as soon as I was hit several people came over to help."

"That's quite a story. Did you ever buy drugs from Sergeant Lender?"

"No, I knew about him, and when the MPs questioned me, I thought I could implicate him and get both of the assholes thrown in jail."

I turned toward Mike and said, "I suspect our Corporal Truman got his funds from the carjacking syndicate he was working for, and he probably told them he agreed to loan Robert a hundred thousand dollars, but he pocketed the money himself."

Mike asked, "Do you think his syndicate buddies killed him?"

"No, I think he was targeted for the same reason as the drug dealers. He was just a really bad guy."

Robert asked, "Am I under arrest?"

"No, I think you learned your lesson. Something tells me you won't ever do anything that dumb again. Have you told this story to anybody else? Please don't lie."

He hesitated briefly and said, "No, I thought about telling my sister, but I never did."

There were two other people on Lender's client list that owed him over a hundred thousand dollars, and I wanted to know if Robert knew them. So, I asked, "Do the names Arron Miller and Bruce Hampstead mean anything to you?"

"No, those names aren't familiar to me at all."

The Fireman

"Thank you for telling us the truth, Robert. We're done for now, but we may be back."

"Okay. It actually feels good not to have to worry about this anymore. I'm happy to help you anyway I can."

After Mike and I were back in the car I said, "He lied about not telling his sister about it."

"Yeah, I know. Should we go talk to her?"

"Maybe, but not today. I want to go through the list of Truman's clients and find out which ones were injured as a result of missing a payment. I also want more information on the other two people who owed him more than a hundred thousand dollars."

"We can do that as soon as we get back. Are we finished in LA?"

"Yeah, let's go back to the airport."

Mike and I arrived at the Honolulu airport by 9:00 PM, and I was back at my hotel by 10:00. Mike promised to come to the hotel the next morning by 9:30.

Jill decided to go shopping and she left a few minutes before Mike arrived. We sat down at the table. Mike handed me the file and said, "The other two big borrowers on Truman's list don't exist. There's no record of them ever living on the base. I also checked with the state, and there are no driver's licenses or voter registration cards for them either. I think Truman added them to his records to get more money from the people who were financing him."

"If you're right, then his carjacking buddies might have wanted him killed, but that doesn't explain the other deaths. I think we're looking for someone who hates drug dealers and had a run in with Corporal Truman."

Mike set up his notebook PC so he could access the public records and we began searching through Truman's client list. It took us several hours, but when we were finished we had four names that warranted further investigation.

"Mike, I want to know about the relatives and friends of these people. I don't believe any of the clients have the technical expertise required to commit these murders. While you are at it, check up on Kidder's aunt and uncle too."

"I'll get started as soon as I get back to the base."

"As much as I like Hawaii, I have a job in Norfolk County I don't want to lose, so let's try to finish this up in three or four days."

"I understand, Frank. I'll try to have the information by the end of the day tomorrow."

Just as Mike was leaving, Jill came back with a shopping bag full of souvenirs. Mike looked at the bag Jill was carrying and said, "It's nice of you to help support the Hawaiian economy."

Jill smiled at him and responded, "I only spent $300."

After Mike left Jill and I spent the next half hour looking at the treasures she bought. Then we had a nice lunch and spent the rest of the afternoon on the beach.

The next morning my leg was much better. I was able to walk without the cane. We decided to rent a car and explore Oahu. Late in the afternoon I received a call from Mike.

"I've checked out all of the people we thought could be potential suspects and it looks like there is only one possibility. Robert Kidder's uncle, Mitchell Kidder, is the director of research and development at Preston Aviation. He has several degrees from Cal Tech, and is certainly capable of building the oscillators."

"I don't suppose he has a criminal record."

"Actually, he does. He was arrested about five years ago with a group that was protesting the decision by a judge to give a six-month sentence to a forty year old guy who raped a twelve year old girl. The group was waiting for the judge to leave the courthouse. When he got into his car, they surrounded it and beat the shit out of it with hammers and baseball bats. All eleven of the protesters were arrested, but the charges were eventually dropped. It turned out the rapist

The Fireman

bribed the judge to make sure he received a lenient sentence."

"So, he's a vigilante. If he's our perp, we're going to have to trick him into taking action against someone acting as a decoy. Do you know someone from the base who would volunteer?"

"I'll do it."

"No, you won't! Robert knows you're a cop. Also, I'm probably going to need your help."

"Okay, I'll ask for volunteers tomorrow morning at the office. I'm sure we'll get several."

"I don't know these people, so you pick the one you think will be best for the job. I think you should also pick a woman to be our victim."

"I can do that. What's your plan?"

"We'll get a story published in the Honolulu paper about a guy on the base who is the base drug pusher and loan shark. He's going to do something really nasty to our victim. We'll also send the story to the local TV stations. Whoever you pick for the bad guy is going to have to go into hiding until Mitchell Kidder makes his move. We're going to have to get somebody to keep track of Kidder's movements and monitor his phone calls. I'll call my friend in Army Intelligence and let him know what's going on and that we need his help."

"I'll call you after I've selected our new base villain and victim. Have a good evening, Frank."

"Thanks Mike, you too."

It was too late to call George, so I waited until morning. When he answered I said, "Hi George. I think we've figured out who the killer is. His name is Mitchell Kidder. He lives in La Jolla where the calls to all the victims originated, has the technical expertise to build the oscillators, and is the uncle of one of Truman's victims."

"Okay, I agree he sounds like a good prospect. Do you have any proof?"

"No, and I need your help."

"What's your plan?"

"Sergeant Ortiz is going to pick someone to be the new base bad guy. He will be a drug dealer and a loan shark. He is also selecting a woman to be the victim. We're going to get the local papers to print a story about him that will make your average drug dealer seem like a saint in comparison. We're also going to release the story to the local TV stations. After the stories have been published, our guy is going to threaten Robert Kidder. I'm sure Robert will tell his uncle and that should spur him into action. What I need from you is surveillance of Mitchell Kidder, including keeping track of his phone calls."

"The surveillance isn't a problem, but the phone calls are more problematic. I'm sure he has an unregistered phone, so unless we know the number, it will be almost impossible to track his calls."

"We already know he's using James Bond's phone. If he doesn't get a new one, we won't have any problems."

"Alright, I'll get things set up so we can start whenever you're ready."

"Thanks George. I'll send you all the information we have on Mitchell Kidder today, but I think it will be several days before we'll need to start the surveillance."

"That will give me more than enough time to get things ready."

Mike called me about an hour later to tell me he picked Sergeant John Mallory to be the new base crook, and Barbara Bentley to be the victim.

I wanted John to do something really awful to Barbara, and decided he was going to throw acid in her face because she was a week late in making a payment. I called Mike and told him what I wanted to do. He thought it was a great idea.

The following morning Mike took Barbara to a friend of his who was a paramedic on the base. He bandaged Barbara's face and hands. They put her on a gurney and took

The Fireman

pictures of her being rolled out of an ambulance and taken into her apartment.

Mike spent the rest of the morning writing a news release that said a woman, who wished to remain anonymous, was warned two days ago that if she didn't make a payment on her loan within forty-eight hours, she would pay in other ways. This morning, as she was leaving her home, a man she didn't recognize threw acid in her face. She survived the attack, but her face was horribly scarred, and she lost the sight in one of her eyes. Mike sent the story and the pictures to the Honolulu Star-Advertiser. He also sent it to the local TV stations.

By early the next afternoon, Sergeant John Mallory was the most reviled person in Hawaii. The Honolulu police announced that although Sergeant Mallory was a suspect in the case, there was no direct evidence he was involved.

The story made the news all over the country the next day.

I decided it was time for Sergeant Mallory to call Robert Kidder. Mike and I were both listening to the conversation. He told Robert he had taken over from Corporal Truman, and with the accrued interest, Robert now owed him one hundred twenty-two thousand dollars. Then he said if he didn't want to end up like the woman in Hawaii, he had to pay forty thousand dollars within a week. Robert, who was obviously frightened, tried to tell him he never borrowed any money from Corporal Truman. Sergeant Mallory listened and when Robert was finished he simply said, "You have one week to pay," and then he hung up the phone. It was a very convincing performance.

I was positive the call would cause Mitchell Kidder to act, so I called George and told him to activate the surveillance. Now all we could do was wait.

It didn't take long. Two days after Robert's conversation with Sergeant Mallory, I received a message that said Mitchell Kidder just boarded a flight to Honolulu. I called Mike and told him what was happening. Mike said he would contact Lieutenant Chan and arrange to have our suspect watched.

Early that evening, I received a call from Lieutenant Chan. He told me the suspect rented a car and checked into a small motel a few miles from the Schofield Barracks. He was still in his room.

I called Mike and told him where Mitchell Kidder was. He said he would have one of his people take over the surveillance. We agreed to meet in his office in the morning.

I arrived at Mike's office about 9:30. He said Mitchell left the motel to have breakfast, then he stopped at a drug store and left the store with something in a small plastic bag. He was now back in his room.

I said, "I wonder if he is going to deliver the package to Sergeant Mallory himself, or is he going to mail it. What do you think?"

"I hope he delivers it himself. That way we can arrest him when he comes onto the base."

"I guess we'll just have to wait and see what happens. If he mails it, and then leaves the island, we'll probably have to wait until he activates the device before we can arrest him."

We didn't have to wait too long. Two hours later the surveillance team called and said Mitchell left the motel and drove to a post office. He went inside carrying a small package. He came out a few minutes later without the package and drove back to the hotel. One of the surveillance team guys went into the post office to find out what Mitchell had just mailed. The package was sent to Sergeant Mallory by certified mail, and the return address on receipt was the motel where Mitchell was staying.

Obviously, he was going to wait in Hawaii until the package was delivered. That would make our job easier. Mike and I went to Sergeant Mallory's apartment to tell him what was going on. When we arrived, Sergeant Mallory said, "Mike, you do know that everybody on this island hates me. I just hope they realize it was just a ruse to catch the killer."

The Fireman

"I promise you we will explain everything to the newspapers. You'll probably be considered a hero when all this is over. This, by the way, will happen very soon. Our suspect just mailed you a package. I'm sure it will be here tomorrow."

"If the package contains one of his devices, can we arrest him immediately?"

I thought about that for a few seconds and said, "Our case would be stronger if we wait until he activates the device. I think we'll arrest him immediately if he tries to leave the island, otherwise we'll wait."

Mike said, "I agree, but while I realize our suspect is a murderer, he is only targeting people the law has been unable to prosecute. He's actually helping the community."

"That's been true so far, but there's no guarantee he won't target other people. He's still a killer and must be stopped," I said.

Mike sighed deeply and said, "I understand."

Then I said, "Sergeant Mallory, when the package arrives, don't open it. Call Mike and we will get a forensics team over here to open it."

"Yes sir."

"Mike, call Lieutenant Chan and let him know we'll need a forensics team tomorrow morning to open the package."

"Okay."

Mike and I left Sergeant Mallory's apartment. Then I went back to the hotel. I told Jill what was happening and our stay in Hawaii was going to end soon. She said that although she really liked Hawaii, she was anxious to get home. We spent the rest of the day together. Now that my leg was better, we were able to spend it really enjoying each other's company.

The following morning, I went back to Mike's office. The mail usually arrived by eleven o'clock. At 11:30 Sergeant Mallory called to tell us the package had arrived. Mike called Lieutenant Chan, and less than an hour later two forensics people arrived at Mike's office. One of them was a man who introduced himself as Lieutenant Miller. The woman who was with him remained silent.

We went to Sergeant Mallory's apartment. Once we were inside Lieutenant Miller put on plastic gloves and picked up the package. The woman opened the large metal case she was carrying. She removed a camera and took several pictures of the package. Then she took a device that looked like a camera mounted on a tripod and set it over the package. She put a plastic square under the package and connected the wire from the plastic square to a notebook PC.

Lieutenant Miller said, "This is a portable x-ray system. We want to check out the contents of the package before we open it."

The woman turned on the device, and on the screen I could see the outline of the envelope. The only thing that showed inside the envelope was a small round object that appeared to be solid and a thin metal chain.

The woman turned off the x-ray and proceeded to check the package for fingerprints. When she was done, Lieutenant Miller opened the package. Inside was the same instruction letter I had seen before, and a round black cylinder that was about an inch in diameter and three quarters of an inch long. It was solid except for a small hole for the chain. The device was checked for fingerprints, but there weren't any, so the woman gave the device to Sergeant Mallory.

The instructions were personalized. It said Sergeant Mallory should pair the device with his cell phone. Once that was done he was supposed to call a number with his phone. When the call was answered he was to key in "3126" and wait for the system to say "Device Activated". Then he should put the device in his right front pocket or attach it to the chain and wear it around his neck.

Mike gave Sergeant Mallory a cell phone to use. He followed the instructions to connect the device to the phone. Then he called the number and activated the device, which

The Fireman

beeped three times. Then he put the device down on a table and said, "I have no intention of putting this thing anywhere near my body."

"I wonder if it has some way of checking to see if the victim is wearing it?" I asked.

"That's certainly a possibility, when the device was activated it could have stored a program on the Sergeant's phone that would validate he was wearing it. But that would be very complex to do. Besides, the instructions didn't say anything about carrying your phone when wearing the device."

"Okay, we're not going to put anyone at risk. Let's put the device into some kind of container that would prevent it from doing any damage."

"When do you think Kidder will make his move?" Mike asked.

"Do we know how long he planned to stay at the motel?"

"He reserved the room for five nights."

"Okay, he checked in two days ago. I suspect he will try to activate the device in the next forty-eight hours."

Lieutenant Miller said, "I have some small metal boxes in my van. I think you should put the device and the cell phone in one of the boxes."

"I agree. Mike, I think you should assign somebody to stay with Sergeant Mallory. When the device is activated he can contact the guys watching the motel and they can arrest Kidder."

"That sounds reasonable."

The woman with the forensics team went back to the van to get the metal box. When she returned she was carrying the box that was about ten inches square and three inches high. It appeared to be made of steel, at least a quarter of an inch thick and had a hinged top with a lock. She put the device and the cell phone in it and closed the top.

I was wondering what they used the box for, but decided not to ask. Mike called his office and a few minutes later a young man arrived. When he walked in, Mike explained to him what was going on. He told him that if the device activated, he should call him immediately. If for some reason he didn't answer, he should call the team watching the motel and tell them to arrest Kidder.

I spoke to Sergeant Mallory that evening and told him to open the box so the phone would be able to make a call. He did that while I waited. He said a few seconds after he opened the box it made a call. I asked him to leave the box open for now and to call me if anything happened.

He called me about five minutes later to tell me he received a text message that displayed some obviously faked health information. I told him to close the metal box again.

I was fairly sure something was going to happen the following evening, so I went back to Sergeant Mallory's apartment at 7:00 PM the next day. The guy who was staying with him left. I opened the box. Then we sat down and we were talking about the case when the cell phone rang once. A moment later the metal box began to vibrate violently. I called Mike and told him the device was just activated. When the vibration stopped I looked at the box. It was smoking, and the metal under the device had actually melted. The table the box was sitting on was burned, but it didn't catch on fire.

Mike called me back ten minutes later to tell me they had arrested Mitchell Kidder and he was being held at the MP office. It was over, but I wanted to talk to Kidder.

When I arrived, Mitchell Kidder was sitting in an interrogation room, handcuffed to the table. I told Mike I wanted to talk to the suspect. I walked in and sat down across from him and said, "Mr. Kidder, my name is Frank Carver. I was here on my honeymoon when I was assigned to this case. Would you tell me why you killed all those people?"

"I have been watching the justice system in this country fail over and over again for the last several years. I had a son who was killed accidentally by a drug dealer when we lived near Chicago. My son was only seventeen; he was

The Fireman

in the wrong place at the wrong time. The jury convicted the drug dealer of drug crimes and second-degree murder. The judge sentenced him to life in prison. Then our government decided that being a drug dealer wasn't a violent crime. After spending less than ten years in jail, his sentence was commuted and he was let out."

"I'm truly sorry for your loss. I can understand your frustration, but I'm sure you realize you can't take the law into your own hands."

"I do realize what I did was illegal, but I'm not sure it was wrong. I guess that will be up to the jury to decide. I'm sorry I messed up your honeymoon."

"Please get yourself a really good lawyer. Perhaps he can get you off. But if you are lucky enough to stay out of prison, please leave the law to those of us whose job it is to enforce it. Believe me when I tell you we all sympathize with you."

I left the room. I walked over to Mike and thanked him for his help with the case. Then I drove back to my hotel. I sent George a text message telling him it was over. The following morning Jill and I went home.

That morning a front-page article appeared in the Honolulu Star-Advertiser that said Sergeant Mallory wasn't a bad guy at all. He was used as a decoy in a plan to trap a killer. The female victim was also playing a part in the plan and wasn't injured.

Three months later Mitchell Kidder was tried on three counts of murder in Hawaii. He pleaded not guilty. The trial lasted only three days. The jury deliberated for five days and was unable to come to a unanimous decision. The judge declared a mistrial, and a month later Mitchell Kidder was tried again. Once again, the jury was unable to reach a unanimous decision. The judge was forced to declare another mistrial.

Four months have elapsed since the last trial. So far, the state hasn't decided if they are going to go to trial for a third time.

There was insufficient evidence to tie Mitchell Kidder to the murders in Chicago and Los Angeles, so he was never charged. He went back to his old job at Preston Aviation when he was released after the second trial.

The Disappearing Man
A Frank Carver Mystery

Prologue

Jason Goldsmith was an airplane fanatic. Since he was a small child, he had been fascinated with airplanes. After graduating high school, he went to speak to the recruiters at all the military services agreeing to join if he could be trained as a pilot. They all told him the same thing. Go to college and earn a degree in engineering. Then come back and ask again about pilot training.

Jason tried, but after two years decided college wasn't for him. Instead, he went to a trade school and became a certified airplane mechanic. He worked for Forest Aviation and loved his job. He never got to fly the planes, but he did get to work on them, and occasionally he would taxi them in or out of the maintenance hangar.

It was Friday, and Jason was looking forward to Monday morning. A new restaurant was opening a few hundred yards east of the east-west runway. They built a glass-enclosed dining area so patrons could watch the planes as they landed or took off. Jason was planning on going there for breakfast.

When Jason went to bed Sunday night, he set his alarm for 5:00 AM, an hour earlier than usual so he would have time for a leisurely breakfast. He arrived at the restaurant at 6:15. The hostess brought him to a table with a perfect view. As usual, there was a light easterly wind, so he knew he would have a great view. His meal was excellent. He was sitting at his table, enjoying his second cup of coffee, when he saw a small business jet make a left turn for the final approach to the airport. It was more than a mile away and Jason watched it as the pilot began to reduce the speed and altitude for the landing. As he watched, he became concerned. He was sure the pilot was too low for a safe *landing. A few seconds later he watched, in horror, as the plane flew directly into the glass-enclosed dining room.*

The restaurant, that had been open for less than an hour, was completely destroyed. Jason was killed instantly, which was a blessing, because most of the others died as a result of burns they received when the plane burst into flames as a result of the impact.

All eleven people in the restaurant at the time of the crash were dead.

The Disappearing Man

My name is Frank Carver. I'm the only homicide detective in the Norfolk County Police Department. My wife, Jill, is the County Medical Examiner.

I had just arrived at my desk when the phone rang. It was the dispatcher.

"Frank, do you know about the new restaurant that just opened by the airport?"

"Sure, they have commercials on every fifteen minutes. Why?"

"It isn't there anymore. A plane crashed into it about ten minutes ago. You need to get over there as soon as possible. I suspect Jill will be there too. There were both patrons and employees in the restaurant when the plane crashed."

"How many people were killed?"

"We don't know yet. The place is on fire. I don't think we'll know who was inside until the fire is out."

"Okay, I'm on my way."

When I arrived, the fire department was still putting out the fire. Calvin, the fire chief, said I would probably be able to go inside what was left of the restaurant in about an hour.

I was amazed at the amount of damage the plane caused. There was almost nothing left except the steel super structure of the building. The fuselage of the plane was mostly intact. The wings were sheared off when the plane crashed into the building. The fuel that was stored in the wing tanks exploded in the fire and destroyed the wings. As I looked around it occurred to me that, although the fire was devastating, it would have been much worse if the plane's fuel tanks had been full.

I noticed something else as I studied the crash site. The plane didn't hit the ground before it hit the restaurant. It flew directly into the restaurant. I was thinking about that when somebody grabbed my right arm. I turned and discovered Jill and her assistant Amanda had arrived on site.

"Wow! This place is really demolished. Do we know how many people were inside when the plane crashed?" Jill asked.

"No," I looked at my watch and then continued, "Calvin said we could get inside in an hour. That was forty minutes ago."

"This place just opened this morning, didn't it?"

"Yeah, I think they were open for less than an hour before the crash.

A few minutes later Calvin came over to us. He had a somber look on his face when he said, "I'm sorry to tell you that there are at least eight bodies in there."

Jill said, "We aren't equipped to handle that many deaths at once. We'll have to have someplace to store them until we can do the autopsies. I'm going back to my car to make some calls." Then she and Amanda left.

"Is it safe to go in now?" I asked.

"Not really, but if you have to go in you'll have to wear a hard hat. Come to my truck with me and I'll get you one."

Calvin and I walked over to his truck. It was one of those trucks paramedics use. The back of the truck had fifty storage areas. Calvin opened one of the larger ones, took out several hard hats, and checked the sizes. Then he handed me one and said, "This one should fit."

I put it on and found it fit reasonably well. Calvin put on a hard hat as well. Then we walked into the remains of the restaurant.

The nose of the plane was embedded at least fifty feet into the structure. The front of the plane was in reasonably good shape. The windshield was broken and it was badly burned, but otherwise intact.

A door was hanging open just behind the cockpit. I peeked through and looked inside the cabin. It was burned but empty, no sign of any furniture at all. I looked into the cockpit and it was burned as well. I asked Calvin, "Can I assume the pilot didn't survive the crash?"

The Disappearing Man

"From the condition of the plane you would certainly assume that, but there's a problem. The pilot wasn't on board. The plane was completely empty."

"Then who was flying the plane? You're not going to tell me the pilot walked away from the crash, are you?"

"No, I don't believe the pilot walked away from the crash. I'm telling you there was no pilot on the plane when it crashed. The plane was empty."

I said nothing, but my mind was going back to my first homicide case. Could somebody be using a transporter again? I know we destroyed the Russian unit, but the United States was developing one too. This stuff was classified, so I couldn't tell Calvin what I was thinking. I decided it was best to change the subject so I asked, "Where were the bodies found?"

"I'll show you."

While Calvin and I were looking at the devastation inside what was a restaurant a few hours ago, my phone rang. I didn't recognize the number, so I answered with, "Lieutenant Carver, homicide."

"Lieutenant Carver, my name is John Gordon. I'm an investigator with the National Transportation Safety Board. Are you currently at the crash site?"

"Yes, I am."

"Please don't allow anyone to enter the plane until I get there. I should be there in less than an hour."

"I'm sorry to inform you that the fire department entered the plane looking for survivors. They didn't find any."

"The pilot is dead?"

"I'm not sure if he's dead, but he's definitely missing."

"Are you telling me the pilot wasn't on board the aircraft?"

"Yes, the plane was completely empty."

"I'll be there as quickly as I can."

I decided I wanted to know who owned the plane, so I called the station. I gave the dispatcher the tail number on the plane and asked her to find someone to trace the owner. Just as I finished that call, Jill and Amanda came over to where we were standing. Jill said she made arrangements with two of the local funeral homes to store some of the bodies until they could perform the autopsies. She also told me the county enlisted the help of a pathologist from Timberlake Medical Center.

I hadn't realized it, but when Jill and Amanda walked over to talk to me, Calvin went back to his truck. When he returned he handed each of the women a hard hat. They put them on and we walked around while Calvin pointed out the bodies they found so far.

Jill examined each body and Amanda took pictures and fingerprints from each victim. Two ambulances arrived and they began removing the bodies from the ruins. After Jill and Amanda had completed the examinations, they left to go back to their lab. Four of the bodies were loaded into the ambulances and they left.

I was surveying the scene again, and as I looked around, it became obvious there were more bodies under the fuselage. I mentioned that to Calvin. He said there was nothing we could do until the NTSB made arrangements to remove the plane.

John Gordon showed up a little later. There were two men with him. He introduced himself and gave me his card. Then all of them went inside the plane. Fifteen minutes later John walked out and came over to where Calvin and I were standing. He said, "The cockpit of the plane is in remarkably good shape considering the amount of damage the rest of the plane sustained. But, I don't believe the pilot could have survived the crash. I did note something unusual; the pilot's harness was still attached to the buckle. It looks like somehow the pilot was just sucked out of the plane. I don't understand how that could happen."

The Disappearing Man

I wanted to say, "I do!" but I didn't. I did say, "That does seem strange. Is there any way the plane could have been remote controlled?"

"I thought about that possibility, but there was no indication of any remote-control hardware in the cockpit. I'm sure somebody was flying the plane."

"John, I believe there are probably more bodies under the plane. How soon can you have it removed so we can check?"

"I should be able to get that done before the end of the day."

"Thank you." Then I turned to Calvin and said, "I'm going back to the station. Please call me if you find anything interesting."

"I will."

I walked back to my car, drove about a mile from the crash site, and pulled off the road. Tim Harris was in charge of our transporter development and helped me during my first investigation as a homicide detective. He was probably the only person who could give me a clue regarding the disappearance of the pilot. So, I decided to call him and ask.

It took almost ten minutes, speaking to various people, before I heard Tim say, "Hi Frank. What's happening?"

"Hi Tim. Thank you for taking my call. I wasn't sure I would ever get through to you. I have an unusual situation that I think, perhaps, you may be able to shed some light on."

"Okay, I'll try to help."

"This morning a plane crashed into a restaurant. The plane burst into flames on impact. Everyone in the restaurant was killed. After the fire department put out the fire, they looked inside the plane for more victims, but the plane was empty. The pilot's harness was still buckled, but he was gone."

"Okay, I understand why you called me, but I can't discuss this with you on an unsecured line. I assume you still have your security clearance?"

"Yes, I do. Do you want me to call you back on a secure line?"

"Yes, I'll send you a text message with the number in fifteen minutes."

"Okay, I have to drive to our local Air Force base and that will take about forty minutes. I'll call you back when I get there."

I arrived at the base about thirty-five minutes later. I showed the guard my ID and told him I needed access to a secure phone. He asked me to wait for a moment while he made a call. When he was finished he said, "They're waiting for you in the communications office. Do you know where it is?"

"Yes, I do. Thank you for your help," I said. The drive to the communications office took a few minutes. When I went inside, a young woman I had met before said, "Good afternoon lieutenant. It's nice to see you again. The room is ready for you." Then she held out her hand and I gave her my cell phone. She led me to the room with the secure telephone line.

I wrote down the number Tim Harris had sent as soon as I received it. When I got into the room I called him. I was surprised when he answered. I said, "Hi Tim, we're on a secure line now."

"While I was waiting for your call I verified that you still have the appropriate clearance. I noticed you have been promoted to colonel. Congratulations."

"That promotion was supposed to be temporary. Anyway, what can you tell me about the pilot's disappearance?"

"I can tell you that by using some of the information from the Russian plans, I was able to complete the design of our transporter system. It's still being tested, but it appears to be completely functional."

"Does that mean you can transport people without killing them?"

The Disappearing Man

"Yes, we can do that now. We also no longer need elaborate sending and receiving platforms."

"So, you can transport anything anywhere. That's a substantial enhancement."

"It's a little more complicated than that. The item to be transported must have a 'locator beacon' attached to it. That enables us to know the exact size and location of the item to be transported. The destination location has to be very precise too. We don't want to transport somebody, or even something, into a wall. To eliminate that possibility, we have established eleven designated receiving areas."

"So, if the pilot was wearing one of your beacons, he could have been transported off the plane just before it crashed."

"In theory, that's correct. However, I can tell you we didn't do that. If the Russians have rebuilt the system we destroyed, it's possible they did it. We no longer have a contact in their group. We have no idea how far they have advanced. Perhaps your friend, Igor, could find out for you."

"I haven't spoken to Igor for almost a year, but I'll call him and ask about it. But, why would the Russians want to destroy a local restaurant? That doesn't make any sense."

"Maybe they weren't trying to destroy the restaurant. Maybe they wanted to kill somebody inside."

"I already thought about that. We haven't identified any of the victims yet, but when we do I'll check them out. Since you have figured out how to enhance the transporter, is there any reason to suspect that the Russians have done so as well?"

"They were ahead of us before, so it's certainly possible they're ahead of us again."

"I wonder if they're still planning to sell the device to one of the radical Islamic terrorist groups."

"What makes you think they haven't done that already?"

"It's scary to think they may have done that, but I'm sure it's a possibility."

"If I hear anything, I'll call you immediately."

"Thanks Tim."

I hung up the phone and sat in the room for a while thinking about my conversation with Tim. I came to the conclusion that I have so little information it was useless to even think about it.

While I was driving back to the station Jill called. She said, "We have been able to identify seven of the eight victims found in the restaurant. Five of them were restaurant employees, including the owner and his wife. The other two were local residents. The last victim isn't in any US data base, so I sent the prints over to Interpol. We're going to try reconstructing his face since most of the flesh is gone. Once we get some kind of drawing, I'll send that to Interpol as well."

"How long will the facial reconstruction take?"

"Probably forty-eight hours. Do you have any idea what happened to the pilot?"

"No, I don't. I'm hoping we can find the owner of the plane, and then we can figure out why the plane was here."

"Do you think the pilot purposely crashed into the restaurant?"

"Yes, I do. But I have no idea why. I assume you're going to be working late tonight."

"I'll try to get home by eleven. I'll call you when I'm leaving."

I really wanted to tell Jill about the transporter, but it was classified. I was going to have to figure out how to discuss the case with her and not tell her about it. When I got to the station I walked over to the chief's office. As soon as he saw me he motioned for me to come in. As soon as I sat down he said, "Tell me about the crash."

I got up, closed the door to his office, and sat down again. He looked at me and asked, "Why did you do that?"

"Because there may be some aspects to this case that are classified."

"I don't have security clearance. You know that."

The Disappearing Man

"Yes, but the information involved in this case is something you're already familiar with, so I don't think discussing it with you will violate any security regulations."

"Now I'm really curious. What's going on?"

"I believe the plane was purposely crashed into the restaurant. I don't know why yet, and that's my first task in this investigation. The pilot of the plane disappeared. I believe that after he set the plane on a course to crash into the restaurant, he was transported off the plane."

"I didn't think that was possible."

"I didn't either, until I talked to Tim Harris again. He said they have improved the capability of the system since we last saw it, and it's now possible to do that. He assured me he wasn't responsible for the pilot's disappearance, but he thought the Russians were a definite possibility."

"Okay, I agree your first task is to find out why. There must have been someone in the restaurant they wanted to kill. But I can't help think there must have been an easier way to kill somebody. How many people died in the restaurant?"

"So far they found eight bodies, but I think there are more under the fuselage of the plane. The NTSB is going to try to remove the plane this afternoon."

The chief sighed deeply and said, "Please keep me informed."

I responded, "You know I will." Then I went to my desk.

The first thing I did was call my Russian contact, Igor. He's in the Russian Secret Service and we worked on my first homicide case together. I didn't expect him to answer his phone, so I wasn't disappointed when I heard a message in Russian. After the beep I said, "Hi Igor, it's Frank. Please call me when you have a chance. It appears that the Star Trek device is working again," then I hung up.

Now I had nothing to do until all the victims were identified, and that wouldn't happen until the plane was moved. I remembered I hadn't asked John about the flight data recorder on the plane, but I thought it might be able to confirm my suspicion that the pilot aimed the plane for the restaurant. I called him, but he didn't answer either, so I left him a message.

While I was sitting at my desk daydreaming, someone tapped me on the shoulder. It was Wendy Cooper. She was recently promoted to Detective. She said, "I'm sorry to wake you. I hope you were enjoying your dream. Anyway, the tail number on the plane that crashed this morning belongs to a plane owned by Emerald Manufacturing. They are based in Houston and make OEM auto parts for all the major car companies. However, their plane is currently being used for a trip to Detroit, so it was obviously not involved in the crash."

"I'm sure I copied the tail number correctly. That's very strange. Thanks for the info."

It was after four o'clock, so I went home. I decided I didn't feel like cooking anything, so I stopped on the way home and picked up a pizza. The evening was lonely. Jill wasn't home and there was nothing I wanted to watch on TV. I put an old science fiction movie in the DVD player and watched that for a while. At some point I fell asleep. I woke up when somebody started shaking me.

I opened my eyes and saw Jill. I said, "I guess I fell asleep. When did you get home?"

"About two minutes ago. It's almost eleven o'clock. After you wake up a little more, I have some information for you."

I yawned and said, "I'm awake. Tell me what you found."

"Interpol was able to identify our mystery victim. His name is Adam Becker, and he was an agent in the Mossad."

"I wonder what he was doing here. I'll have to call George tomorrow and ask him if he can find out what Becker was working on. Did you find out anything else?"

"Yes, the plane has been moved. There were three more bodies under the fuselage. Also, John told me to tell

The Disappearing Man

you the flight data recorder had been disabled. He also said the fuel tanks were opened just before the crash, and he was positive the pilot wanted the restaurant to be destroyed."

I called George Dyer when I arrived at my desk the next morning. After he answered I said, "Good morning, George. I need your help with something."

"Of course you do, that's the only time I ever hear from you."

"You know that's not true, and don't forget the task I did for you in Hawaii."

"Okay, I apologize. So, what can I help you with?"

"Before I get to that, I thought you should know the Army still has my rank as colonel. Anyway, there was a plane crash here yesterday. So far the facts indicate the pilot purposely crashed his plane into a restaurant. Everyone in the restaurant was killed. As strange as that may sound, there are two other facts in this case that are even stranger. First, one of the people killed in the crash was a Mossad agent named Adam Becker. The second is, the pilot of the plane has vanished."

"Now I know why you called me. I'm really sorry Adam Becker was killed. I met him for the first time several years ago when he was helping us rescue somebody from Iran. Our paths have crossed about once a year since. He was one of the Mossad's best, and he'll missed. I'll call my contact at the Mossad and let them know. You said the pilot vanished. Do you have any idea where he went?"

"Since this isn't a secure line, all I can tell you is that I believe a 'Star Trek' device was used in his disappearance."

"That's interesting. When I call my Mossad contact I'll ask if he knows what Becker's assignment was. Have you discussed this with Tim Harris?"

"Yes, he said it was a definite possibility the device was used. Apparently, there have been some substantial enhancements since my last encounter with it."

"Give me a couple of hours. I'll call you back."

"Thanks George."

"You're welcome. By the way, the reason you're still a colonel is because my boss decided you should retain the rank because of the job you did for us in Hawaii."

The three new victims of the crash had yet to be identified, but I was positive the target was Adam Becker. He had to be involved in something important. Otherwise, why destroy a restaurant, a multi-million-dollar airplane, and kill ten innocent people just to kill Becker?

Late that afternoon George called me back. He said, "I spoke to my contact at the Mossad. He told me Adam Becker was investigating a possibility that Iran was attempting to buy electronic triggering devices that are used for nuclear weapons. He was in your area because the primary manufacturer for the devices is Parker Engineering. Their manufacturing facility is located near the airport."

"Yeah, I know where it is. It's only about a quarter of a mile from the crash site. I guess Becker must have discovered something that got him killed."

"You're probably right, but the person I spoke to told me that they haven't spoken to Becker since he told them about the triggers three days ago. It's possible he found something and was killed before he could report it."

"That's certainly a possibility. But why kill him at the restaurant? I wonder if he was supposed to meet an informant there. I'll check the other victims and find out if any of them had a connection to Parker Engineering."

"That's a good idea. By the way, because I believe the target was an Israeli agent, I had to inform the CIA. I suspect you'll be hearing from them shortly."

"I expected that. Unless they tell me otherwise, I'll keep you informed regarding my progress in the case. Thanks for your help."

"You're welcome."

I called Jill and Amanda answered the phone. I asked her if they identified the last three victims yet. She said they

The Disappearing Man

just finished and would send me the complete list of victims in a few minutes.

I received the list in an e-mail message that arrived just before five o'clock. I thought about waiting until morning to check out the victim list, but decided not to wait. I was going to check out their social security files to see if any of them worked for Parker Engineering, but I decided to call Parker Engineering instead.

It took me less than two minutes to get connected to the director of personnel. I told her who I was and that I needed to know if any of the people who were killed at the restaurant were employed there. Before I could read the list, she said they only employed sixty-three people, and everybody was at work today.

I decided to read her the list anyway and one name, Jeffery Haskell, was an employee there, but he resigned several months ago. He was a design engineer. I asked her what he worked on and she said she didn't know because the work he was doing was classified. I thanked her for her time and the information.

I guess Jeffery Haskell worked on nuclear weapon triggers, but I had to find out for sure. I decided I would visit Parker Engineering in the morning.

While I was driving home I received two calls. The first one was from Jill to tell me she would be home around 8:00. The second one was from the CIA. After I answered my phone a man said, "Good evening Colonel Carver, my name is Morris Easton. I'm with the CIA. I understand you're working on a case involving the murder of Adam Becker. Is that correct?"

I'm not sure why, but I didn't like the tone of his voice, so I responded, "You're only partially correct. I'm not a colonel, I'm a lieutenant. Also, I'm not at liberty to discuss any information regarding police investigations over the phone."

"I understand your reluctance to discuss a current investigation over the phone. Could we set up an appointment to meet early tomorrow afternoon?"

"Yes, I have something to do in the morning, but I'm sure I'll be at my desk by one o'clock."

"Okay, I'll see you tomorrow afternoon."

I thought the call was strange. I was sure CIA agents receive similar training to what I received before I started working for Army Intelligence. He should have known I would never discuss a case with someone I don't know over the phone, even if they do claim to be a CIA agent.

I arrived at Parker Engineering at 9:30. I stopped at the receptionist's desk, showed her my ID, and said I needed to speak to whoever was in charge regarding a former employee. She said she would get the personnel manager. I told her I spoke to the personnel manager yesterday and she didn't have the information I needed.

Then she said, "I'll see if Mr. Parker is available to speak to you. Please sit down, this may take a few minutes."

About five minutes later a man walked into the reception area, spoke to the receptionist, and then walked over to me. He extended his hand and said, "Good morning, lieutenant. I'm Bradley Parker. How can I help you?"

I shook his hand and replied, "I need to speak to you regarding one of your former employees. Is there somewhere we can talk in private?"

"Of course, please follow me."

I followed him through the door and into a small conference room. As I passed him, he closed the door and motioned for me to sit down. "This room is soundproof and electronically shielded. What would you like to discuss?"

"I'm sure you're aware of the plane crash that destroyed the restaurant down the street."

He appeared to be annoyed when he replied, "Of course I'm aware of it! What does that have to do with me?"

"Jeffery Haskell was killed in the crash."

The Disappearing Man

He paused for a few seconds and then he said, "I'm sorry to hear that. Jeffery was an excellent engineer, but he resigned his position several months ago. How is Parker Engineering involved?"

"There was another man killed in the crash. His name was Adam Becker. He was an agent in the Mossad. There is evidence indicating the crash was intentional. I believe Adam Becker and Jeffery Haskell were the intended targets. I'm sorry to say, the other nine people killed in the crash were collateral damage. They were just in the wrong place at the wrong time."

"Do you know why Adam Becker was there?"

"He was investigating an attempted purchase of nuclear weapon triggers by Iran."

"We would never sell anything we produce to Iran. I believe Iran is the greatest threat the free world has faced since the defeat of Germany and Japan. Iran possessing a nuclear weapon is unthinkable."

"I wasn't suggesting that you were selling the triggers to Iran. My question is, did Jeffery Haskell have the knowledge to build them?"

"I'm sure he did. He was our chief design engineer. But I've known Jeffery for a long time. I can't believe he would use his knowledge to help Iran."

"Do you know why he resigned?"

"Actually, no, I don't. I asked him why he was leaving and all he would say was he needed time to think about his future. He didn't need money. His father died several years ago and Jeffery inherited a substantial amount of money and a controlling interest in Haskell Enterprises. It's a very large company, but not very well known. They make a variety of building materials and private label the stuff for the big hardware and home store chains. I'm sure Jeffery was worth millions."

"So, Iran wouldn't have been able to tempt him by offering him money. Did Jeffery have a family?"

"He wasn't married, but he did have a younger sister. I believe that she was in a doctoral program at Cal Tech. She wanted to earn a PhD in physics."

"Do you have any contact information for her?"

"I'm not sure. We would have to look at his personnel records. We ask all of our employees to let us know who to contact in case of an emergency. If she was his contact, the information should be in the file."

"Would you please check on that for me?"

"Of course," he responded. Then he got up and said, "I'll be back in a few minutes," as he left the conference room.

I wasn't sure why, but I felt certain Jeffery was involved in building the triggers for Iran. While I was deep in thought, Bradley Parker walked back into the room carrying a file folder. He closed the door, sat down at the table, and slid the file to me.

"This is Jeffery's file. I checked and there's an address and phone number for his sister. Please feel free to look through the file. I want to find out if Jeffery was involved with Iran in any way."

I said, "Thank you, Mr. Parker." Then I opened the file and began to read it. Jeffery was also a graduate of Cal Tech. He had advanced degrees in electrical engineering and physics. He also had a bachelor's degree in mechanical engineering. He was apparently very bright because he earned all of his degrees before he was twenty-six.

After I finished going through the file, I wrote down the contact information for Jeffery's sister, Christina. I thanked Mr. Parker again and then left Parker Engineering.

By the time I got back to my desk, it was about eight o'clock in California, so I decided to try to contact Christina Haskell. There were two phone numbers for her. The first number I tried rang for more than a minute before I gave up. I tried the other number and it immediately gave me a message that the mailbox was full.

The Disappearing Man

I decided to call Cal Tech. After several minutes I got through to the registrar's office. I told the woman who answered who I was and that I needed to get in touch with Christina Haskell because her brother just died. She was far more helpful than I expected. She said she would ask Christina's counselor to tell her to contact me. She also said there were only eleven other students in the postgraduate physics program, and she would ask them to tell Christina as well. I thanked her for her help.

I looked at my watch and realized it was almost time for my meeting with Morris Easton. I was hoping that he might have some information regarding Christina.

I received a call from the dispatcher saying Mr. Easton was here at 12:55. I told her I would be there in a minute. When I walked into the lobby there was a man speaking to the receptionist. He looked like he was in his mid-forties, he was tall and thin, but looked very muscular. As I walked toward him he turned in my direction, smiled, and said, "Good afternoon Lieutenant Carver, I'm Morris Easton." Then he reached into his pocket and showed me his ID.

I looked at the ID and asked, "How can I help you, Mr. Easton?"

"I would like to discuss the crash at the restaurant. Is there somewhere we can talk privately?"

"Sure, we'll use one of the interrogation rooms." He followed me to the room. When we were both seated he said, "I'm not sure how much you know about the people killed in the crash, but we think Adam Becker and Jeffery Haskell were the intended targets."

"Yeah, I already figured that out."

"Good, were you aware that Jeffery has a sister?"

"Yes, I tried to contact her but she isn't answering either of her phones."

"That's because she is no longer in the country. She was kidnapped by terrorists about three weeks ago. The terrorists contacted Jeffery and told him they would rape and kill her if he refused to help them."

I was fairly sure I knew the answer to the question I was going to ask, but I asked anyway, "What did they want him to do?"

"They wanted him to build some key components of nuclear weapons for them."

"How did you find out about it?"

"He stalled them for a while by telling them he didn't have the components he needed and it would take several days to get them. Then he contacted us and told us what was going on. We asked one of our people in Iran to find out where his sister was being held. He called us the next day to tell us that Christina was injured in the kidnapping and died as a result of her injuries."

"What did Jeffery do when you told him?"

"He said he wanted to kill the kidnappers, but we convinced him to work with a Mossad agent instead. We arranged the meeting at the restaurant. We now know we have a security breach. Unfortunately, it took the death of eleven people to make that apparent. We contacted Adam Becker directly, so nobody at the Mossad was aware of the meeting. There were only four of us who knew about it. None of us would have said anything to anybody about the meeting. We did discuss it amongst ourselves, but there was nothing written. We think our office must be bugged. We never thought Islamic Terrorists were that sophisticated, but we were obviously wrong. By the way, if you gave me any information about the case on the phone yesterday, I wouldn't be here now."

"I was wondering if you were a real CIA agent because of that. How can I help?"

"We know the pilot wasn't among those killed in the crash. Do you know what happened to him?"

"Not exactly. He disappeared from the plane right before the crash."

The Disappearing Man

I could tell from the look on his face that Morris was confused by my answer. After a few seconds he asked, "How is that possible?"

Now I was in a dilemma. I didn't know if Morris' security clearance was high enough to discuss the transporter with him. I said, "That information is highly classified. I'm not sure if I can discuss it with you. My first case as a homicide detective involved the device that makes the pilot's disappearance possible. Had that not happened, I suspect my security clearance wouldn't have been high enough either. Give me your ID and I'll make a call to verify whether or not I can discuss this with you."

Morris gave me his ID and said, "I understand. I have no problem waiting for you to verify my security level."

I said, "I'll be back in a few minutes." I went back to my desk and called George. I explained the situation to him. He told me it would only take a few minutes. True to his word, about three minutes later he called me back. He said he verified the security clearance for Morris and it was okay to discuss the device with him. I thanked George for the quick response and went back to the room where Morris was waiting.

After I walked into the room and closed the door I said, "You've been cleared. I think you need a little history first. My first case as a homicide detective involved a series of murders where all the victims were found in locked motel rooms with part of their bodies missing. Additionally, all of the victims were residents of a prison near Moscow and were awaiting execution."

"How did they end up here?"

"Did you ever watch Star Trek?"

"Yeah, of course. Didn't everybody?"

"Well, the Russians invented a transporter. It worked for inanimate objects, but wasn't exactly ready to transport people yet. The victims were actually killed before they were transported, but every one of them was missing part of their body. The primary designer of the system was a professor at the college here. After the initial design was completed, he came back here and built a receiving station. Then he went back to Russia and began sending people here."

"Wow! That's some story! What happened?"

"Without going into a lot of detail, it turns out we had a transporter expert of our own. He came here and realized it would be possible to activate the transporter and send a bomb back to Russia. So, he got the biggest non-nuclear bomb we had and sent it back to them. Their transporter was destroyed. One other thing you should know, although the development of the device was done in Russia, it wasn't built for them. The people building the device planned on selling it to terrorists for a lot of money. They were going to use that money to overthrow the Russian government."

Morris didn't say anything, so I continued. "I spoke to our transporter expert two days ago. He said they have a fully functional device now. It no longer requires special sending and receiving stations. He felt the Russians could have rebuilt their device and it's probably similar in capability to ours. I believe the people who developed the device have perfected it and sold it to one of the Islamic terrorist groups."

"Why couldn't they transport a killer to the restaurant and then transport him back? Why use a plane?"

"Apparently the receiving places have to be predefined, otherwise there's a potential for transporting somebody into a solid object."

"I'll bet that would be unpleasant. So, do you have any suggestions how to proceed?"

"I think the plane is the key. If we can find out more about it, maybe that will give us a clue to the pilot's identity. I'll call John Gordon from the NTSB. Perhaps he has some information regarding it."

I took my cell phone out of my pocket and called John. He answered on the first ring.

"Hi John, it's Frank Carver. I was wondering if you had any information about the plane."

"Yes, I received a report a few minutes ago. The plane was at a maintenance facility in Stockton, California. It was scheduled to be completely overhauled, inside and out. That's why the cabin was empty. It appears the plane was stolen sometime Friday evening or early Saturday morning. The maintenance facility is normally closed on weekends. However, when the other airport workers arrived on Saturday, the hanger door on the maintenance facility was open. They contacted the manager of the maintenance facility. When he arrived, he noticed immediately that the plane was missing. He called us and the local police to report the theft."

"So why didn't you know the plane was stolen when you first saw it at the crash site?"

"Because whoever took the plane changed the tail number. The number matched the plane model, so it wasn't immediately obvious."

"Do you think they took the plane someplace else to repaint the tail number?"

"No, I think they did it at the facility in Stockton. That plane has a maximum range of sixteen hundred miles, so they had to refuel somewhere. We're checking now with airports along the probable route to find out where they stopped. I'm hoping somebody will be able to identify the pilot. But there's something else you really need to know. The plane was owned by Parker Engineering."

"That is interesting. Bradley Parker failed to tell me it was their plane that crashed into the restaurant when we met this morning. Is it possible he didn't know?"

"I suppose it's possible, but unlikely. I'm sure the maintenance facility manager contacted somebody at Parker Engineering to report the theft."

"Can you confirm that for me?"

"Sure, it will probably take a while, but I'll call you as soon as I know."

"Thanks, John."

As soon as the call ended Morris asked, "What did Bradley Parker not mention this morning?"

"That it was their plane that crashed into the restaurant."

Morris was silent for a few moments. Then he said, "Either Parker Engineering is involved in this or they're being framed."

"I believe they're being framed. I think if Bradley Parker knew it was their plane that crashed into the restaurant, he would have been a little nervous when we met this morning. He wasn't nervous at all, but he certainly did express genuine concern when he found out Jeffery Haskell was one of the targets. I think I'll go visit Bradley Parker again."

"Is it okay if I go with you?"

"Sure, let's go."

Morris and I arrived at Parker Engineering a half hour later. We went in and the receptionist recognized me immediately. She said, "If you looking for Mr. Parker, he left about an hour ago. He looked upset, so I asked him if there was a problem. He ignored me and just walked out."

"Can you call him for me?"

She said, "Sure." She picked up her phone and called him. A minute later she said, "He's not answering. The call went to his voice mail."

"I need his cell number."

The receptionist wrote the number on the back of one of Parker's business cards and handed it to me. Then she said, "I've worked here for about three years. I've never seen Mr. Parker act like this. He's always so friendly and nice. I'm sure something is wrong."

"Thank you. If you hear from Mr. Parker please ask him to call me immediately."

"Yes, sir."

Morris and I left. When we got back into the car I said, "I think it's now pretty obvious Parker is involved in

The Disappearing Man

this thing. Something must have happened since I met with him this morning."

The next thing I did was call the station and ask them to have the cell phone company locate Bradley Parker's cell phone. I knew that would take a while, so Morris and I headed back to the station. When we were about half way there my phone rang. It was John Gordon. I answered the phone and said, "Hi John. I hope you have some news for us."

"Yes, I do. The plane stopped to refuel at a small airport near Springfield, Missouri. They have a security system there that films everyone who buys fuel. They remembered our thief because he was the only one who paid for his purchase with cash in the last several weeks. They're sending me pictures by e-mail. When I get the message, I'll forward it to you. It should be within the next ten minutes."

"Thanks John. I hope this is the break we need."

"What happened?" Morris asked.

"John is sending me pictures of the pilot. He was videotaped by a security system at a small airport. I should have the pictures by the time I get to my desk."

"That's great news! I hope we'll be able to identify him."

"We'll know shortly."

We arrived at my desk about twenty minutes later. I checked my e-mail and, as promised, there was a message with attachments from John. I opened the first picture and immediately Morris said, "I know that guy. He's wanted in probably half of the civilized countries in the world. His name is Kamal Abbas. He's a freelancer and works for whoever pays him the most. I'm somewhat ashamed to tell you that he has done work for us in the past as well. However, now he's wanted for murder. He killed a CIA agent about four years ago."

"Is he a pilot?"

"Yes, and from all accounts a very competent one. It's very likely he was paid to do this job."

"So now we have to find him and make him tell us who paid him."

"It won't be easy. To the best of my knowledge this is the first time he has actually been spotted in five years, and if we are lucky enough to catch him, he'll never tell us who hired him."

I was thinking of how we could find him when the dispatcher called to tell me that either Parker was in an area that had no service or his phone was turned off. The last time his phone was detected was in the area of the airport.

"The phone company is unable to locate Parker's phone. It's beginning to appear that every path we take is a dead end," I said with a note of sarcasm in my voice.

"There's something else we have to consider. If Iran is looking for trigger systems for nuclear devices, we have to assume they either have the nuclear device or will have it shortly. That makes this a national security issue. I have to report this."

"I understand and agree. There's something else to think about too. They killed Haskell, so now they have to find somebody else. What if that person is Parker? I'll bet he's an engineer and is probably capable of building the triggers as well. I don't believe he would work for Iran unless he was forced to do so, but maybe they have some leverage to force him to do it."

"Does he have a wife and family?"

"I have no idea, but I'll find out."

I called Parker Engineering and spoke to the receptionist again. I asked her if she had heard from Mr. Parker and she said no. Then I asked her if Mr. Parker had a family. She told me he lives with his wife, Lynn, and they have two children away at college. Their son, Daniel, is a junior at UCLA. Their daughter, Kate, is a freshman at Yale. I asked her if she had contact information for Daniel and Kate and she gave me their cell phone numbers. She also gave me Parker's home number.

The Disappearing Man

I called Lynn Parker first. She answered immediately, like she was waiting for the phone to ring. She sounded apprehensive when she answered, "This is Lynn Parker."

I managed to say, "This is Lieutenant Carver with the Norfolk County Police," when she started to scream and cry at the same time.

Then she stammered when she said, "Please don't tell me they killed her already!"

"Please calm down, Mrs. Parker. I don't know what you're talking about. I'm looking for your husband."

Several seconds went by. I could hear her sobbing. Finally, she softly said, "We were warned not to speak to the police."

"Mrs. Parker, please tell me what's going on."

It took a while before she answered, "They took Kate and told Bradley that if he wanted to keep her safe he had to follow their instructions exactly."

"Do you know what the instructions were?"

"I don't know other than we couldn't contact the police and Bradley had to take the next flight to JFK. He would get further instructions after he arrived."

"Mrs. Parker, it is absolutely imperative that I speak to your husband before he puts himself and your daughter in danger."

"I don't believe he will call. He said they were monitoring his phone."

"I'm hoping he's smart enough to buy a disposable phone at the airport."

"He was very upset. I doubt he's thinking very clearly."

"I hope you're wrong. Mrs. Parker, I would like to come over there and wait for your husband to call. I don't believe your house is being watched, but just to play it safe I'll use a county maintenance van. I'll also stop at several of your neighbor's houses first."

"Okay, but please be very careful. We live in a gated community and there are patrols constantly checking the homes here. It would be almost impossible for somebody to be watching the house, but I still don't want to take any chances."

"I understand completely. I'll see you in about an hour."

I went to the chief's office. He was on the phone. Using hand signals, I made it apparent I had to speak to him immediately. He hung up his phone and motioned for me to come in. As soon as I got inside his office I closed the door and told him what was happening. I said I needed a county maintenance van immediately and asked him to requisition one for me as soon as possible. He picked up his phone and placed a call, spoke to someone about the van, and hung up. Then he said, "The van will be out in front in ten minutes. Keep me informed."

"Thank you, sir. I will."

When I got back to my desk Morris looked at me and said, "Do you want to tell me what the hell is going on?"

"Somebody kidnapped Parker's daughter. They ordered him to take the next flight to JFK and not to tell anybody except his wife what's going on."

"They're using his daughter as the leverage to force him to build the triggers."

"Obviously, I'm going over to meet with his wife. Do you want to come?"

"Yeah, of course I do."

"Lose the coat and tie. We're supposed to be county maintenance people."

I left my coat and tie on my desk too. I also took off my shoulder holster and put my gun in my front pocket. Then we both walked out the front entrance. Less than two minutes later a van pulled up that had the county seal painted on the side. Under the seal it said, "Norfolk County Water & Gas".

The Disappearing Man

The driver walked over and said, "It's all yours. Don't wreck it. It's our only new one."

Morris and I got into the van. Inside it was filled with tools and pipe fittings. There was also a tool box. I put my gun in the tool box and we drove over to the Parker's house. We stopped at the gate house and the guard walked over to my window.

The guard said, "Good afternoon. How can I help you guys?"

I took out my ID and showed it to him. Then I said, "We're here undercover. Don't tell anybody."

He looked around and said, "Some guy paid me fifty dollars to tell him if anybody unusual or suspicious asked to go into the development. I had no intention of doing it, but it was hard to turn down an easy fifty."

"Do you have his phone number?"

"Yeah, I'll get it for you."

He went back inside the gate house and came out a few seconds later with a piece of paper. He handed it to me and I asked him, "Did the guy express any interest in a specific resident?"

He nodded his head and said, "The Parkers."

I said, "Thanks for your help."

The guard opened the gate and we drove through. We stopped four houses down from the Parker's. I picked up the tool box and got out, walked up to the front door and rang the bell. A young woman answered the door and asked, "May I help you?"

"One of your neighbors reported a possible gas leak. Have you noticed anything?"

"No."

"I'm sorry to have bothered you."

The same thing was repeated at the next three houses. When I got to the Parker's door Mrs. Parker opened the door before I could ring the bell. She said, "Are you Lieutenant Carver?"

"Yes, I have a CIA agent with me as well." I turned around and waved to Morris. He got out of the truck and walked up to the door. Then we went inside.

"I'm sorry. I was hysterical when we spoke on the phone, but I'm really scared."

"That's perfectly understandable. This is Morris Easton. He's an agent with the CIA. We were both investigating the crash at the restaurant. Some information we uncovered indicated that a former employee of Parker Engineering may have been involved in the situation. I went to see your husband this morning and he was very helpful. A few hours later I found out the plane that crashed was owned by Parker Engineering. I went back to speak to your husband again, but I was told he left and refused to tell anybody why he was leaving or where he was going."

"He didn't tell me it was his plane that crashed into the restaurant. I don't think he knows."

"Please excuse me for a minute. I have to call the station."

I walked into another room and made my call. I gave the dispatcher the phone number I received from the guard and told her to have someone check it. I also told her to tell the chief that I was at the Parker residence. Then I used my phone to check the airline schedules and found there was only one flight to JFK in the afternoon.

I rejoined Morris and Mrs. Parker and said, "If your husband is going to call, it should be soon. His plane was scheduled to land twenty minutes ago."

We all walked into the kitchen. Morris and I sat down at a counter. Mrs. Morris decided to make a fresh pot of coffee. When it was done she asked if we wanted any and we both said "Yes". We were sitting down drinking it and talking for almost a half hour when the phone rang.

Instantly Mrs. Parker became frightened. She could barely speak when she answered the phone. It was her husband. She talked with him for a moment and then handed me the phone.

The Disappearing Man

"Mr. Parker, this is Lieutenant Carver. Both you and your daughter are in serious danger. Since we spoke this morning I found out that Jeffery Haskell's sister was kidnapped in order to force him to work for whoever was blackmailing him. She was injured in the kidnapping and died as a result of those injuries. We believe Jeffery found out about her death and reported the incident to the CIA. They set up the meeting with Adam Becker at the restaurant. Someone leaked the information concerning the meeting to the Iranians. An agent named Kamal Abbas was hired to kill both Becker and Haskell. He stole a plane from a maintenance facility in Stockton, California and crashed the plane into the restaurant."

"Parker Engineering had a plane at that facility being refurbished. Was it our plane that was used?"

"Yes, it was your plane."

"The pilot must have been killed in the crash. Why would he agree to a suicide mission?"

"The pilot didn't die in the crash. He managed to escape. Did you already tell them you could build the triggers for them?"

"No, they haven't asked me to do anything except take a flight that leaves in about an hour for Paris and to contact them again when I land."

"I want you to tell them you don't know enough about the triggers to build them, but you know somebody who does."

"And who would that be?"

"That would be me."

"How could that possibly work? If they ask you any questions, your lack of knowledge would be obvious."

"First, you should know I have a degree in electrical engineering. Second, I have high level security clearance so I would be able to study the plans for the device and learn enough about them so I would be able to fool them if it became necessary. Finally, I have a plan I think will end this whole mess, but for the plan to work I have to take your place."

"I have an engineer working for me who is similar in appearance to you and also knows how to build the triggers. In fact, he was hired to replace Jeffery. He has a big bushy beard and moustache, so his facial features are hidden. I'll bet you could pass as him. His name is Peter Thompson."

"That sounds good. I'll go meet him tomorrow morning and tell him to take some time off and disappear."

"I'll call you again when this is over. Tell Peter I'll cover all of his expenses and continue to pay him his regular salary while you are taking his place. I hope they believe me when I tell them I can't build the triggers."

"I don't really think they have a choice. We'll be waiting for your call."

I turned toward Morris and said, "I need a passport and driver's license with the name Peter Thompson on them. I'm sure you can do that."

"I'll have them for you by tomorrow morning. I know we have a picture of you in our files we can use. Are you sure you can pull this off?"

"Yes, I'm sure. I just have to spend some time tomorrow with Peter so I can appear knowledgeable about the triggers."

I turned to Mrs. Parker and said, "Thank you for your cooperation. If you like, I can get someone to stay with you until your husband returns."

She thought about it for a moment and said, "I think having someone to talk to would be a good idea."

"I'll take care of it," I said. Then I called the station and asked if Wendy Cooper was available for an assignment. The dispatcher said she was and she would have her call me. Five minutes later Wendy called. I explained the assignment to her and she said she would be here in less than an hour.

"Mrs. Parker, an officer named Wendy Cooper will be here soon. She will stay with you until this situation is

The Disappearing Man

over. She's a very capable officer and will be able to offer you both companionship and protection."

"Thank you, lieutenant."

"You're welcome."

Morris and I left shortly after Wendy arrived. I drove Morris back to the station. He said he would come to Parker Engineering as soon as he received my new passport and driver's license.

By the time I got home Jill was waiting. I explained the situation to her and told her I would be gone for a few days on an undercover assignment. She wasn't pleased, to say the least, but she did understand the nature of my job, so she accepted it. Her final comment on the subject was, "I think you should quit the police department and join the CIA!"

I replied, "That's not a bad idea. I'll consider it," she screamed several obscenities at me, walked up to our bedroom, and slammed the door.

I decided I should wait for a while and let her calm down before I went to smooth things over. I called the chief and he wasn't exactly happy with the situation either, but in the end, he agreed it was the only reasonable course of action.

My next call was to Tim Harris. I knew we weren't on a secure line, but I had to take a chance we weren't being monitored. After he answered I explained the situation to him. I said, "I want one of your locators. I'm hoping I'll be able to get close enough to the Iranian scientist who is building the bomb to grab him. When I do, I want you to transport both of us out of Iran."

"That's an interesting idea. We've never tried transporting two people with a single locator. I'm positive it would work for you, but I'm not sure if the person you are holding on to would survive unharmed."

"To be perfectly honest with you, I don't care if he doesn't. I think this may be an excellent opportunity to derail the Iranian nuclear program. How big is the locator?"

"It looks like a key fob for a car. There's a button on it. When you push it, that will tell us to activate the transporter."

"Send me one overnight. Send it to the station because I won't be home. I'll pick it up after my nuclear training is finished."

"Sometime you will have to tell me what kind of nuclear training you're receiving. Anyway, it'll be there in the morning. After you get it, call me."

The next morning, I arrived at Parker Engineering at 9:30. The receptionist didn't look happy to see me. She said, "Good morning lieutenant, I'm sorry to tell you that I still haven't spoken to Mr. Parker."

"That's okay. I spoke to him last night. Right now, I need to speak to Peter Thompson. Please ask him to come here."

She said, "Okay." Then she picked up a phone and called Peter. "He'll be here in a minute," she said. She looked like she was going to ask me something, but decided not to.

A short time later a man about my age and size, but with an enormous beard and moustache, walked into the lobby. We made eye contact and I said, "Mr. Thompson, I'm Lieutenant Carver. It's imperative we speak immediately about an urgent and classified matter. I spoke to Mr. Parker in the conference room yesterday morning. I would like to go back there with you and I'll explain everything."

He looked at me with a very confused look on his face, but said, "I guess we can do that. Follow me."

I followed him into the conference room and closed the door. I sat down across from him and said, "First, what I'm about to tell you is classified. As you are probably aware, Mr. Parker left here yesterday and refused to tell anybody why he was leaving, where he was going, or when he would be back. I spoke to him last night and we both believe you're the key to resolving the current situation."

The Disappearing Man

Now he looked even more confused than before. He asked, "What situation?"

I spent a few minutes explaining what was going on. Then I said, "Since the Iranians killed their source for the triggers, they decided to try again. This time they kidnapped Mr. Parker's daughter. Then they ordered him to fly to Paris where he would receive further instructions. Both Mr. Parker and I are sure they're going to try to force him to build the triggers. He's going to tell them he's not capable of doing that, but you are. Obviously, we don't expect you to do that. What we want you to do, is to spend today teaching me the basics of building the triggers. Then, I will take your place here. Also, we want you to disappear until this situation is resolved."

"The triggers are very complex devices. I'm not sure how much you could learn in one day. Additionally, to understand how they work, you need a background in both electrical and mechanical engineering."

"I don't need the details. All I need is enough information to prove to them I know how to build the triggers. I have a degree in electrical engineering, and have a basic understanding of mechanical engineering as well. Once I get into their nuclear facility, I have a plan to put them out of business for a while."

"If they find out you really don't know how to build the triggers, they will kill you."

"I realize that, but I do have a plan, and that doesn't include my death."

"Why did Mr. Parker pick me for this task?"

"Because you and I are about the same age and build. Also, nobody really knows what your face looks like because of your beard. Without your beard, we may look fairly similar."

"Where do you want me to go?"

"It doesn't really matter where, but it should be at least a few hundred miles from here. I'll use your car and stay in your house until this is over. Mr. Parker said he'll pay all your expenses for your forced vacation, and continue to pay you your regular salary."

"Okay, let's get started. Stay here and I'll be back in a few minutes with the design specifications."

I never realized how complex a nuclear trigger was until I began to study the specs. Peter told me that if we had the triggers we use now, the bombs we dropped on Japan at the end of World War II would have been ten to twenty times more powerful.

Around noon, Morris stopped by with my new identification. It all looked perfect. I now have a driver's license, passport, and an American Express card that identifies me as Peter Thompson.

By the end of the day, I felt I knew enough that I would be able to answer any questions I was likely to be asked. In any case, I planned to continue studying the plans until the last moment.

I followed Peter back to his apartment and went inside. Peter packed a suitcase and we exchanged car keys. He was about to tell me where he was going, but I stopped him and told him I didn't want to know. That way I couldn't tell anybody where the real Peter Thompson went in case I was caught.

Peter left to begin his vacation and I went back to the station. There was a package from Tim Harris on my desk. I went to the chief's office and spent a few minutes telling him what happened during the day and that I wouldn't be back until this case was resolved. Then I picked up the package and drove home.

Jill and I had a quiet supper. I knew she was worried. I understood, because if it was her who was going, I would be worried too. I did my best to convince her that everything would be okay. I was about to leave and assume the role of Peter Thompson when my phone rang. It was Bradley Parker. He said, "You were right. They believed me when I told them I wasn't able to build the triggers. How did your training go with Peter today?"

"I think it went well. I'm confident I'll be able to prove my capability."

"I hope so, because they refused to release my daughter until you're in their custody."

"I plan on refusing to cooperate until they release her. Where are you?"

"I'm in Arlington, Virginia. You won't believe how I got here."

"Yes, I would. I know exactly how you got there."

"You knew they have a transporter?" he asked excitedly.

"Yes, that was how the pilot managed to escape before the crash into the restaurant."

"Why didn't you tell me?"

"The information is classified. When will you be back here?"

"I missed the last flight so I'm going to drive. I'll be at the office by nine o'clock tomorrow morning."

"Good, I'll be there too. I want you to quietly tell your people I will be replacing Peter temporarily."

"I'm not sure that will be necessary. You won't be there very long. They gave me a device to give to you that will allow them to transport you to their location in Iran. They will be expecting you sometime tomorrow."

"Okay, I was expecting that. But I want you to make a modification to the plans for the trigger before I go there."

"What did you have in mind?"

"I want the trigger to detonate the bomb as soon as it's attached. Can you do that?"

"That's an interesting, although very nasty, idea. However, I like it. There are several safety protocols built into the design, but I think I may be able to bypass them. I'll think about it on my way home."

"Good, I'll see you in the morning."

I arrived at Parker Engineering just before nine o'clock. The moment I walked in the receptionist said, "Mr. Parker is waiting for you in the conference room."

She unlocked the door. I said, "Thanks," as I opened the door and walked through. The door to the conference room was open. I peeked inside and saw Bradley Parker sitting there.

I knocked softly and walked in. He said, "Good morning, lieutenant."

"Please call me 'Frank'. I don't see any need to be formal."

"Okay Frank, you can call me 'Brad'."

"Perfect. The first thing I would like to know is, how did it feel to be transported?"

"Needless to say, I was more than a little bit apprehensive about it. But after doing it, I think it's the perfect way to travel. Suddenly you find yourself surrounded by bright white light. It was disorienting because you have no frame of reference to tell up from down. It only lasts for a few seconds, and the white light begins to dissolve. In its place, you can see your new location."

"Okay, now I know what to expect. Did you make any progress on the change I requested to the trigger?"

"Yes, and it turns out to be very easy. It requires only three wiring changes."

"Would the change be obvious to somebody studying the schematic?"

"No, I don't think it would even be discovered by somebody familiar with the design."

"That's excellent. I want a set of modified plans before I get transported."

Brad said, "Already taken care of." Then he handed me a thumb drive and said, "The file is password protected. I wanted something easy to remember. The password is 'bond007'."

"Thanks, I'm sure I can remember that. I would like to spend some time studying the plans with you before I go to Iran."

"That sounds like an excellent idea."

We spent the next five hours going over the modified trigger design. By the time we were done, I felt confident I would be able to bluff my way through any questions the Iranians were likely to ask.

Brad handed me the locator and asked, "How are you going to get back?"

I put my hand into my pocket and retrieved the locator Tim had sent me. I showed it to him and said, "With this."

Brad smiled and said, "Good luck."

I double checked to make sure I had nothing with my real name on it. Once I was sure I was ready, I pushed the button on the Iranian locator.

Nothing happened for several seconds. Just as I was beginning to think my plan failed, I found myself surrounded by bright white light just as Brad had described. Moments later I found myself in a large office. There was a man sitting down behind a desk that was about twenty feet in front of me. There were also three guards, with guns drawn and aimed at me. As soon as I became fully aware of my surroundings, I raised my hands and said meekly, "I'm Peter Thompson. Bradley Parker sent me here. I'm not armed. Please don't shoot me."

The man behind the desk said, "Show me your identification," with a strong accent I couldn't identify.

I slowly reached into my back pocket and got my passport. I gave it to one of the guards who took it and handed it to the man behind the desk."

The man behind the desk said something I didn't understand, but one of the guards began to pat me down looking for a weapon. I still had the locator in my hand so I showed it to the guard and said, "Is this what you're looking for?"

It apparently wasn't because he continued to pat me down. He found my cell phone and took it out of my pocket. Then he stood up and said something to the man behind the desk. The man behind the desk said something to the guards.

The guard who had my phone put it on the desk. Then the guards holstered their guns and left the room.

The man behind the desk said, "My name is Abdul-Qadir. I would like to ask you some questions. I assume you brought the plans with you?"

"Yes, I did, but I won't answer any of your questions until it's confirmed that Mr. Parker's daughter has been released."

"What's to stop me from killing you and taking the plans off your body?"

"The file is password protected. But even more important is that the plans are designed to trigger US weapons. They will have to be modified to work with the weapons you've designed. Without me it would be impossible for you to build a working trigger."

"You seem very sure of yourself. We have excellent engineers here. Many of them are graduates of US universities. I'm sure we could do it without you."

"Perhaps, but it will take a lot less time with my help. I promised Mr. Parker that I wouldn't help you until his daughter is released. You already have me, so you really don't need her."

He said, "I suppose you're right." Then he picked up a phone and made a call. It took several minutes before he hung up. Then he said, "She will be released immediately. Somebody will take her to a police station that's close to where she is being held. She will be instructed to call her father and tell him to call you. Please sit down while we're waiting for Mr. Parker to call."

I sat down across from Abdul-Qadir. After I was seated he said, "You seem willing to help us. Why?"

"Because I'm somewhat sympathetic to your cause. I had a neighbor who was Muslim. He and I spent a lot of time together, and after a while I began to understand why he felt the way he did about the western world."

"So, you don't have a problem with us having an atomic bomb?"

The Disappearing Man

"As long as you don't use it. There are Muslim countries that have atomic weapons. As long as they're used as a deterrent to war, I believe that simply levels the playing field."

"That's an interesting opinion, and one I'm sure isn't shared by the majority of people in your country."

We talked for another ten minutes when my phone rang. It was Brad. As soon as I answered he told me his daughter had been released and was okay. She was waiting to be picked up at a police station near downtown New Haven. Then he thanked me.

Abdul-Qadir asked, "Was that Parker?"

"Yes, he confirmed his daughter had been released and she was unharmed. So now you can ask me any questions you would like."

For the next half hour, we discussed the technical aspects of the trigger device. Apparently, he was satisfied because he said, "You will be taken to your quarters. We will provide you with food, something to drink, and clean clothes. Tomorrow you will work with our chief engineer. Please give me the drive with the plans and the password."

I handed him the thumb drive and said, "The password is 'bond007'. I don't think it will take more than three or four days to make the necessary changes. If possible, please have the information in the file printed. It'll be much easier to work with in that format."

Abdul-Qadir said, "It'll be ready for you tomorrow morning." Then he picked up his phone and had a brief conversation I didn't understand. Less than a minute later a guard walked into the room. He said, "Follow me."

I followed him through a long hallway to an elevator. When the elevator arrived, we stepped in and the guard inserted a card key into a slot and pushed a button. The elevator went up for a while. When the door opened I stepped into large room that had a big bed, a desk, a sofa, and a TV. The guard said, "This is your room. I will bring you food and drink from Boof. That's our version of

McDonalds. You can't leave the room without a guard. You need a key to call the elevator and you're on the fourteenth floor of this building, so don't try to jump."

"Food from Boof will be fine. I have no intention of trying to leave the room. I made a commitment and plan to keep it."

The guard didn't say anything. He just walked into the elevator and left. I explored the room. The view of the city was excellent. There was a very nice bathroom as well. I turned on the TV, but there was nothing in English, so I turned it off. I sat on the sofa and played games on my phone until the guard returned. He walked in and placed the bag of food on the table in front of me and said he would be back at eight o'clock in the morning. He would bring food and clean clothes at that time.

The bag contained a big hamburger, fries, and a coke. It was actually much better than I expected. Eventually I got tired. I took off my clothes except for my underwear and went to sleep thinking about how surprised they'll be when they discover that both me and their chief engineer are both gone.

I woke up at 6:00 and spent a half hour walking in circles inside the room for exercise. I played a few more games. Just before eight the elevator door opened. The same guard came in with another bag from Boof. He also gave me a bag that had clean clothes and said he would be back in a half hour. Then he left.

I ate my breakfast, which wasn't very good. I took a shower and put on the clothes they provided. They seemed to fit perfectly.

The guard came back and told me to get into the elevator. He pressed a button and the elevator went down several floors. When the door opened the guard said, "Follow me."

I followed him through a long hallway that had offices every fifteen feet or so. After we passed a lot of small offices, we arrived at a much larger one. The guard unlocked

The Disappearing Man

the door, opened it, and told me to sit down. Then the guard left and locked the door again.

I sat in the office, alone, for about twenty minutes. The lock clicked and a middle-aged man with a full beard walked in. He walked over to me and said, "Good morning, Peter. My name is Jarir. We'll be working together for a while. Although you're a prisoner, I promise you won't be mistreated."

"Thank you Jarir. Your English is perfect. Where did you learn to speak it?"

"I was raised near Atlanta and graduated from Georgia Tech. I've been speaking English for as far back as I can remember. After I received my master's degree, I returned to Iran."

"So, after living in both the US and Iran, which do you prefer?"

"There are positive and negatives with both locations, but overall, I prefer Iran. I spent some time studying the drawings you brought and have some questions for you, so let's get started."

He walked over to a large drawing table and I saw the printed plans laying there. He pointed to a few things and asked me a couple of very technical questions. Fortunately, I was able to answer them intelligently. But I was worried that any second he would ask me something I wouldn't be able to answer. I had to act as soon as possible.

We were both hunched over the table looking at the drawings. I suddenly stepped back from the table and began coughing. I put my right hand in my pocket and took out the locator. Jarir turned around and asked, "Are you okay?"

I put my left hand on his shoulder, pushed the button on the locator, and said, "I will be shortly." A second later the room faded out of view and we were surrounded by bright white light. Several seconds went by before the light began to fade. A few seconds later we were standing in a laboratory. Tim Harris was a few feet in front of me, smiling.

I felt fine. I looked at Jarir and realized immediately that the trip didn't go as well for him.

The only part of him that looked normal was his shoulder where I was holding him. He was on the floor next to me. The skin on most of his body had turned a blueish gray. His hair, which was black, was now white and covered his head in patches. His eyes were gone. His arms extended from his shoulders at a weird unnatural angle. He was dead.

Tim walked over, looked at Jarir's body, and said, "I told you we never tried transporting two people with one locator."

"He was the chief engineer in the Iranian nuclear program."

"This will probably set them back for a while."

"We did a little more than just capture their chief engineer. If I'm correct, their entire nuclear program will become history soon."

"How did you do that?"

"We gave them a design for a nuclear trigger with a nasty surprise inside."

"Would you like to elaborate?"

"Sure. When they attach the trigger to their weapon, it will immediately cause the weapon to detonate. It'll be a low-level explosion, by nuclear standards, but will produce excessive amounts of radiation."

"That wasn't very nice," Tim said with a smile.

"What can I say? I'm just not a nice guy. By the way, where am I?"

"You're in Mountain View, California."

"Good, I can get a flight home from San Francisco." Then I thought for a moment and asked, "What time is it?"

Tim looked at his watch and said, "It's almost two o'clock in the morning."

I said, "You know, travel by transporter is going to bring new meaning to 'jet lag'."

Then I called Jill. She was a little groggy when she said, "Hello."

The Disappearing Man

"Hi Jill, I know it's a little early but I wanted you to know the case has been resolved. I'm in Mountain View, California now, but I will be home by tonight."

She asked, "How did you end up there?" But before I could answer she said, "It's probably classified, so don't tell me. I'm just glad you're alright. Call me and I'll pick you up from the airport."

"As soon as I know when I'll be back, I'll call you. I love you."

"I love you too."

After I hung up Tim said, "You know you don't have to fly back to the east coast. I can get you to New York in a few minutes."

"I'll have to think about that. Where is the receiving location in New York?"

"It's in what looks like an abandoned hangar at LaGuardia."

"Can somebody check and see what the first flight is to Norfolk County?"

Tim replied, "We can use the computer in my office."

I followed Tim over to his office, which was very impressive. It was probably four hundred square feet. There was a conference table, a large desk, an additional desk with several computers on it, and a half round sofa with a round marble table in front of it. Tim walked over to one of the computers, and a few seconds later all the flights for the day between LaGuardia and Norfolk County were listed. There was a flight that left at 8:10 and arrived at 10:20. I told him to book the flight using the name Peter Thompson and handed him Peter's credit card to pay for it. He returned my card and said, "Uncle Sam will pay for this flight."

"Uncle Sam would have paid for it with this card too. How do I get from the hanger to the passenger terminal?"

"I'll have one of my technicians drive you over. We'll send you over there at seven o'clock."

"That sounds perfect. When is the existence of the transporter going to be made public?"

"If it was up to me, I would do it immediately, but the military wants to keep the transporter a secret for a while. They want us to build twenty-five more systems and set up receiving stations all over the planet. Then they want to test the system to see if it would be feasible to use it to transport large numbers of troops instantly to trouble spots anywhere in the world."

"That actually sounds like the perfect application for the transporter. But I wonder how you get a receiving station to a remote location. Could you set up one inside an empty cargo plane?"

"We did think about that, but until we do some additional refinements to the system, it wouldn't be possible. Now the receiving stations need an area that's at least fifteen feet square and twelve feet high. Additionally, the latitude and longitude of the receiving station must be accurate to four decimal places and the height accurate to one quarter of an inch. That would be impossible to do with an airplane, even if it was big enough. We do intend to set up receiving stations on two of our aircraft carriers, but with the current technology, it would be useless unless the ocean was at a dead calm."

We talked for a while. At a few minutes after six my phone rang. I didn't recognize the number so I answered by saying, "This is Lieutenant Carver."

"Hello Frank, I'm sorry it took so long to return your call."

It was Igor. "Hi Igor, I had a problem I wanted you to be aware of. Apparently, the people in Russia that were working on the transporter got it completed and sold it to Iran. I can personally attest to the fact that it's now capable of transporting people."

"They transported you somewhere?"

"Yeah, I was transported from a place near the Norfolk County airport to a building somewhere in Iran."

The Disappearing Man

"What was it like?"

"It was a little disorienting, but otherwise okay. Personally, I think it's a great way to travel. You can go anywhere on Earth in a few seconds."

"This is very disturbing. I wonder if they have the money to start a revolution."

"I have no idea, but I wanted you to be aware of what's going on. I wouldn't worry too much yet. The system requires a receiving station, so unless they manage to set up one in the Kremlin, I think your government is safe."

"My concern is that if Iran is able to build a nuclear weapon they could use it to send a bomb to Moscow."

"I believe that problem may be resolved shortly. I can't discuss it on an unsecured line."

"How about if I come and visit you next week? Then I could meet Jill too."

"Okay, I would like that. We have a big house with a couple of guestrooms. You're welcome to stay with us."

"I'll call you tomorrow."

After the call was over, Tim asked, "Is Igor coming to visit you?"

"Yeah, sometime next week."

"Maybe I'll drop by too. Anyway, it's time for your trip to New York. You do still have the locator in your pocket, right?"

"Yes," then I reached into my pocket, took out the locator, and showed it to him.

"Give it to the technician when you get to New York."

I followed Tim back to the area where the receiver was. Tim spent several seconds programming the transporter. Then he said, "Push the button."

I did, and a few seconds later I was in the hanger in New York.

The technician said, "Hi, I understand you need a ride to the passenger terminal."

I guess I was getting used to travel by transporter because I didn't feel any discomfort at all this time. I responded, "Yes, Tim said you would drive me there." Then I handed him the locator.

He said, "Thanks. Let's go."

Twenty minutes later I was checked in and waiting by the gate for boarding. I had a half hour to wait, so I called Chief Mitchell and George and brought them up to date on the case. Then I called Jill. This time she was awake. I said, "Hi honey, I'll be arriving on a flight from LaGuardia at 10:20."

There was a definite note of confusion in her voice when she asked, "LaGuardia? How did you get there in a few hours?"

"I'm sorry to tell you..."

She interrupted me and said sarcastically, "I know, it's classified. I'll be there to pick you up. Bye."

"Bye."

That afternoon, after I got home, I called Peter Thompson and told him it was safe for him to return because the case was solved, and I wanted my car back. I know I lied about the case being solved because we didn't catch Kamal Abbas, and it was unlikely he would be caught.

Then I called Morris and told him the mission appears to have been a complete success. He didn't know about the modifications to the trigger design. I was trying to decide if I should tell him, because I knew there was a security leak. Then he told me they found the mole. It wasn't somebody in his department. The mole worked in the records section and had access to all the reports, regardless of their classification level. The woman admitted to passing information about the meeting to her "handler", whom she refused to identify. I decided not to tell him because I was still not certain how safe the information would be if the CIA was aware of it. It seemed likely that there was probably more than one mole.

The Disappearing Man

Igor came over from Russia the following week and spent four days with us. We had a great time. He was very pleased with the method I devised to set back the Iranian nuclear program.

Four months later a large explosion was reported in a remote area of Iran. The Iranian news agency issued a statement that said the explosion occurred at an experimental nuclear power generating facility and there were several fatalities. They also said the area was contaminated by excessive radiation and it was unsafe to be within ten miles of facility. The report made me smile.

Made in the USA
Columbia, SC
11 November 2024

45608573R00140